All's Fair *in* Love *and* Pickleball

ALSO BY KATE SPENCER

In a New York Minute

One Last Summer

All's Fair in Love and Pickleball

Kate Spencer

FOREVER
New York Boston

Forever
Hachette Book Group
1290 Avenue of the Americas, New York, NY 10104
read-forever.com
@readforeverpub

First Edition: June 2025

Forever is an imprint of Grand Central Publishing. The Forever name and logo are registered trademarks of Hachette Book Group, Inc.

The publisher is not responsible for websites (or their content) that are not owned by the publisher.

Forever books may be purchased in bulk for business, educational, or promotional use. For information, please contact your local bookseller or the Hachette Book Group Special Markets Department at special.markets@hbgusa.com.

Print book interior design by Jeff Stiefel

Library of Congress Cataloging-in-Publication Data

Names: Spencer, Kate, 1979- author.
Title: All's fair in love and pickleball / Kate Spencer.
Other titles: All is fair in love and pickleball
Description: First edition. | New York : Forever, 2025.
Identifiers: LCCN 2024060282 | ISBN 9781538771068 (trade paperback) | ISBN 9781538771075 (ebook)
Subjects: LCGFT: Romance fiction. | Novels.
Classification: LCC PS3619.P4653 A79 2025 | DDC 813/.6—dc23/eng/20241223
LC record available at https://lccn.loc.gov/2024060282

ISBNs: 9781538771068 (trade paperback), 9781538771075 (ebook)

Printed in the United States of America

CCR

10 9 8 7 6 5 4 3 2 1

For anyone who's ever been too scared to try something new out of a fear of failing or looking stupid.

I've been scared too.
May you and I both always remember
that it's still worth it.

(And that we all *fail or look stupid at some point.)*

AUTHOR'S NOTE

Dear Reader,

All's Fair in Love and Pickleball is a love story with a happy ending, but it also contains some sensitive subject matter, including grief and losing a parent to cancer. I write about these things from a place of personal experience and aim to do so with sensitivity and respect. Please take care of yourself if any of these topics are difficult for you.

Love, Kate

1

Saturday, April 1

I KNOW INSTANTLY that the man rushing into the hospital emergency room ahead of me is an asshole.

Even though he clearly sees me just steps behind him, he does not pause to hold the door. Instead he shoves it open with a grunt, letting it swing shut just as we make direct eye contact. It's a fraction of a second but long enough to register two swirling dark storm clouds below eyebrows that arch skeptically against his olive skin. He glances down at the bubble I've blown between my lips, grimaces for a split second, and then hustles inside as the smudged glass door closes in my face.

I'm not hung up on chivalry or antiquated, sexist gender rules. I'm fully capable of taking care of myself. Hell, I've been running the Sunset Springs Racquet Club completely on my own for the last two years, since my mom passed away. I have no problem opening a door for myself.

It's just the principle of it all. When you're born with a mom whose life mantra is "How you treat strangers is a direct reflection of who you are as a person," you learn to pay attention to this stuff. You become acutely aware of who speaks kindly to servers in restaurants and who presses the Open Door button on elevators as people rush toward them, and who does not.

So far, this guy's scoring a zero on Mom's scale of "How Not to Be a Jerk," and he's only making an already hard day worse. It's like he somehow knows my car battery just died minutes ago after barely making it to the hospital, and he's decided to really rub it in.

"Thanks a lot," I mutter sarcastically under my breath, which is minty-fresh, courtesy of Trident, but short-winded from jogging the entire way from the parking garage. I've sped here from Santa Barbara, where I was attempting to do the last thing my mom had written on her "What to Do After I Die" wish list: *Sprinkle my ashes somewhere that means a lot to both of us.*

Now is not the time to complain about my mom's lack of specific details when it came to her posthumous requests. The last month of her life had been a dark, miserable blur, and I will be forever honored to carry out these requests. But if I'm being honest—and really, when am I not?—I would have appreciated some details. The last thing I wanted was to get her wishes wrong.

I'd agonized and hyper-fixated on this one and finally landed on Santa Barbara, her home during college and the place she'd met my dad. I was literally about to twist the lid open when a phone call from Deb, the club's part-time receptionist, interrupted the moment.

"Bex, it's Deb, calling from the club," she'd hollered in her thick Long Island accent.

"Deb, I have caller ID. I know it's you," I'd replied, trying not to chuckle. Deb is super savvy about social media, but her boomer vibes really come out every time she calls me on the phone.

"Loretta fell on the court playing pickleball," she said, and my smile dropped. "With one of those snowbirds from Michigan. You know, the guy with the terrible hair plugs?"

"Michael?" I asked, trying to nail down exactly who she was talking about. Sunset Springs is a retirement town; there are a lot of questionable hair plugs.

"I don't know. Michael, Steve, they're all the same." She sounded panicked. "The X-ray shows her wrist is broken in two different places."

Even as an eternal optimist, it's hard for me to spin this injury. Deb is Loretta's best friend, and she said it's bad, a complicated break. Surgery will be required, followed by months of physical therapy. There is no bright side to be found—except when I hustled off the beach and bumped directly into a police officer cruising along on a Segway, who eyed the plain wooden urn suspiciously.

"You know it's against the law to scatter ashes on California beaches?" It was a half question, half accusation, and I nodded convincingly.

"Of course," I lied. Satisfied, he gave me one more skeptical, stern look and then rolled on his merry way.

Once I was inside my car, I hurriedly checked Google on my phone and discovered that Loretta's injury—and Deb's phone call—had saved me from incurring a five-hundred-dollar fine and possible jail time. It was the smallest of silver linings, but I'd take it.

The racquet club and its members are my entire world. I've always felt this way to some degree; growing up in a family business will do that to you, I think. I worked the front desk long before it was legally permitted, handing out fresh towels and charming members with tales of elementary school shenanigans. I learned to ride my bike on the empty courts and snuck my high school boyfriend in after hours to make out in the upstairs office that is now my apartment.

Still, it feels different today, as the sole owner. The members are the closest thing I have to family, and I always try to be there for them during an injury. But Loretta, who I've been teaching for the last four years, has been like a wise, nurturing grandmother figure, especially in the months right after my mom passed away.

I don't make a habit of playing favorites, but Loretta is undeniably the one I adore the most—not that I'd tell any of my other students that. Anyone who thinks older folks don't get pissed about trivial stuff has never seen four seventy-year-olds go up against each other in a pickleball match. In my world, the older you are, the fiercer you are—even if your bones and bodies don't always cooperate.

Just about everyone who frequents the club is sixty or older; hell, the entire town of Sunset Springs is qualified to be in the AARP except for me. I've spent just about my entire life there, so I am well versed in the kind of injuries that befall seniors. A broken wrist in your seventies is a massive pain in the ass. And, you know, the arm.

Back inside my beat-up old Prius, I buckled my mom's urn into the passenger seat and patted the lid affectionately. Grief sure as hell makes you do weird things, and for me, that includes talking to her like she's still right here, alive and next to me.

"I promise I'll find somewhere really good to sprinkle you," I said to that small box. "But I know you'd want me to try to go help Loretta out."

Mom devoted decades to the club and its members and left it all to me in her will. I'm not just honoring her legacy in this moment, but trying to walk in her footprints all the darn time. She was pure goodness, and she would have immediately loathed this handsome asshole, who was still steps ahead of me inside the hospital.

I watch as his very attractive backside storms the reception desk with a demanding energy, leaning his elbows on the counter without greeting the older man behind it.

"My aunt," I hear him say, but I miss the rest. I study him as he impatiently taps his long, tanned fingers along the lip of the counter. Deciphering what people are like based on their clothes is one of my innate skills, and this guy is an easy read. He's giving casual vibes in loose-fitting joggers, a crisp white T-shirt, and spotless sneakers. But each item clings to his body just so, like every thread had been told exactly where to land. The simplicity of it all highlights how impeccably in shape he is. The lines of his body are entirely lean, tight muscle. Even his tousled dark hair seems perfectly in place. The only thing that is even the slightest bit imperfect about him is the very faint hint of a five o'clock shadow on his face.

He rushes off down a corridor to my left, and then it's my turn to check in with the front desk of the hospital. Every time I come here, my body clenches like a fist about to land a punch. I know this place well because it's where I got stitches at eight years old after slipping and slicing my forehead open in the dry riverbed behind my house. When I was twelve, I walked out of here with a fractured arm decked out in a neon-pink cast after I hit a curb on Annie Paige's skateboard and went flying.

But these childhood memories have all been overshadowed by Mom's cancer.

Now, every time I'm here, I feel the weight of her illness like a boulder against my back. She's been gone for two years now, but time isn't the healer we all make it out to be. Even now, the grief—already raw and reignited from this morning's activities—eats away at me, grating at my skin like a scratchy wool sweater.

"I'm here to see a patient," I say with a smile, ignoring his confused look as I place Mom's urn on the counter. "Loretta Karras."

The silver fox behind the desk checks me in and waves me down the same nondescript hallway as the guy before. I take a quick detour to use the restroom. The drive from Santa Barbara to Sunset Springs is a good five hours with traffic, and I hadn't stopped once. Lucky for me the vending machine is directly next to the bathroom, and I grab a Diet Coke and some extra-spicy Takis and set off to find Loretta's hospital room.

After navigating my way through endless hallways, I finally pass the nurses' station and come to her room. The door's cracked just so, and I pause, listening to an angry voice inside rant on about something. I make out only a couple of words, like *unacceptable* and *lawsuit*.

Something about the low rumble of the person on the other side of the door is familiar, but I can't place it, and when I hear Loretta's sharp laugh cut through the air, it makes me grin. She's the epitome of no-nonsense, and I take that as my cue that it is safe to go inside.

"Knock-knock," I say in a singsong voice. Just inside the door is Loretta, propped up in her hospital bed, and she shifts her face toward me with a broad smile as I walk in.

"Bex!" she exclaims in that raspy voice I've grown to treasure. Her eyes are the color of black coffee, and they sparkle like gemstones. Even though her hair's a shocking grayish white, her brows are dark and thick, and they match those of the tall man hovering just by her bedside, contorting his handsome face into a scowl. The same one who had so unceremoniously barged into the hospital just before me.

Of all the people in the world who could claim Loretta as their aunt, did it really have to be this guy?

2

"AGAPI MOU," LORETTA says as she reaches out and taps his arm. The words are in Greek, but I can tell just by her voice that it means something affectionate. "This is Bex. She owns the racquet club."

"Hey," I say quickly. There's no way to miss the glowering look the guy's giving me, like he could laser beam me into space with just the force of his eyes, but I do my best to avoid his death stare and focus all my attention on my friend. "Loretta, I'm so sorry. When Deb called me, I thought she was playing an April Fool's joke on me."

"You should be sorry," he says flatly, and I am irritated to find out that his low, gruff voice is as attractive as his face. "It happened because of your cracked courts."

"Bex," Loretta says, and the patience she exudes with just that one word tells me she's had to take this tone with him before. "This is Nikolaus, my nephew. Can you believe my luck that he just happened to be in Los Angeles this week?"

She focuses her attention back on him, with a sour, exaggerated glare. "And to think you said your trip was too short for you to come visit, and now here you are."

"It's almost like you planned this," he teases, and his face softens up just enough to allow an affectionate smile to appear for a split second.

"I always tell you that family is the most important thing," Loretta replies before turning to me. "I always tell him that. But does he listen?"

"Theia, you're extremely important to me," he assures her, his eyes still gentle. "I just have a tight turnaround this week with training."

"Niko's going back out on tour," Loretta says. "You've seen him play before."

"Wait," I say, as the pieces fall into place instantly. "This is Niko the tennis player?"

Of course, I should have made the connection, but the chaos and emotion of today has clearly impacted my ability to put two and two together. I've watched him play tennis on the TV in Loretta's living room a few times, and I gasped in horror when he stumbled on the court after losing a point in the first round of the French Open two years ago, shattering his knee.

"Yes, her nephew," he interjects. Clearly he's the kind of man who thinks he can speak for a woman, and his elder at that. What an insufferable jerk.

Of course, this behavior totally tracks with what little I know of the guy. He'd been a world-ranked tennis player, somewhere in the top 100 at one point, if I remember Loretta's past gushing correctly. But one fact has stuck in my brain: The man earned the nickname Karras-hole, not because of how hard he hits the ball—which, from what I've seen, is very hard—but how often he tosses his racquet in a toddler-like fit of anger. As far as I can tell, the moniker fits him perfectly.

"And Theia," he says to Loretta. "I'm not back on tour. Yet. I'm just going to play in a qualifier in Miami Memorial Day weekend. I have to make it through that to even get a draw in the tournament."

She brushes him off with a frown and a shake of her head. "They should just let you back on the circuit."

"That would be nice, but that's not exactly how it works," he says.

"Nice to meet you." I stick out one hand, and he shoots me a peeved look, like he'd forgotten I was in the room and then was annoyed that I'd spoken up and reminded him. After a beat, he begrudgingly shakes it with a solid, firm grip.

"Is that..." His eyes narrow for a moment, and his face creases with confusion as he lets go. "An urn?"

I hug it against my chest protectively. "Yes." He deserves only a one-word answer, so that's all I give him.

"Huh," he says, brow furrowing as he scours my face for more information. I change the subject instead.

"Your aunt is one of my best students."

"And friends!" Loretta chirps from the bed.

"And friends," I repeat. Over the last couple of years, we'd become close, thanks to her daily devotion to pickleball and our book club, of which I am the youngest member by roughly forty-five years.

"You didn't have to drive all the way back from Santa Barbara for me," she says, as she tries to adjust her blanket with her one working hand. Loretta and I had delved into grief intensely throughout our friendship, and she knew what my trip was for.

"I know," I reply. I bend to help her, tugging the thin cotton up to her waist, and folding the edge over neatly like my mom taught me to do as a kid. "I wanted to."

Niko interjects, oblivious to the unspoken conversation I'm having with his aunt.

"Well, I would hope any friend of my aunt would care about the courts she's playing on," he grumbles, the muscles in his neck flexing as he speaks. It's a true shame he's this attractive, because his attitude completely spoils his ridiculously good looks.

"Settle down, Nikolaus," she scolds. "Bex is the only reason I'm not cooped up at an old folks' home somewhere. Pickleball is why I get out of the house. You should be thanking her, not yelling at her."

She clucks under her breath and pats my hand apologetically. "He's very protective of me," she explains, as if he wasn't standing inches away from both of us.

"Because you're hurt," he says defensively, running a hand across his furrowed brow with a sigh. "You shouldn't even be playing pickleball at your age."

"Why?" I shift to stand a little straighter, puffing up my chest. It isn't easy to make five-foot-two seem tall, but damn it, I try my best. "Pickleball is actually very accessible for people of all ages and abilities."

"So accessible that she's broken her wrist in two places and is going to have to get surgery tomorrow?" he huffs. "Cracked courts are dangerous."

"And I've already called a couple of contractors to come review all of them, so I can get an estimate for repairs. They just can't get here for a couple of weeks."

Repairs that hopefully won't cost too much, because I'm not sure I can afford them. But I'll figure it out. The club is my family's legacy, my beating heart. Keeping it open will always be my top priority, no matter the cost.

"Or you could tear the whole place down," he grumbles, a cocky smirk unspooling across his face.

"Excuse me?" I take a step forward and feel the weight of his eyes grazing my body, taking in the cropped pink tank that I'd fashioned out of a thrift store find. His insult might as well be directed at me, my character, my very being, and it stings like it's personal, because it is.

"Oh, come off it, Niko," Loretta snaps, ending our standoff. She may be injured, but that doesn't diminish her air of authority, and we both turn to face her, standing at attention. "You sound like a snob. Maybe I don't want you staying in my guesthouse after all."

She says this like a threat, and I watch as Niko pauses and processes her words for a moment before leaning in and planting a kiss on the top of her head.

"Theia, I can't stay. I just told you I'm flying back to Miami tomorrow."

"But you could train at the racquet club," she insists. "Couldn't he, Bex?"

"Um." It's my turn to now be taken aback by the stuff coming out of Loretta's mouth. Surely this is the pain medication talking. "I don't think he'd like our courts, based on what he just said."

Niko nods, relief passing across his face. "Exactly," he agrees. "The qualifier is in eight weeks. Everyone I train with is in Miami."

"Is your family there?" she asks, both pointed and polite all at once. I have to give Loretta some credit; I've never seen this side of her before, and it turns out she is an expert guilt-tripper. "And you just told me you fired your coach."

"I did," he says, and I can hear the patience in his voice waning. "And no, I don't have any family there anymore, as you know."

He's interrupted by Loretta's phone buzzing on the side table pushed up next to her bed. She gives it a quick glance and then looks back up at Niko. "It's your father."

"I'll get it," he says, grabbing the phone and pressing the screen to pick up the call. "Ya, Baba."

He cradles the phone to his ear and wanders off toward the window, muttering quietly in a mix of Greek and English. Loretta relaxes back into the mound of pillows behind her, grimacing as she adjusts her injured arm, which is bound up in a sling.

"He's not normally this cranky," she says apologetically. "I think he's worried about me."

"Isn't he the guy who got famous for smashing his racquet in, like, every match?" I ask. "It seems like cranky would be his default, from what little I know."

"Ah, I hate that that's his reputation," she grumbles, like only a doting aunt can. "I've wiped his tush more times than I can count. He'll always be that sweet little boy to me."

The thought of this prickly, irritable man as a goofy, smiling toddler, being chased around by Loretta, diaper in hand, seems almost impossible to imagine.

Niko finishes up on the phone and comes to stand at the foot of Loretta's bed.

"How's my little brother?" she asks.

"Worried," Niko says, in a tone that tells me this is a common emotion for his dad. "He's going to call you before he goes to bed."

She nods.

"He wants me to stay here, with you, for a little bit," he adds, and Loretta lights up at this. "Until the qualifier, anyway."

"That's my boy." She reaches up and pats his cheek affectionately. "The bed is all made and ready for you in the back house. Now, go ask the nurses if I'm allowed to eat yet. I'm starving."

"Yes, Theia," he agrees and then glances up at me, giving me a stern look that obviously signifies that I'm to follow him outside.

"I'll go call Ed and fill him in," I offer, and she nods. He's another one of my students, the club's oldest member at eighty-one, and Loretta's other best friend. The two of them lost their spouses in the last ten years and have formed an alliance with Deb and her wife, Maureen. They are their own sort of found family and have welcomed me into the fold with open arms.

Niko moves from the room with purpose and shockingly doesn't let the door slam in my face this time. Instead he holds it open and then ushers me out into the hallway. I trail behind him and notice how each step he takes down the hall and away from Loretta's room feels deliberate, like he thinks through every single movement his body makes.

Once we're out of her hearing distance, he spins around to face me. The yellow overhead lights cast him in a strange, unnatural glow, like he's some sort of beautiful, melancholy ghost.

"I could sue you, you know." I shouldn't be taken aback because he certainly isn't the first person to threaten litigation against the club in its nearly thirty years of existence. But this isn't just any man; it's Loretta's nephew. She's one of the warmest people I know, and if they didn't have the exact same eyebrows and dark fringe of lashes, I'd be shocked that they're related.

"No, you couldn't." I say this brightly, with a chomp of my gum, which has lost all its flavor since I popped it in an hour ago. I've met my share of men who think they can push me around, and pushing them right back is one of life's greatest pleasures. "Every client has signed a very detailed waiver. And the club is insured up the ass."

He scoffs at this, but it shuts him up.

"Look, I love Loretta—" I start, and he cuts me off.

"I love her, too. She's literally the only relative I have left here in the States now that my parents are back in Greece. She's practically my entire family."

Niko crosses his arms and paces away from me, grumbling

under his breath. "I can't believe she hurt herself so badly playing such an idiotic sport."

He's loud enough so that I can hear every single word.

"Excuse me." I grab his arm, forcing him to look directly at me. "Aren't you the person who cracked his entire knee open a few years ago while literally having a tantrum on a tennis court?"

The look of disbelief he gives me makes me chuckle.

"What, you don't think I know your whole story? Even if Loretta wasn't constantly talking about her 'amazing nephew Nikolaus'"—I make sure he can hear the sarcasm in my voice and make quotation marks with my fingers just to really drive home the point—"it would be pretty hard not to know who you are. She just didn't mention you were a jerk *off* the court, too."

Niko used to be everywhere in the tennis world. He surprised everyone when he qualified for the US Open as a lower-tier player on UCLA's varsity team. This underdog story rocketed him to micro-stardom, and even though he never made it very far in a Grand Slam tournament, he remained a favorite in the game and moved in and out of the top 100 ranking players in the world. That was until two years ago, when he blew out his knee and his whole career.

"She's probably the only person who doesn't think that," he cracks with a slight twist of his lips, cocking one of those pitch-black brows at me.

I decide there's no point in bickering with this man, and I say a silent vow to myself that I will avoid him at all costs after today.

"Well, good luck finding a place to train while you're here." I give him a polite smile. "It was nice meeting you."

He quiets for a moment, staring down the hall toward Loretta's room, and then back at me. "You're the only private club close to Loretta's house," he says finally. "I googled. The next closest one is Starlight."

"Yeah, I'm well aware," I snap. Starlight's remodeled club lounge and state-of-the-art pickleball courts are a big reason membership is down for us. It seems like the perfect place for Niko, who clearly thinks the club and our cracked courts are beneath him. "It's very fancy. You'll love it there."

"I need something close if I'm also taking Loretta to doctor's appointments," he says, and a knot materializes in the center of my stomach as it dawns on me what he's saying and not saying.

"I thought you wouldn't dare set a foot on my crappy courts," I counter.

"Yeah, well, it's not like I have a choice," he says, and he sounds just as annoyed by this as I am.

"I'll need my own court every day, from about eight to five." He says this as if it's nothing, like he's ordering a Crunchwrap Supreme at Taco Bell.

"Wait, you're serious?" I narrow my eyes at him, making sure I'm following what he's saying. "Oh god, you *are* serious."

Niko ignores my groan and glares off over my shoulder.

"I'll need a ball machine too," he says finally.

"It'll cost you," I reply, and he just nods.

"I have the money. I just need some space to practice for a few weeks while I'm here."

"Whatever you wish, Tennis Prince." Today I'm wearing one of the first athletic skirts I've ever upcycled—a white Wilson number from the eighties I've added patchwork to, and I lift it slightly, giving him a mocking curtsey. "I'll tell my staff at the club to have your throne installed tomorrow."

Joke's on him, I think to myself. I *am* the staff.

And with that, I spin on my heel and march back down the hallway, away from the most arrogant man I've ever met.

I'm almost back at reception when I remember that my car's dead, stuck on the second floor of the hospital parking garage, and I stopped paying for AAA last year. Deb's covering the desk at the club, so I can't call her for a ride, and I'd rather not pay for a taxi if I can help it. I freeze, debating for a moment what the best course of action is, and then realize I have no other choice. I turn around, shoulders sunk in defeat, and walk back toward Loretta's room to find Niko still lurking, now angrily tapping out a text message on his phone.

Before he can see me, I sneak back around the corner and start mapping a path home on my phone. Two miles walking in the desert sun, clutching the remains of my mother? It will suck, but it is better than groveling at the feet of that jerk.

There's nothing I hate more than asking for help, though Niko Karras and his perma-frown are now a very close second.

3

Friday, April 14

MY MOM HAD a very simple philosophy for winning at pickleball.

1. The game is always played defensively, no matter which team is trying to get the point.
2. You don't need to move fast; you only need to think fast.
3. You must, at all costs, try to ignore the extremely sexy sounds Niko makes when he's playing tennis on the court next to you.

Jesus, what? That's not it at all. Get it together, Bex.

Ahem. The third rule is *Think of the paddle as an extension of your arm.*

It's just kinda hard to remember Mom's coaching advice with Niko grunting aggressively mere feet away, his damp black hair swept back away from his face with a white sweatband as he pounds the tennis ball with his racquet over and over and over again—

"Ten, eight, two!" Deb hollers the score of our lesson scrimmage from the other side of the court and snaps me out of my lusty daze. The neon yellow ball rockets over the net, demanding I pay attention to my actual job of teaching pickleball and not the way Niko's snow-white collared shirt sticks to his broad shoulders in the sweltering Sunset Springs heat.

"Nice serve!" My paddle connects with the ball with a satisfyingly audible crack, a sound I instinctively know, after two weeks of playing next to him, that Niko can't stand. He's constantly whining about how loud pickleball is, and the thought of possibly chipping away at his serial killer focus reinvigorates me. I dash the last few steps toward the net, my bright pink skirt fluttering in the arid wind, as I stop just in front of the white line that marks the part of the court known as the kitchen.

Ed is already up at the net, and he dinks the ball—the pickleball term for a low lob over the net—back at me. It should be an easy shot to return. It's one I've nailed a thousand times since my mom first dragged me out to play back in junior high, right after she herself painted the regulation lines of a pickleball court in almost the exact spot where I'm standing today.

Taking my time, I extend my paddle back behind me confidently, and for a moment, I can't believe I was ever worried for a second about Niko distracting me today.

Clear eyes, full heart, can't—

"*Uh!*" That voice rumbles low and deep somewhere off to my left, a guttural sound that drips with so much raw sex appeal that my whole body twitches in response. Unfortunately for me, this includes my arm, which is, as Mom always said, part of my paddle. It's almost like she's here right now shouting it in my ear.

Almost.

I whiff the ball awkwardly and pop it high up in the air, an amateur move. After Loretta, Deb is one of my most seasoned students, and she reminds me of this by smacking the ball with the kind of vigor I did not realize seventysomethings possessed until I started coaching pickleball. It whizzes by me like a bullet, and I miss the return shot completely, handing her and Ed the final point.

"Ugh, you guys win again!" I fall to my knees dramatically, play-acting like the sore loser tennis players I used to watch with Mom on TV as a kid. According to the tennis message boards I've picked through over the last two weeks, it's the exact kind of move Niko was notorious for when he played on the professional circuit. Not that I'm surprised; no one who scowls as much as he does could possibly lose gracefully.

"That's it, lesson over. I can't handle this humiliation." Groaning, I flop onto my back, the ancient, faded court warm with the seasoning of the sun as I blow a giant bubble of gum through my glossed lips. I'm a Trident Wintergreen obsessive, and there's nothing my dentist can say to get me to stop chomping it constantly.

With a whoop, I fling my giant straw sun hat in the air,

splaying my arms wide out by my side in defeat. My outfit has the air of a preschooler's painting project—lots of color, minimal thought—just how I like it. Cropped vintage Rod Stewart T-shirt and the pink athletic skirt that I sewed specifically to complement the new fuchsia streak lighting up my otherwise bland, straw-colored hair. I'm pretty sure my socks are mismatched too, but luckily they're low and barely visible from the electric-blue sneakers I scored on super sale at Tennis Warehouse in Riverside.

When I finally swing back around to sit, elbows on my knees, I find Deb packing up her bag and Loretta chuckling from the bench as she watches me, tipping a giant water bottle to her lips. She stayed away from the club immediately after her surgery, but on Monday, she texted me "I'm so bored!" and then next thing I knew, Niko was pulling up in front of the center, unloading her from the passenger seat of his rented Audi.

Niko. He peers at me from the adjacent court, and even though his eyes are unreadable, I can tell from the way his brows furrow downward that he's judging me, as usual. I've diligently studied his movements since he showed up in Sunset Springs, hunting for some glimmer of something in him other than pure, unfiltered arrogance. My research thus far has been fruitless, even though his reputation as a difficult, stubborn a-hole on the court precedes him, especially after the video of his career-ending knee injury went viral online. "Temper-tantruming tennis star trips and busts knee after tossing his racquet, in a sure sign that karma is indeed real," read one mocking internet headline.

And there were plenty more like that, an endless supply

of Instagram posts, TikTok videos, and news articles that detailed everything from the fast rise of his professional career to one poorly played match he blamed on the quality of his socks. His socks! Almost every single one mentioned his moody, grumpy demeanor both on and off the court. A few even alleged that he planted such items himself in an attempt to craft his own notorious image.

But he was Loretta's nephew, and I adored her, so how bad could he possibly be?

That bad, it turns out.

"What's wrong, Nikolaus?" I hop up and offer him my most obnoxious grin before bending over to dust the fine desert sand off my knees. The stuff is everywhere out here. "Not used to seeing someone exhibit pure, unbridled joy before?"

His gaze slides down the length of my body, and a shiver runs through me despite all my better instincts. I would never admit it out loud, but these days, I feel desperate for any sort of hungry glance in my direction, even if it comes from the most miserable man I've ever met. My love life since moving back home after college is sadly a lot like Sunset Springs: a literal dry spell. My hometown may be a retiree's paradise, but it's a nightmare for a twenty-six-year-old single woman with a healthy sex drive.

Not that I didn't want to be here. Moving back in with my mom immediately after graduating from college hadn't exactly been part of my life plan any more than cancer had been a part of hers. But we were all each other had, and there was nowhere else I'd have rather been than by her side throughout the entire journey.

It was never a question of if I would take over the center. During that final summer of her life, before she entered hospice, we'd sit out on court 8—her favorite—in two old lawn chairs, watching the sunset over the jagged mountains. We'd talk about mundane things, club business mostly, but I knew that she was trying to set me up, in her own way, so that I could handle things when she was gone.

I just wish I had known then how much work it was going to be, how in over my head I would feel at times.

"God, your dad and I had no idea what we were doing when we redid the courts with asphalt," she said to me on one particularly good night, just after the sun had melted into the horizon, leaving behind a trail of orange-pink sky. "We should have thought more about what would last long-term."

"Yeah, but you guys didn't have any money when you bought this place. That's just what made the most sense at the time," I said defensively, protective of the family lore I'd heard my entire life. "It was either asphalt or concrete."

"Well, there's nothing we can do about it right now." She put on a rosy face, but it looked less like genuine optimism and more like masked panic. "We still don't have the money."

"You could always sell pictures of your feet," I joked, and she recoiled with a horrified laugh.

"You've seen my bunions, Bex," she huffed. "You're just lucky you didn't inherit them."

"I just got your height and humor." I stood up and slid my chair closer to hers, so that I could wrap an arm around her, my head tucked into her shoulder like a puzzle piece, proving my point. The exact same size, each topping out at a whopping five foot two.

"I like this," she said, tugging at the strand of blue hair that framed my face. "But then again I like all your colors."

"How did I end up with a mom who encourages experimenting with hair dye? I thought you were supposed to try to talk me out of such things."

"Bex, you have always been colorful, and I wouldn't have it any other way."

There was a pause, a brief moment of sad stillness, and then she'd added, "Your dad too, I just know it."

Sunset Springs Racquet Club was small but mighty, my parents' pride and joy—and let's be real, their other child—for almost thirty years. Mom once made a crack about how I was conceived on one of these courts after they celebrated closing on the place with a bottle of champagne, and judging from how in love my mom always described the two of them, I believed it.

My throat clenches ever so slightly as I try to let go of the memory of her, still so tender and raw. Just then Niko saunters over, pointing his racquet at the long crack that zigzags the length of the net, directly under my feet. "The court's getting worse."

"Yeah, well, we can't all have U-C-L-A's gold-star facilities," I mug, deliberately dragging out the syllables of his alma mater's name as slowly as possible. "Some people think it adds charm."

"You would," he says with a grimace, as he stretches a long, tanned arm across his chest, muscles flexing, and I feel that surge of frustration that always surfaces whenever I try to talk to him.

"I'm sorry, what's that supposed to mean?" Sometimes he is such a classic, pompous jock that, if you told me he'd walked directly out of an eighties movie and right into present day, I'd believe you.

"You dress like a fireworks display," he says with an aloof shrug.

Every time his eyes land on me, I feel the weight of his disgust hit me like an ocean current. It's been obvious since day one what he thinks about me, the pickleball player stuck in her hometown, always a little too noisy, too bright, and too much. I like this about myself; I'm not ashamed of who I am or how I act. But I was mortified that I'd somehow allowed this random man, a mere stranger to me weeks ago, to have the power to make me feel like I should be.

I retaliate by doing something I know will drive him nuts and blow a bubble in his direction and then pop it loudly, delighting when he winces at the sound.

"So what you're saying is that you'd rather I dress like..." I trail off, hands on my hips as I pretend to examine his outfit. "A human tablecloth? A virginal bride on her wedding day? A—"

"They're *tennis whites*, Bex." He shuffles on his feet, and when I look back up at his face I notice his brows shifting as he watches me. For a moment he even looks nervous. Good.

"They're *boring*." It's not the best insult, but it'll do.

"I think you're just not used to seeing people in things that match." He rubs a hand along the edge of his jaw, scratching at the shadow of a beard that somehow makes the angles of his face look even more razor-sharp.

"Rude!" I reply with a roll of my eyes. "Retta, did you hear what your nephew said?"

"Typical tennis player!" Loretta jokes, giving Niko a playful look. She adores him, but I chalk it up to them being blood relatives. No one on earth could voluntarily like Niko otherwise, especially someone as warm as she is.

"It's almost five o'clock! We better hit the road," Ed says with a smack of his hands on his thighs, as he slowly rises off the bench next to Loretta. "The grocery store calls."

"I am expecting a charcuterie board tonight, Ed," I tease. "You know I can't play mah-jongg unless I'm stuffed full of cured meats, and I have a ton of emails to get through before I can come over. Expect a ravenous competitor."

The words come out sounding overeager and excited to be invited, which, honestly, I still kind of am. When Loretta invited me to join their weekly game last winter, it had been my first social interaction since…well, forever.

"You know you're welcome to join us," he cajoles Niko, who's still hovering a few feet away, arms across his chest. "I'm sure Bex is dying to beat you."

Niko shakes his head, and I feel a twinge of embarrassment as he's reminded of the fact that a group of septuagenarians picked up on my glaring lack of a social life and took pity on me.

"I've got conditioning tonight." He gestures to the basket of tennis balls next to him. Conditioning, as I've learned in the two weeks that he's been here, is something he does most nights, when it's cool and crisp outside. It involves him doing a bunch of speed drills on the court, and then setting up the automatic ball machine and playing against it for hours, sometimes until the court lights shut off at eleven. "And then I have a call with a reporter who's doing a story on me for the *LA Times*."

This piques my curiosity, but I don't indulge it, knowing it would almost surely crank up his ego another notch. Instead, I give him an overly pleasant forced smile. "Remind me, how many more weeks do we have the pleasure of you being here?" I ask.

"Six," he says, giving me a wolfish scowl. "Are you already sad I'm leaving?"

"No, just counting the days and wanted to make sure I mark my calendar accordingly."

The two of us pause as Loretta, Ed, and Deb leave the court, and it's quiet for a moment, a silent standoff.

Niko is the first one to break. "Have a great time with your fellow old folks."

He cracks into a smile that's anything but warm.

"And *you* enjoy your hot date with the ball machine," I quip, turning on my heel with a wave. "I hope you get lucky."

"At least that'll be one of us," he mutters back at me, jogging off before I can get the last word in. I spend the rest of the walk to the front office trying to think of a comeback to put him in his place but come up empty and instead fixate way too long about the sounds he must be making out alone on the court.

4

"YOU'RE LOOKING AT four thousand, maybe more, depending."

Travis, the first contractor to come survey the damaged ancient courts, crouches on his knees, studying the faded asphalt with a toothpick dangling from his mouth. He got here just as Ed and Loretta left, and he's spent the last hour nailing down an estimate for repairing the courts. I try desperately to ignore the dreaded tightening across my shoulders as he walks me through the cost of everything.

"Total?" I ask, leaning over his shoulder. For a split second, I feel naïvely optimistic. Four thousand dollars is shockingly low, and while it would hurt financially, it wouldn't totally torpedo our already depleted budget.

He lets out a low chuckle and then tilts his straw sun hat up to get a better look at me through his mirrored, knock-off Ray-Bans. When he slides them down his nose, his eyes—both kind and matter-of-fact—tell me everything

I need to know: I sound inexperienced at best and delusional at worst. "Per court, I hate to tell you. And that's if we don't need to do extra patching on the crack repair. Four thousand is on the low end, really."

Four thousand dollars, multiplied by eight courts. The number sinks to the bottom of my stomach like a coin dropped into a well, but there's no luck to be found here. If only I had something I could wish on right now, some magical, moneymaking genie in a bottle that could swoop in and save the day.

"Oh shit," I mutter, the panic evident in my voice. Just a few weeks ago, I finally finished paying off Mom's medical and funeral bills, and that took two years. The club's membership is down, and we are barely breaking even. I've struggled with the learning curve that comes with taking over a small business, on top of doing it while grieving my mom.

There is no way in hell I can scrape up enough money to cover thirty-two thousand dollars' worth of repairs.

A memory that has played over in my head for the last couple of years resurfaces. Mom, tucked into the hospital bed we installed in her tiny living room, turning to me and saying, "You could always sell the club. Wilson Hood is interested."

"Absolutely not," I said with a teary shudder.

I feel the same today as I did then. Letting go of the club wouldn't be just letting go of a business; it would be like losing my mom all over again. Not to mention the countless members and players who have come to see the club as a second home. This place is so intrinsically a part of her, of me, of them, that it feels unnatural to even consider it, especially handing it over to Wilson, who owns Starlight Tennis Center, our main competitor.

But now I get why she suggested selling the place. The courts aren't the only things in need of repair; the bathrooms are outdated, the plumbing finicky, the building structure in need of a serious paint job and earthquake-proofing. The club is close to veering into money pit territory.

Still, there is no way I can let it go. It isn't fancy, or perfect, but it had been my parents', and then my mom's. And now, it's mine.

Thirty-two thousand dollars.

I'm overcome by a very strong urge to vomit all over Travis's head.

Somehow I manage to grit my teeth and hold it together. "I still need to get some estimates from a few other companies. And then I'll let you know!"

This façade of confidence has carried me through the last two years of managing the club on my own. Most of the time, I'd successfully faked it until I made it, but something about this current situation felt different. Scarier.

That evening, alone in front of the computer at the front desk, I feel anything but self-assured. I chew on the tail end of my braid as the sky settles toward sunset and scan the detailed budgets from past years that my mom had meticulously kept in QuickBooks. Coaching clients and keeping members happy comes naturally to me, but juggling the numbers is something I'm still trying—and most often failing—to master.

Even though I was raised in this business, it still seems like I have no clue what I'm doing, and I loathe the feeling. It triggers pangs of shame and inadequacy that first bloomed in me as a little kid. I spent all of my childhood thinking I was simply super disorganized and scatterbrained, until one of my college professors wisely suggested that I be tested for ADHD during my freshman year. *Ding-ding-ding!*

My diagnosis was clarifying and freeing, and with proper medication and the right tools and systems, I learned to work with my ADHD, not against it. Executive function has always been hard for me, and so now I handle it by being extra on top of things. While most people have one personal calendar, I have two (digital and paper), plus a to-do list on my bed-side table and at the front desk, just in case I miss something. I've always joked that I am Type A(DHD), but the tag does kind of sum me up perfectly. I pay extra attention to details because it's so hard for my brain to hold on to them. Not that my ADHD is a hindrance, or something I feel bad about. It's my superpower, really. I may miss some stuff or have a hard time processing directions, but I'm exhaustingly creative and wildly passionate about the things I love.

All of these traits went into overdrive when Mom got sick, which is a thing I've learned happens when you become a caregiver for someone. The skills you once channeled into other parts of your life are redirected and beamed like a spot-light onto the person you're caring for. This leaves all your other responsibilities lingering in the shadows, collecting dust, until the caregiving is, well, done.

And with Mom gone, I jumped right into running the club just like I did tending to her. I was all action, funneling all my churning, heavy sorrow into taking care of this place.

The racquet club wasn't just where I'd grown up; it was the beating heart of my family. The few memories I have of my dad all involve this place, and the unconditional love of our family is woven tightly into the very soul of the club, just like the strings of a tennis racquet.

I love it here because it's a part of me that I can't live without, as vital to my existence as my organs.

But lately, work is all I do.

Take today, for example. I spent the day coaching lessons, which I've been doing since two days after my college graduation. In between sessions, I restocked the towels, filled up the water coolers, and checked in with members playing out on the courts, making sure everyone was happy. This had been my routine for years, but taking over Mom's side of things meant that I spent my nighttime hours handling all the emails, the marketing, and the drafting of our next club newsletter.

And the finances. God, the finances. I desperately need to hire a bookkeeper. "Add it to the list!" I say out loud, to no one. And then, "With what money?"

A swell of despair bubbles up through my chest, engulfing me. It feels like I've been playing a constant game of catch-up ever since assuming responsibility for the club, and no matter what I do, I never get ahead. There's no way the courts are getting repaired anytime soon. We have no money to spare, and the revenue we'd lose during construction would only put us deeper in the hole.

I was so certain that I'd have no problem taking over the reins that I am only now realizing just how in over my head I am.

A tap on the front door startles me out of my panicked daze. "What the hell?" I mutter, blood racing.

Wilson Hood's face peers at me through the glass, and I press my lips together, trying to hide my annoyance. Being the owner of the ostentatious Starlight Tennis Center, just twenty minutes away, made him our competition, and so I'd always viewed him as a thorn in our club's side. He'd come to pickleball years after my mom, once he realized what a cash cow it could be. Of course, Wilson didn't half-ass it; the guy doesn't half-ass anything. Instead he'd gone full-hog—installing brand-new, cutting-edge courts with a special bouncy surface that supposedly makes game play better. His latest gamble—a members-only spa and café—earned him way more press than I'd expected, and I'm terrible at hiding my irritation and envy when it comes to this man.

Wilson has been expanding his pickleball empire in the last few years and picked up another center closer to San Diego a few months ago. He's stopped by a bunch since Mom died, to pay his respects, sure, and to "check in" on me. But I'm positive he's sniffing around this place, trying to see what's happening now that I'm in charge. If he catches on that we're in financial trouble, there's no doubt he'll try to swoop in and snag the club. *My* club.

I warm with a heated, carnal urge to protect this place; fierce mama bear energy, like I'm the only person who can save it.

"Well, this is unexpected," I say, after unlatching the lock on the door.

"Hey there, Bex," he says, with a scratch of the gray

stubble on his face, a wide gold band with diamonds glinting on his middle finger. "Just popping by on my way home after dinner downtown with some friends. I was hoping you'd hang this up for me."

I hadn't noticed the flyer in his hands, but now he's dangling it in my face, close enough that I have to shuffle back a step to read the bright-green lettering.

THE STARLIGHT TENNIS CENTER
PADDLE BATTLE—MAY 20

"Starlight's stepping in as the host of this new tournament next month," he explains. "Amateurs only, so I thought some of your members might want to enter. We're sponsored, so the prize money is..." His hands fly up to his head as he flutters his lips to make a sound like an explosion, like he can't believe the number. "And we're auctioning off a chance to double up with a big celebrity player for an exhibition match, with a hundred percent of that going to the food bank downtown. Lots of press coming, too. Should be the biggest pickleball tournament in the desert, so far."

"That's nice," I say, scanning the paper. "Mom used to volunteer there. She'd like that." My voice is forced but polite. Mom would expect me to be respectful of Wilson, someone our family's known for years. But she's not here anymore, and the independent streak that runs through me pounds like thunder. I waffle between wanting to honor her wishes and make my own decisions.

"You know, maybe you might want to get in on the

tournament, give those old folks a run for their money?" he asks. I prickle as he playfully punches me on the shoulder like I'm still the little kid he knew years ago. "You and your mom used to kick some butt."

"Oh god, I don't know. I haven't played competitively in so long," I say, as I fiddle with the edge of the flyer. "Not since college, anyway. And I don't have a partner. Or time."

"Well, if you want to sign up, do it soon," he cautions, but it comes across like boasting. "I've never had this much interest in a tournament before. People are clamoring for chances to play pickleball competitively. Especially amateurs. It's going to be huge."

"I'll spread the word," I say, and then slip back around the desk to my spot in front of the computer.

Wilson studies me for a moment, his face switching into something a bit more condescending or, if I'm being generous, parental. "How's the dink life treating you these days, kid?"

"I mean, I work eighteen-hour days, but otherwise, pretty great," I say with a laugh, and Wilson chuckles. His skin seems smoother than I remember, and I wonder if he's gotten some secret cosmetic procedure to help him age backward. He appears shiny and freshly polished, just like all his clubs.

"You know, Bex, your mom and I talked about me stepping in and taking over the club a few years back, before she even got sick. I'm looking to expand, and I've been around this block a few times. I know how hard it is to handle a place like this on your own, especially at your age. I could make a good offer, take this all off your hands so you could go live your life."

"I really appreciate that," I say with a nod, giving him my most professional face. "But I'm doing great."

"And the club?" His face is light, but I can see his brows twitch just a little, revealing his skepticism.

"Oh, fantastic," I lie, my tone so convincing that I almost believe it myself, despite what a bunch of spreadsheets say.

There's no way I'd ever consider selling, much less to Wilson, whose clubs resemble bloated, ornate McMansions. Just the thought of him putting an organic juice bar in the lobby here makes me shudder. I wouldn't even be able to afford a cold-pressed beet juice if Wilson ran the club, much less a membership.

Determination settles in my chest, pushing all the worry and anxiety out for now. I'm going to figure this out on my own to prove to myself that I can, truly, handle this. Wilson gives me a dubious look, and I grind my teeth together and flash him the brightest, most assertive smile I've ever forced onto my face. "Trust me," I say, crossing my arms. "I've got everything under control here."

Now I just have to figure out exactly how the hell to do that.

5

"WHAT'S WRONG, BEX?"

I've been so engrossed in plotting how to come up with a pile of money that I don't hear Niko prowl into the office until he's hovering above me, elbows on the counter, his giant dark eyes glowering.

"Huh?" I say, disoriented by the stress of number-crunching.

"You look like you just found out there are only seven colors in the rainbow," he replies with a flat smirk, his lips forming a plateau on the horizon of that perfectly angled face.

"Very funny," I deadpan, watching the way his neck muscles ripple as he gulps from a massive water bottle the size of his head. He is drenched in sweat, black hair tousled under that stupid white sweatband, and even though he's no longer on the court, his chest is panting slightly like he's still recovering from an intense practice.

He looks like a wild animal caught on someone's doorbell

camera in the middle of the night, and his eyes linger a second too long on my face. "Seriously, are you okay?"

"Yes, I'm fine, Niko. Thank you for asking." I try not to ever let on with him, or anyone, really, that I'm struggling, but I can hear the exasperation evident in my voice. Tonight everything just feels like too much, and I can't hide it. "Have a good night."

He glances down at his watch and scrubs a small white towel against the back of his neck in thought, before eyeing the flyer Wilson left, still on the reception desk.

"Paddle Battle," he reads off the paper. "God, even the names for pickleball tournaments are ridiculous."

"Well, it's a good thing you're leaving us soon." I tuck my hand under my chin, giving him a giant, fake smile. "You'll never have to think about pickleball again."

"The thought devastates me."

He matches my absurd, toothy grin with his own, his teeth as shockingly white as his head-to-toe outfit. It's obvious he's as full of shit as I am.

We stay like that for a quiet moment, the two of us locked in yet another staring standoff, and it's enough time to register just how golden his skin has gotten playing outside these last two weeks. Every part of him not covered by clothing glistens, like he's purposefully trying to highlight all the deliciously strong parts of himself. It's not just his muscles; his cheekbones are so cut they look like they could bench press two hundred pounds. It would be so much easier to loathe him if he wasn't so shockingly attractive.

And I'd never admit it, but our little moments of bickering

have become the most fun part of my day. I love to act like I hate Niko, but it is becoming harder and harder to convince myself that I actually do.

"How are you getting to Loretta's for your mah-jongg game?" he asks, breaking our connection and effectively ending our latest duel.

"I'm walking," I say haughtily. I spent a ridiculous chunk of money getting my car towed to the mechanic, where it is sitting, pathetically waiting for me to be able to afford repairs.

"Come on. I'll give you a ride," he says, nodding toward the front door. "It is literally on my way home."

"Nah, it's fine." I wave him off. "I need to move my body. I've been behind this desk for too long anyway."

"It's nine o'clock at night, Bex." More glowering.

"I know how to tell time, Tennis Prince."

"Right." He gives me a look of pure exasperation. "So let me give you a ride, *Pickleball Princess*."

"Fine!" I growl, as I hop up and grab the flyer. I press it up to the bulletin board and stab it with a push pin. "*Fine.* I will accept your incredibly generous offer."

And that is how I end up in the passenger seat of Niko's car.

The inside of his rented Audi two-door is immaculate. Of course it is. Clean black leather, spotless vacuumed floors. Meanwhile, even when it's functioning, my ancient Prius looks like a family of raccoons threw a three-day-long rave inside it. It is a museum devoted to wrappers and crumpled tissues, and every coffee cup I've ever used can be found wedged somewhere under its passenger seat.

But his car is serene, like it could double as a meditation studio. It smells faintly of pine and cleaning solution, and there's even a tiny little trash can in the cup holder.

"How fancy," I cluck and tap the lid with my fingertip as he pulls out of the parking lot. "I love your devotion to cleanliness. And in a rental, of all things."

His eyes stay locked on the road because he's incapable of anything but linear, relentless focus, but he lets out a little laugh, a soft rasp that sounds sexier than it should. What is it with this man and the noises that come out of his mouth? I grew up hanging around the racquet club, listening to players groan and grunt for years without the faintest hint of attraction. But for the past two weeks, the sounds he makes have lodged under my skin like a painful, sexy splinter. Something is seriously wrong with me.

"You know what they say about people with clean cars, right?" He asks this with a hint of a smile, and if it were anyone other than Niko, I'd assume he's attempting to flirt. But I cancel that thought immediately because I'm confident his feelings toward me hover somewhere around barely tolerable on a good day.

"That they're serial killers?" I taunt, and I study his profile as it flashes in and out of darkness thanks to the streetlights along the road.

"That they're perfectionists," he corrects me. "Your car is a reflection of the rest of your life. The theory is that if your small space is disorganized, so is every other aspect of your world."

"How predictable," I huff. It sounds like something he

learned on some stupid bro wellness podcast. "I thought for sure it would be something like 'people with clean cars have dirty mouths.'"

My attempt to get a rise out of him fails, so I change course.

"I've always thought disorganization was a sign of creativity and imagination," I tell him. "My apartment is covered in scraps of cloth, but I made this skirt last night, so I must be doing something right."

"You made that skirt?" he asks, and this revelation is enough for him to flick his eyes toward me for a brief second.

I wait for a beat before replying, expecting some other dig to roll off his tongue. But the silence just stretches, and his face looks expectant and patient, all lit up by the constellation of tiny lights on his dashboard panel.

"I did," I say, considering how much information to offer. "I make a lot of my pickleball clothes. It's relaxing."

I trail off, not wanting to give him too much ammo to work with. We spend hours together every day at the club, but our conversations are either filled with polite chitchat or mindless bickering, and this admission makes me feel oddly vulnerable. Concocting designs and sewing up pieces has been my main form of self-care since Mom died, the best escape at the end of a long day. I love the feeling of my brain zoning out, my hands working as if in a trance. It is creative and soothing and has come to mean more to me than I first realized.

In the last six months, I've become especially invested in scouring the desert's overflowing thrift stores and making new garments out of people's discarded clothes. There's something magical about breathing new life into an old skirt or ratty pair of pants, finding a piece of clothing someone deemed useless, ready to be tossed, and discovering an entirely new identity for it. The process strikes me as beautiful and hopeful, an antidote to my stress and sorrow. I do it solely for myself, to keep my mind off the harder things.

"That's cool" is all he says, and I take that as an opening for more conversation.

"You know, I like that about pickleball," I add. "That it's a sport that embraces its weirdness. No one cares what you wear on the court."

This is what had finally convinced me to start playing in eighth grade, when Mom started offering lessons at the club. She'd let me play in my Vans and torn skinny jeans, and I'd fallen in love with pickleball instantly, wholeheartedly, with my entire being.

Tennis had never quite clicked for me as a kid, and my mom's disappointment had been evident, even though she'd never said a word. She'd always encouraged me to follow my own interests, but that didn't mean that I still couldn't sense her persistent hope that I'd one day become even a fraction as obsessed with tennis as she and my dad had been. But everything about the sport had bored me out of my mind. It felt stuffy and pretentious, and I could barely focus on one match, much less play a whole set.

But god, how pickleball had worked with my excitement-seeking brain. Quick matches, constant movement, and rules that just made sense to me. Chitchat wasn't just allowed on the court—it was encouraged! Picking up that paddle was the first time I felt truly at home in a sport, like it was my second skin.

Niko snorts a kind of half laugh, half objection, and whatever softness I felt for him moments ago is shoved aside by familiar irritation.

"What?" My shoulders tighten, the defensiveness an old friend. "You can't handle the weirdness of pickleball?"

"It's not that," he says, with a shake of his head. "What I can't handle is when people call something a sport even though it's clearly not. I'd say pickleball is maybe a hobby, and that's on a good day."

"Excuse me." I turn in my seat to stare him down. "Playing mah-jongg with a bunch of seventy-year-olds is *a hobby.* Pickleball is literally the fastest-growing sport in the United States."

Sure, this is a stat thrown around by every pickleball fanatic at least forty-five times a day. But it is also true. Pickleball's popularity is undeniable. We get twice as many requests for pickleball lessons and court rentals at the club as we do for tennis, a fact that I could easily rub in his face right now if I wanted.

"I know," he says, "but it's also *literally* a game a couple of old drunk guys made up to play with their kids when they couldn't find the right racquets for a round of badminton."

"Paddles," I correct him, grasping for any easy way to annoy him.

He shoots a peeved look in my direction—mission accomplished—and then stares forward without saying a word. With a flick of his wrist, he yanks off his sweatband and tosses it in the back seat behind him, dragging one of those giant, calloused hands through his hair.

The air in the car suddenly feels hot despite the AC blasting.

"Do you know how self-righteous you sound?" I mutter, crossing my arms in front of my chest. "You're like every other tennis snob who thinks they're too good for pickleball."

"I don't think I'm too good for it." His voice is a low grumble, and I hate how much I like it. "I just don't want to play a game that requires you to stand in something called the kitchen. It's immature."

"It's *fun* is what it is, Niko. I know you're not familiar with the concept, but fun is this thing people experience with other people, where they socialize and have a good time."

Maybe it's the surprise appearance from Wilson or the stress of the club's dwindling finances, but I'm extra raw tonight, and his insults about pickleball stab at something deeply personal. "And you don't stand *in* the kitchen," I add. "That's a penalty. Unless the ball bounces in it first."

"See?" He waves a hand up, arguing his point. "That doesn't even make sense. Tennis is a logical game. And it requires actual athletic skill."

His tone is straight-up high school debate captain, all smug and knowing.

"Wow. Do you have any more compliments you wanna throw my way?" I snap. I know, somewhere in the rational part of my brain, that this anger isn't really about Niko at all or my undying devotion to the game of pickleball. It is about the longing I feel for my mother's presence, the way my fingers still itch to dial her number. It's about how much I love the racquet club and how much I fear losing it. How life feels fraught and terrifying and completely out of my control.

But it's way easier to funnel it here, to dump it all on this person next to me.

And so that's exactly what I do.

"I'm just saying, it's not a real sport." He lets out a chuckle, and the sound is both sexy and cocky. I'm not sure which makes me more annoyed. Or turned on.

"Yeah, it *is*," I protest, and I feel impassioned, galvanized, like I'm arguing on behalf of every person who's ever so much as glanced at a pickleball. "There are professionals, rankings, tournaments. People are beating down the doors of tennis clubs, but it's not to play tennis. One day, you might even want to play, but no one will want to be your partner with that attitude. Though I guess I shouldn't be surprised that someone who's known for being an *ass* on the tennis court would be the same about pickleball."

He slows the car as we near Loretta's angular, sixties-style house, pulling into the curved driveway that cuts like a U through the cactus-covered front yard. I'm fuming and silent as he shifts into park, before turning to look at me as I unbuckle my seat belt.

"Well, luckily, I don't plan on ever playing pickleball," he says in a monotone voice. His entire gaze is on me, but it's equally unreadable.

"That's too bad," I say, gripping the handle of the door. "Because I bet you'd be really, really good. Maybe even better than at tennis."

I don't mean it as a dig, but a flicker crosses his face, almost like it's hurt him unintentionally. He's been mostly quiet about his training, not talking much about whatever this mysterious qualifier is in Miami. But I know enough about his past career to know that Niko was once an incredible tennis player. He'd been good, good enough to be labeled a "rising star" by news outlets, to rack up tens of thousands of Instagram followers, and to land an endorsement deal with an energy drink, before disaster struck his knee and put a stop to all of it.

I know all of this, but I feel an inkling of guilt for poking a painful part of him without meaning to, and so I say nothing except "Thanks for the ride."

I reach down to pick up my bag off the floor just as Niko leans over and grabs something from the console between us. It takes me a second to realize it's a pack of gum. My gum. Trident Wintergreen, as I live and breathe, there pinched between his fingers. But Niko *hates* my gum. He constantly complains about the sound of me popping bubbles and has shooed me off more than once when I've offered him some.

"Want a piece?" he asks, and I don't know how we got here, from us arguing about the merits of pickleball and tennis to Niko offering me my favorite gum that he most definitely despises. And yet, this is happening.

I watch as he creases open the pack slowly, precisely, like he does everything else. He slides his finger along the tidy row of perfectly packaged pieces and pulls one out, offering it to me. Suddenly, the space between us seems incredibly close, too close, and I squint in nervous thought, my mind racing as

I hold out my palm. This should not be a big deal. So what if Niko has a pack of Trident Wintergreen gum in his car, something that can be purchased at literally any gas station in the United States and probably—though I don't know this for a fact—the entire world? This is a normal thing, a typical thing, not something to fixate on.

But it feels odd, not quite right, like a clue to a mystery I haven't even come close to solving.

My brain is stuck on this as our hands touch for a split second before he pulls back and tosses the pack on the dashboard. I unwrap the shiny silver paper and roll it into a tiny ball between my fingertips before pressing it into his stupid little trash can cup. We lock eyes as I slowly bring the gum to my mouth, placing the rectangle on my tongue.

I am charged at one hundred percent, lit up, a nuclear power plant of energy.

And then Niko does the most Niko thing he could possibly do at this moment: He lets out a small, low sigh, almost a hum really, from the depths of his chest. And despite all of his stupid, blathering opinions about sports, his arrogant gloating about the merits of tennis, and all the other things that make me utterly, completely despise him, I feel the vibration of his voice run down my body like a caress. My nipples harden ever so slightly, and I squeeze my thighs together without thinking, like clenching my body will somehow convince my brain to stop playing this game with me.

"I should go inside," I say quickly, and my voice is breathy and wanton. I'm horrified, certain that he can tell that I'm lit up, on fire. That there's something about this entire maddening interaction that makes me want to grab his hands and press his palms against my breasts, to grind myself against the hardness of his body. To whisper, "Do you see what you do to me?" in his ear, and hear the sounds I could make come out of his mouth.

Before he can reply, I shove the door open and leap out of the car, dashing up the short walkway to Loretta's front door.

I do not look back at Niko until I'm face-to-face with Loretta, who stands in the doorway and greets me gingerly with a one-armed hug. She lets me go and peers over my shoulder and then looks back at me, brows hitched upward, asking me a silent question.

"He gave me a ride," I explain as I turn and catch a glimpse of Niko still there in his Audi sedan, a moody silhouette in the front seat. "And now he's brooding."

"Jeez, I wonder why," she says with a chuckle, as if she knows exactly why her nephew is in perma-scowl mode all the time. I want to ask, but instead I crack a forced smile and turn my attention toward the night ahead.

I've wasted too much time on Niko already.

6

"HEY, GUYS!" I say, my voice entirely too lively for this time of night. The car ride with Niko landed somewhere between thrilling and enraging, and it's harder to shake than I realize. I can feel myself overcompensating: My smile is wide and toothy, the wave of my hand is enormously broad, and four pairs of skeptical eyes study me from around the open kitchen and dining room. Normally, I come with something in hand—a bottle of wine from Trader Joe's or some pita crackers and a hunk of that truffle cheddar Deb likes—but tonight I show up with nothing but rattled nerves, my body still electric and prickling from my car ride with Mr. Dagger Eyes.

"Well, what on earth has gotten into *her*?" Deb asks with a sly smile, eyeing me through her bejeweled purple glasses. Her wife, Maureen, smacks her forearm.

"What?" I ask, though I know I've fooled none of them. I drag a hand across the damp expanse of my neck and smooth my braid, twirling the ends nervously as I slide into the empty chair across from her. "I'm sorry I missed the game."

Deb's coral-pink lips twitch into a smirk as she studies me, manicured nails tapping on the rim of her can of peach-flavored seltzer. "Don't change the subject. We saw who drove you here."

"Got a little private tennis lesson after work, did you?" Maureen teases, shooting an amused glance at Deb, who looks like she can't wait to get in her next comment.

"I thought you hated tennis," Loretta says as she settles back into her chair at the table and pops a cracker into her mouth. "Has something changed?"

"Loretta, he's your *nephew*," I say with a snort. I'm somehow both starving and too wound up to eat, and I pick around the tray for some stray grapes.

"Which is why I can tease you about him," she says, twisting the stem of her wineglass between two fingers as she stifles a laugh.

"You three are hilarious." I narrow my eyes at them, but my glare is bullshit and they know it, and it's met with a titter of pleased laughter.

"Ignore them, Bex," Ed calls from the island in the kitchen, where he seems to have made himself at home. "They turn into teenagers when they drink." He lifts a bottle of Chardonnay out of a crystal ice bucket and raises a questioning brow. "Speaking of, can I offer you a glass?"

I nod eagerly. I'll take anything to quell the avalanche inside me.

"Excuse me, old man." Deb deliberately waves her can of

seltzer in the air as proof of her sobriety. "May I remind you who was the first person to run to the window like a puppy and then called the rest of us over?"

Ed gives me a sheepish look as he shuffles over and hands me my glass. "Okay, fine. It's not just them."

I throw back a gulp before surveying my nosy, eager audience. "It's like you're all begging me to make some ageist crack about you all losing your minds or something. I'm not interested in Niko."

Except that isn't entirely true. The thought of jumping on top of Niko and ripping his clothes off for what would almost definitely be the world's most glorious hate-fuck is, well, kind of interesting.

"No offense, Loretta," I add hastily, pushing all fantasies aside for now.

"None taken," she says with a shrug, but her face is still smug, like she has a front row seat to the dirty thoughts in my brain.

"He was leaving the club, and he lives here," I insist, and I pray the nonchalance in my voice doesn't sound forced. "He offered me a ride so I didn't have to walk."

"Maureen and I could have swung by and grabbed you," Deb says. "You just have to ask."

"I know," I reassure her. "But I like walking."

These four people in front of me are the closest thing I have to best friends here in Sunset Springs, and we've become especially tight over the last year. Still, it's hard for me to rely on anyone but myself, even with people who feel almost like family now.

Game night inevitably turns into hours of stories and sharing; in the past we've dug into everything from Deb's double mastectomy to the time in the seventies when Loretta almost had a threesome with one of the original cast members of *Saturday Night Live*. (She still won't tell us who.) And yet I can't quite bring myself to share about the things that seem to take up most of my thoughts these days, my anxiety over the club's finances being one of them.

Then again, I'd probably rather discuss that than get into my tormented hate-crush on Niko, even though it is—from most angles of analysis—completely logical.

1. He's practically the only other person my age within a twenty-mile radius.

That is basically my only requirement for a date these days.

"He's a fine young man," Ed says with authority, not letting it go. "And a damn good tennis player. Every time I hit the ball around with him it's like being in the presence of a master."

"With damn good looks." Loretta winks back at Ed, who looks as close to blushing as I've ever seen him, and I catch something happening between the two of them that seems a bit more intense than normal. They almost look like they're flirting with each other. "Which, again, I can say, because he's my brother's son. I'm complimenting my own genetics."

"Loretta!" I give her a horrified look, but she's one white wine in and loving my reaction. "Should you be drinking on pain meds?"

"Oh, relax. I'm only on, like, a couple of ibuprofen a day," she says, swatting in my direction, as if she can wipe the concern off my face. "Let me make you a plate. You must be starving."

"I'm fine," I say. She ignores me and stacks some crackers and squares of cheese onto a plate, along with a big pile of sliced vegetables, and slides it in front of me.

"Even I find him appealing, and I haven't been with a man since Woodstock," Deb cracks. "God, that guy was hung."

"Deb!" I shriek, and I consider scooping up a bunch of the game tiles and tossing them at her head.

She hacks at the triple-cream cheese Ed places on the table, her lips curled into a satisfied smirk as her wife just shakes her head with a chuckle. Maureen, of all people, is used to Deb's antics.

"The four of you are worse than the entire frat system at ASU," I scoff, hoping they don't notice the Niko-induced goose bumps on my arms that refuse to stand down. "I thought we were here to play a game, not gossip."

"Honey, you know gossip is ninety-five percent of what we do during game night," Maureen says. "And book club."

"And you sure ran in here like you'd been lit on fire," Loretta says.

"Yeah, well." I clasp my hands on the table and lean back in my chair. "It's been a shitty day."

Deb shoots me a tender, concerned look, shifting effortlessly from nosy gossip to grandmother mode. She reaches a hand across the table and squeezes my wrist affectionately. "What's going on?"

"It's taken me a while to pay off some bills," I say with a resigned sigh. "I had no idea funerals were so freaking expensive."

Loretta shifts in her chair and gives me a knowing look. "When Terry died, I was so deep in my grief that I practically handed my credit card over to the funeral home. Those places can take advantage of you."

"Sorry to bring up such a morbid topic," I say, fiddling with the glass Ed's put in front of me.

"We're all old here. This is what we talk about," Deb cracks, but her face is gentle, open, and waiting for me to continue.

"Okay, see? *That's* morbid," I reply.

"You know what I'm saying," she adds. "You can talk to us."

"Thank you," I say, pausing to gather my thoughts. "It has to do with the courts. They're all in dire need of repair."

"Honey, if this is about Niko giving you a hard time when I broke my wrist—" Loretta starts.

I shake my head. "He's not wrong. It's something we should have done a while ago. And I definitely don't want anyone else to get hurt. I just need to figure out a way to fund it."

I can feel the avalanche of panic inside me subsiding, but now it's as if my body is made of petrified wood, hardened from centuries of exhaustion.

"What about a fundraiser?" Maureen brainstorms. "Something online?"

"I considered it, but we did that when Mom got sick, and

I feel strange asking people to donate more money," I explain. So many people had gone above and beyond with their generosity back then. I don't doubt that they'd show up for me again. But something in me—Pride? Stubbornness? Oh, who am I kidding, it's a fifty-fifty mix of both—longs to figure this out all on my own.

"TikTok," Deb says matter-of-factly, finger gliding across her phone screen like it's the answer to all of life's problems. "You only have like, what, six hundred followers? Build your platform. The last thing you want is a *mid* social presence."

"Okay, first of all, I can't believe you're insulting my follower count," I joke. "You know I am not on there to chase clout."

"You leave the clout chasing to me," she says. "Did you know my last video got over a hundred thousand likes?"

I give her an impressed face. "Also, your use of Gen Z slang is very impressive," I say, and she brushes me off with a playful wave.

"Oh, come on. I learn everything on TikTok. Do you know what ethical nonmonogamy is?" She leans closer, obviously eager to discuss her latest discovery.

"I do," I say with a laugh, as Maureen gives her wife a loving eye roll.

"Wait, I don't know what that is." Ed shoots the two of us a confused look as Loretta clucks at him.

"I'll explain later," she reassures him, and again I see his face light up, bright and youthful.

Maureen begins laying out the tiles, and I ponder Deb's advice for a moment.

"I don't know if I even have the time to make a million videos for social media right now, much less do it well," I say finally. "It takes me, like, an entire week to learn one viral dance."

"Well, then I'll just have to put you on my page," Deb says with a nonchalant shrug. "And I can teach you dances, obviously."

"What about a gala?" Loretta exclaims. "Oh god, I'd love an excuse to get dressed up. Put on a fun outfit."

"I'd love that, if I had the time to figure it out," I say. "I just need something fast. Maybe I should drive over to the casino and dump all my savings on the roulette table."

Except I can't even drive myself to the casino. Or afford to get my car repaired, much less the courts. God, what a mess.

I drag my hands across my face in frustration, blowing out a tired sigh.

"Keep at it," Ed says encouragingly. "You'll come up with something."

I give him a confident nod, masking the tornado of anxiety roaring through my body. There has to be a solution, some way to turn the future of the club around.

When I lift my head from my palms, they're all watching me with kind, concerned faces.

"I'll figure it out," I assure them. It's the kind of promise that might have satisfied friends my own age, optimistic twentysomethings that naïvely still believe things just work out, but these four know better, wizened by life's ups and downs, challenges I can't yet fully understand as someone fifty years younger. Even in my panicked state, I'm buoyed with gratitude for them. This group feels like a treasure I stumbled upon, and even though this wasn't what I thought my life would look like when I graduated from college, I love my little retirement community.

I just wish I could solve this financial conundrum in front of me…and get laid by someone who isn't on Medicare. Or Viagra.

Out of nowhere, my brain teases me with an image of Niko from earlier tonight, sweaty and out of breath. No matter how much he gets under my skin, there is something undeniably attractive about him, his energy, and the way he carries himself, like he can conquer the world just because he believes he can.

Like he could conquer me, if I let him.

I quickly shove the image aside before I let it set off hormonal explosions throughout my body.

You've had some good ideas today, I remind myself. But sleeping with Niko is *definitely* not one of them.

7

Saturday, April 15

I WAKE UP with a start, my neck sweaty, as the alarm pounds out a steady, piercing beat. I blink, and the neon numbers stare rudely back at me—6:30 a.m.—which means Deb is going to be here in exactly ninety minutes for a lesson. She always comes just before the club opens on Saturday and then handles the front desk while I coach.

Groaning into the pillow, I reach a hand up to my ribs to rub at the indent imprinted by my sports bra. I stayed up until almost 2:00 a.m. in hyper-fixation mode, researching how to print my own T-shirts, so theoretically I should be exhausted. But my brain starts churning the second my eyes flutter open, and I know there's no way I'll be able to fall back asleep. Already the thoughts are circling—I need money; I need to save this place; I need to prove I can do it, somehow—and I stumble bleary-eyed to the bathroom. I feel like a zombie who hasn't totally turned yet, and I don't even wait for the shower to warm up, choosing instead to boldly step under the piddling icy stream of water, the rest of my body jolting to attention.

Figuring out how to save the club feels like a second chance at life for this place, or maybe it's a first chance, an opportunity for me to forge my own path. This mission gives me a small spark of optimism, and I skip conditioning my hair, even though the water is finally at a temperature fit for humans, and bolt from the shower, hustling through the rest of my morning routine.

I grab my water bottle and a hard-boiled egg that I hope is still edible from the fridge, and I bound down the stairs and burst into the lobby, letting out a shriek when I find Niko bent over the reception counter, flexing in a runner's stretch.

"Jesus, Niko!" I clutch a hand to my chest, my fingers digging into the faded, tie-dyed, cropped tank I chose especially for this morning. I gave him the key code to the door—a special perk normally reserved for longtime members who like to come in and play before regular hours—but I'd never seen him use it, until now. "What the hell are you doing here this early?"

He doesn't even bother to bestow a glance in my direction, his gaze fixed on his palms, which are planted flat on the desk in front of him.

"I run on Saturday mornings," he says, as he lets out a long, audible groan, dancing somewhere between pleasure and pain, before switching the position of his legs. He's breathing into the tightness of his muscles, willing them to release, and it needles at the soft spot I have for him and the harder, lusty spot hidden directly behind it. "So I decided to run here, shower, and then practice. Stefan's meeting me today."

Stefan was one of the best tennis players at the club, a former college tennis coach who retired in Sunset Springs to be closer to his grandkids in nearby Temecula. Niko had roped him into playing on a weekly basis, though their matches appeared completely one-sided. Niko was like a spider, trapping unsuspecting members in his web of vicious serves and rocketing volleys that gave me whiplash every time I tried to follow the ball across the court.

"Yeah, but it's only, like, seven a.m.," I grumble through a mouth full of dry yolk. It's bad enough that he's been squatting in my brain all night, but seeing him in the flesh like this now prickles at me and sends a sheen of hot annoyance radiating across my skin.

It's not just attraction that has me charged; it's the distinct realization that, even on my best days, I'm overcome by the relentless feeling of loneliness. I'm not even thirty, and I'm the only person I know my age who has lost both parents. I run a business solo, surrounded by people generations older than me who I adore but don't totally get. Even though Niko is a pain in the ass, he's also a default ally of sorts just due to his age, and part of me likes having him around.

"And I just finished my run," he says in that matter-of-fact, slightly irritated tone of his. "So now I'm coming to shower and then play."

"A perfect day for Sunset Springs' own Tennis Prince," I

tease, as I desperately focus all my attention on firing up the computer, giving myself something to look at other than him. I squint at the dark screen like it's a calculus equation. Maybe if I stare hard enough, I'll will the computer to turn on faster just with the power of my brain. It doesn't work, and my eyes drift back over to the man in front of me.

He finally lifts his gaze, still leaning on those taut, sun-kissed forearms. He's near enough that I can make out the way his hair has curled into short, soft ringlets from his sweat, and I tap at the mouse impatiently, begging it to save me.

"How'd you get back here last night?" he asks, and there's a protective edge to his voice that disarms me, tricking me into thinking he might actually care. "I could have given you a ride."

"Deb and Maureen drove me home," I croak, reaching for my water bottle. It feels like a thirty-pound barbell in my hand. I need to do something to distract myself, and so I hop up from behind the desk and move past him to the shelf of towels by the door that exits into the court area, trying not to mentally measure the inches between his ass and my thighs. I grab a stack and bring them back to the desk, where I yank one off the top and begin unfolding and refolding it with painstaking attention.

His gaze leaves my face, moving slowly down the length of my body. It doesn't feel like he's undressing me with his eyes, not exactly. More like he's studying me, taking silent notes, memorizing what he sees now to use in some sort of future review.

"Did you make those?" He points to my purple and white

bike shorts, which match the scattered, circular tie-dyed pattern of my shirt.

"I make a lot of my pickleball clothes," I say, nodding, exhausted by what feels like his constant scrutiny. Why does this have to be so hard? "I told you that last night."

Niko moves closer, one step, then two, until he's a foot away, near enough that my eyes can trace the smudge of dirt that lingers just above his right eyebrow.

He opens his mouth like he's going to say something, the hardness of his gaze shifting into something that seems almost kind, or as close to kind as Niko can get. He reaches a hand toward me, pinching the shoulder of my tank top between his fingers for a brief moment, like he's marveling at it, even, until he remembers that we don't especially like each other and recoils with a grimace.

"What?" I ask, lowering my voice to mimic him, lips curled. "Let me guess. I look like the cross between a clown and someone who follows the Grateful Dead?"

I cross my arms in front of my chest, awaiting whatever insult he's going to sling my way. But he just drops his chin to stare down at me, and goddamnit, I instantly see the path I could take directly to his lips if I were to kiss him.

Which I'm not.

"I should be the one asking you what you're doing here," he says, ignoring my comment as he drags the side of his hand against his upper lip.

"You know I live upstairs," I reply.

"You don't seem like the type to be up early on a weekend," he says, and then avoids my eyes when I give him an offended look as I fold one edge of the rough white towel and then the other. "Sorry," he says, giving me a rare win. "That came out wrong."

I resist the urge to gloat and continue with my folding. "I'm trying to figure out some way to raise some money for club repairs. I couldn't sleep. My mind just started planning."

This catches his attention. "Planning what?"

He shifts upright, arms stretching overhead so that his crisp white tee rises up a couple of inches. My chest flutters at the sight of his belly button and the pitch-black hair that travels down across the expanse of his muscular stomach, sneaking into the top of his shorts.

Goddamnit.

"I don't know, exactly," I say slowly, my voice echoing that of a no-nonsense kindergarten teacher. I'm trying to portray a sense of confidence, like I totally have this all figured out. "Maybe a T-shirt? Something advertising the club?"

He nods but doesn't say anything.

"Or maybe something about pickleball. 'Stay out of my kitchen'? 'Give a dink, take a mile'?"

I'm spitballing. These are all slogans I've already dismissed. "I need something catchy."

He lets out a laugh, an honest-to-goodness, full-throated guffaw, and for the first time, I notice that when his smile is wide, two tiny, barely there dimples dot the edges of his cheeks.

I've never seen Niko laugh, not this loud, and it disarms me, knocking me off my perch where I'm always training my eyes on him like a sniper.

"Oh, I'm sorry. Do you have a better idea?"

"I'm a professional athlete, Bex," he says. "I have no creative bones in my body."

Only broken ones, I think.

"Then why are you laughing at me?" I ask pointedly.

"I'm not laughing at *you*, Bex," he says, and the look he gives me says he's downright hurt that I'd think that. "I'm laughing because it's kind of perfect timing."

"For what?" I rack my brain for a more confusing, maddening person, but I don't think I've ever met anyone like Niko.

His biceps ripple as he lengthens his right arm overhead. "I've decided that I'm going to play pickleball."

I snort. Somehow his arrogance still shocks me despite being up close and personal with it for a while now.

"You." I say this kindly, as if maybe he misspoke and doesn't realize it.

He nods like it's no big deal.

"You," I repeat slowly. "The man who's been scoffing at the sport for the last two weeks. Are going. To play *pickleball*."

Niko's face doesn't change, unfazed by my attitude. He just nods again and points at Wilson's flyer up on the board. "In that tournament. And I need you to be my partner. I've seen you coaching your lessons. I know you're the best player here. Besides me."

Stunned, I buy myself some time by yanking the scrunchie from my wrist and wrapping it tightly around the end of my hair until there's no give left in the elastic.

"Wow, and here I thought you weren't funny," I scoff

with a laugh, grabbing the refolded stack of towels and walking over to the white IKEA shelves, stacking them carefully like Jenga pieces, before I have to return his gaze. "Turns out you're hilarious."

"Bex, please," he says quietly, and the hint of desperation in his voice catches my attention. I turn back toward him, and he's staring at me, his lashes flattening against the dark shadows under his eyes as he blinks. "I'm serious. I could really use your help."

I freeze because the smoldering look he's giving me has faulted the wiring of my brain. I'd expected a healthy round of teasing, because surely he can't be serious. He's only ever spoken of pickleball with a sneer, but right now he's practically begging me, eyes pleading. There's something else that mixes with this out-of-left-field ask, almost like desire is a part of it, even though he doesn't want it to be.

It makes no sense. How can he loathe me and look at me like this at the same time? Then again, I claim to be annoyed by him, but I also can't get him out of my thoughts. I remember the gum in his car and how he seemingly cared how I got to Loretta's house last night, and nothing computes. It's like I have a bunch of puzzle pieces in front of me that almost fit together, but not quite.

"Absolutely not," I say finally, once I determine that he is, in fact, entirely serious about this request.

"Come on, Bex," he says, his voice still teetering on the edge of desperate, which is not a place I've ever witnessed him go before. "A favor, for me?"

"Niko, I'm already doing you a favor by letting you have

a full-time membership here," I huff, even though, technically, he is the one helping me out. It's not like the club didn't need the money.

"I thought that was a favor for my aunt, not for me," he counters.

I let out a loud sigh to let him know that I'm not convinced. "I don't have the time to train for a tournament, much less teach you how to play pickleball."

"I know we could win," he says confidently, taking a step toward me. "And we could split the prize money. We'd each get fifteen thousand dollars."

"Wait, what?" I ask, startled by the size of that number. Good lord, I knew people were investing in pickleball, but this is triple what I won the last time I played in a tournament back in college.

Somewhere in the distance, the bells above the front door jingle. I spin on my feet like an Olympic skater, turning to greet Deb with a tight grin, escaping Niko and his devouring eyes.

"Well, hello there, Coach!" she coos at me, adjusting the giant white visor resting on her cropped slate-gray hair. "And...Loretta's *nephew*."

The door swings closed behind her as she stops abruptly and eyes us both, the lenses of her glasses shifting color as they adjust to the brightness of the room.

"Are you both coaching me today?" she asks playfully, and I know exactly what she's thinking as she watches us.

Niko scoffs at this, like the mere suggestion of him stepping near a pickleball court is absurd, even though he just had the audacity to ask me to play with him. "I was just on my way to shower," he says. I'm so irritated by his constant high-and-mighty-tennis-player routine that when the horny corner of my brain tries imagining the soapy water mixing in with the tuft of dark hair along the firm sloped ridges of his stomach, I push the thought aside.

"Bex, think about it." He tents his fingers in a prayer that lingers at his chest for a split second. It's a flash of a movement, but for Niko, this is full-fledged begging.

"I already told you no," I say in my most chipper singsong voice.

He throws up his hands and storms off toward the small, gender-neutral dressing room, and I don't stop staring at him until Deb smacks me on the thigh with the flat side of her paddle.

"He had the nerve to ask me to partner with him for a pickleball tournament," I tell her, grimacing.

"I know he's a little bit salty," she says, smirking when she catches a look at my frustrated furrowed brow, "but I do think you'd make a good pair."

I give her a look that says *absolutely not.* "As doubles partners? Hell no."

She tilts her head at me with a wise, knowing look. "Well, how about as a couple, then?"

I shudder, putting on my best disgusted face. "When hell freezes over, and even then, no."

It doesn't matter how attractive he is, or how being in his presence somehow feels like both being rocketed into space without an oxygen tank and sinking into a warm bath at the end of a long day. The only thing worse than dating Niko—with his pompous, moody attitude—would be being his pickleball partner.

Not even for fifteen thousand dollars.

I shake my head no.

Not even then.

8

YOU'RE LOOKING AT around 50k. Another email from another contractor, quoting me even more than Travis's estimate.

But that's not even the worst thing in my inbox. Just below it is a message from Wilson, the subject Selling the club. I click through and scan the first few lines, and immediately regret it.

> Please see attached contract my lawyer drew up. Obviously, all can be discussed and modified, but I have a new investor on board who's hungry to start a pickleball empire and brings cash equity and experience to the table. Plus he comes with a built-in brand.

I drag Wilson's message to the folder I've titled "Stuff to Deal with Later" and drop my head into my hands. Dread doesn't so much feel like a pit in my stomach as it does an endless tsunami, crashing over and over and over against my heart. It's a violent shake of the earth, a roar in my ears, so loud I almost miss the familiar thud of one of the doors closing nearby. Growing up at this place means every sound is a core memory, imprinted on my soul. I know without looking that it's the heavy door that leads out to the courts. What I don't know is who just opened it.

"Bex?" Niko bellows, and I have my answer. Of course. A bunch of members are attending a seventy-fifth birthday party in town, Deb, Ed, and Loretta among them, and so we are probably the last two people left here.

"Yeah?" I ask, not looking up from my screen. Niko shuffles around the reception desk awkwardly and then comes to stand next to me, giving me no choice but to glance up at him. He's so close that I make out the faintest hint of freckles sprinkled across his cheekbones like stars just starting to twinkle at dusk.

"You forgot your racquet out on the court," he says, thrusting my trusty old Selkirk steed at me. I open my mouth to chastise him, but he beats me to it. "*Paddle*," he adds. "Excuse me."

My eyes widen, lips twisting into a genuinely pleased smile. "Good catch."

"Well, when you won't shut up about something, I have no choice but to pay attention."

I catch the hint of affection in his voice as he stands there unmoving, eyes fixated on my face. "Have you thought about what I asked earlier?"

I have thought about it, all day actually, as much as I am loath to admit it. And I've thought about other things, too, all of them involving Niko and very bad decisions. My mind does one of those sped-up movie montages of all the things about him that irritate me—the cocky swagger, the persistent erudite vibe. The way he just casually assumes he'd be "the best" at pickleball.

But then my thoughts switch to all the times I've ogled him from afar, watching him battle the ball machine like it's filled with his own personal demons. The way he so patiently coaches Ed on his serve when he doesn't know I'm looking, and how Deb told me he made his aunt chicken soup from scratch last week. His insistence that he drive me to Loretta's, and the way the concern had etched across his face when he asked how I'd gotten home.

Somehow, the way he irks me also attracts me; maybe, I'm realizing, they're one and the same. It's like it doesn't matter how he gets under my skin as long as he's there. As much as I hate to admit it, there is something tender under all the hardness, and I can't look away from him.

And I'm so tired. I can feel the ache of exhaustion deep in my marrow, all the way to the surface of my skin. Of feeling unsure and worried and perpetually forcing optimism and sunshine out of every pore of my body, as if my positive attitude could somehow save this place. I just want to feel something that isn't the weight of grief or responsibility for once.

Before I know what I'm doing, before any intelligent thoughts can send a signal to my hands to keep them from moving, I'm standing and reaching for his face, gliding my fingertips up the damp, smooth arch of his neck and into that thick, silky hair, bringing our mouths dangerously near each other.

His eyes are so dark that I can barely make out his pupils, and he watches me with the same quiet intensity I've observed on the court, as if he's calculating all the many directions the ball could go in before he decides the precise way he's going to attack it.

How, exactly, is Niko going to play out this game in front of him?

I get my answer when he drops his head to mine, a low sigh escaping his lips.

"Fuck, Bex." He utters the words like he's in pain, and he brings one hand to cup my cheek as he drags the other through my hair.

But he doesn't kiss me, not immediately. Instead his lips go for my neck, because of course this brooding man is part vampire. He sucks at the skin there, grazing his teeth over the tense muscle, sending electric currents straight down my spine. And then he does the thing that drives me absolutely fucking crazy: He lets out one of those low, growling moans like he does on the court, and I lose it.

I'm greedy, and I reach for his chin, pulling his lips to mine. He's delicious, all salt and sweat and pent-up frustration, the most clichéd version of manly I've ever had the pleasure of tasting. He doesn't hesitate or seem to overthink what's happening right now between us. Instead he strokes my bottom lip with his tongue, and I match him eagerly, ready to learn everything about the way he kisses.

I know, rationally, that this is a very, very bad idea. But screw all my better instincts. Right now I am an A+ student sitting in the front row of Niko Karras 101, and all my senses pay attention. There is the firm grip of his hands on my waist, the gruff sounds he makes that set off fireworks inside me. The gentle way he almost pulls me closer with his lips alone, devouring me with a hunger I've never seen in his serious, steadfast day-to-day. His hands travel down my ass, and there's another groan against my mouth. I whimper in response. I cannot get enough of this, and then he leans closer and lifts me straight upward, pressing me tight around his waist.

If I was hungry for him before, I'm now ravenous, a starved animal who's just been let out of their cage to feast. My legs twist around him as if on command, and he lifts me higher until I'm touching the edge of the desk, never once breaking our kiss as he slides me onto the counter. Somewhere behind us something falls to the ground—the computer mouse, probably—but neither of us pauses. I wouldn't stop this moment even if it had been a priceless crystal vase shattering all over the floor. I lock my legs even tighter, pulling him so close that the hard press of his erection against the inside of my thigh brands my skin, and I reach down for the edge of my tank top and yank it up to my neck. He laughs quietly when he figures out what I'm doing, his fingertips grazing my ribs.

"You have no idea what you do to me. Do you know how many times I've thought about doing this, when I see you here?" he says, nipping at my ear with wet, tender kisses as he traces his fingertips up to cup my breast through my sports bra. "You and your wild clothes, and your smart-ass mouth."

I groan loudly now, wildly turned on by every word coming out of him. It's been ages since someone has touched me like this. My life lately has been full of sympathetic hugs and pats on the back, but nothing else. I brighten remembering what it feels like to be wanted, a flashlight with brand-new batteries switched on in the dead of night.

And god, do I love it.

"I think about it, too," I confess, and I'm so euphoric my body practically levitates off the counter. "About you behind me, bending me over, and—"

Niko slams his mouth on mine, and all tenderness has been washed away by unfiltered, greedy lust. He squeezes my breast again, using his thumb to trace the outline of my nipple through the thin material, and now it's my turn to let out a guttural, animalistic sound. I want to be devoured by this man. I don't even care that he's an arrogant tennis snob who never leaves home without a sweatband around his head. Right now, he's *my* arrogant tennis snob, and I want to inhale him, eat him for breakfast, lunch, and dinner.

"Oh my god!" a startled voice I don't recognize says behind me. "I'm so sorry to intrude."

Apparently, my doglike hearing evaporates when Niko's mouth is on mine because I completely missed the trill of the door chimes, and now a stranger is hovering just a few feet away. I watch in real time as she processes what she's just stumbled upon, her mouth frozen in a perplexed O shape.

"Niko?" she says, giving us a shocked look. "I'm Angela

Rakkas, with the *LA Times.* We had a preliminary interview scheduled for…"

The stranger—*Angela*—glances down at her phone and then back up at the two of us. "Right now."

Niko pulls away from me like I'm poison, his eyes wide with horror. Leaping off the counter, I yank my tank top down as he adjusts himself behind the desk.

"Yes, hi." He strides forward, hand outstretched. "Angela. It's so nice to meet you. I completely lost track of time. I'm so sorry about that. I'm so honored that you're going to do this profile."

There's no more trace of the dominant sex god that was just in the room, ravishing me. Instead he is all business while I am a sweaty, heart-thumping mess. I slide onto the stool and smooth out my hair, hoping I don't look as disheveled as I feel.

Angela's bright-red glasses match the color of her short pixie cut, and a delicate nose piercing sparkles against her ivory-white skin when the light hits it. She strides toward me, still looking slightly caught off guard, offering her hand. "Nice to meet you…"

"Bex," I say, still unclear about what's unfolding in front of me. "I'm the owner of the club."

"And Niko's…girlfriend?" Angela asks cautiously, her eyes darting between us. Without thinking, I nod, and I can almost feel the horror creep across Niko's face.

"Oh, yes," I agree a little too eagerly as Niko dashes around the desk and comes to stand next to me, wrapping an arm around my shoulder. I catch a hint of his scent—sweat, musky deodorant, hot skin—and it sends my libido sizzling.

"Bex has kindly given me a place here to train while I'm taking care of my aunt. And she's my partner in the pickleball tournament I told your editorial assistant about last night."

I immediately scrunch my face in confusion, and he gives me a squeeze, signaling I'm supposed to do something. I look up at him, and the answer is right there on his panicked face: *Play along, follow my lead.*

"A former tennis pro turned pickleball player." Angela sounds excited, and she nods eagerly as she talks. "Finding a new path after a career-ending injury. Dating his doubles partner."

I can feel Niko wince against me at her words. "Well, I am training to try to return to the pro circuit eventually."

"Right," Angela says, seemingly less pumped about this bit of Niko's story.

"Hopefully," he adds, and only then does it dawn on me that I have no idea the extent of Niko's injury and whether it's actually possible for him to compete like he used to.

"And Bex, I'd love to chat with you as well, seeing as you're..."

"So many things! Like seriously, how many hats am I even wearing? I'm Niko's number one fan, his pickleball partner."

I'm babbling, overwhelmed by the explosive kiss we just shared and this new reality he's somehow roped me into. I feel his fingers grip my shoulder, like he's physically trying to hold the words back, but they keep pouring out of me, a half laugh, half shriek.

"It was love at first pickleball lesson," I add, because I

can't stop my lips from betraying me. "Instant! Like, a wave crashing into me."

Why can't I shut up? It must be because that kiss has caused my brain to short-circuit, and I'm operating purely with some sort of human cruise control turned on. I turn and give the new love of my life a wide-eyed stare that I hope looks more like adoration than it does panic.

"Absolute infatuation," he says stiffly, and I can tell it's hitting us both at the same time: We've entrapped ourselves in a giant lie, and if we don't turn this sinking ship around now, we're going to be so screwed.

But before we can concoct a way out, a grin spreads across Angela's face. "The pickleball-playing owner of the Sunset Springs Racquet Club and a former tennis underdog turned pickleball amateur. This profile is already writing itself."

Angela looks downright delighted, and she presses something on her phone before laying it on the desk in front of us. "I'm going to start recording so we can get this all on the record." A little red dot appears on her screen; she gives it a gleeful tap and then looks back at us. "So, Niko, tell me—which did you fall in love with first, pickleball or Bex?"

9

"UPSTAIRS," I HISS to Niko the second Angela's car pulls out of the club parking lot. "Now."

We're the only two people here in the lobby, but this feels like a conversation we need to have in private, especially after we both rambled into Angela's phone for twenty minutes. "Shit, shit, shit," I mutter under my breath. What had we just told her?

I lock the door to the club and frantically march up the stairs to my apartment as Niko follows behind me. We don't say a word to each other, and I watch as he blinks, taking in the chaos of my teeny living room. He's eyeing the stacks of secondhand T-shirts on the dining room table, Mom's ancient sewing machine taking up the rest of the cluttered space. I turn away from my little shoe-strewn entryway and face him, seething. It's as if someone has heated me up in the microwave, and I'm about to explode.

"What the hell was that?" I squeak, throwing my hands up in the air. "Why did you tell that reporter we're playing in the tournament together? I don't get the sudden one-eighty when all you've done is tell me how stupid you think pickleball is!"

"Oh, I'm sorry." He storms toward me and then stops abruptly when he's barely a foot away, like he doesn't want to get too close to me despite the fact that he was practically ravaging me not half an hour earlier. "I was too busy pretending to be in love with you to think straight."

I push past him, weaving around the table and pacing toward the kitchenette. Once I reach the counter I circle back. I don't stop moving. I might be engulfed in a full-on panic attack at any second.

"You need to call her tomorrow and tell her we broke up, and that we're not playing in any tournament together, ever."

"Bex." He exhales audibly, eyes blazing. There's that desperate look again, though now I see it more clearly for what it really is: fear.

"I told you I needed your help. She's doing this whole profile on me and my time at UCLA, their tennis program and my career. And I have nothing to show for myself other than being an injured, washed-up tennis pro living with his seventy-year-old aunt."

"So you told them you were entering a pickleball tournament?" I spin around and yank open the fridge, grabbing a can of sparkling water from the bottom shelf. I make a point of not offering one to my new boyfriend. He'll quickly learn that I don't wait on anyone, especially fake lovers.

"I just..." His eyes search the ceiling like he isn't sure how to explain himself. "I just wanted to seem interesting.

An injured tennis player known for a shitty temper, now taking the pickleball world by storm before trying to break back into the pros seemed...better."

"Better for you!" I say, pointing my finger at him. "But what about me? I can't believe you roped me into this without even asking me first! I guess this tracks for a guy who used to plant anonymous stories about himself."

"What?" he asks with a flustered wave of his hand. "I tried to ask you, this morning! And it's not like you helped the situation by telling her we're a couple."

"She walked in on us kissing!" I sputter, circling the room as I take giant gulps of the fizzy water. "It's kind of hard to talk ourselves out of that."

This shuts him up for a moment, and the pause allows me to observe him again. I see he's still sweaty, glistening with nerves and adrenaline, his hair slicked back to reveal those devilishly dark eyelashes, capped by thick, severe brows. Every hair on his body is jet-black, and I have no idea why this realization sends a shiver through me, but it does, sharp and direct.

"Well, you were the one who initiated that," he says finally.

I throw my hands up in frustration. "With your consent, I believe?"

He gives me an exasperated look but doesn't argue otherwise.

"I'm sorry that I was desperate to kiss someone and you just happened to be the person standing in front of me." I survey him with a wave of my hand, trying to gain my composure. "And you were all...you know."

"I was all what?" he asks slowly, his eyes never leaving my face.

"Saying all those things." A flush creeps up the back of my neck, threatening to turn my entire face bright red.

"What about it?" he replies, cocking one luscious brow at me.

He's calling my bluff. He knows I'm flustered by his words, that it makes me blush to repeat them out loud. It's almost like he's holding something over me, something I cannot for the life of me remember until he opens his mouth again.

"*I think about it, too?*" He taps the tip of his index finger to his chin in feigned thought, the corners of those rose-colored lips crooking up into a smile that's as dark as the hair on his head. "Oh no, wait. Those were *your* words, not mine."

He knows he's won, and he's gloating.

"I'm sorry you're the only other person under sixty years old for miles around," I scoff. "My options for people to make out with are fairly limited here. And you're leaving in six weeks, so it seemed like a practical decision."

"Well, same," he says with a quick shrug of his shoulder. "And I have thought about it. Though I mostly like to imagine Deb."

He pauses, almost like he's setting up a punchline. "Me, behind her…"

"Can you stop?" I groan, pacing again. I don't know what to do with my limbs, with this pent-up tension inside me. I truly cannot believe that the one time I let my hormones take over control of my body, this is what happens. "And please don't get all cocky just because I kissed you. You're basically like a yogurt sitting in my fridge that I needed to eat before it expired."

"Wow, Bex. What a compliment." He gives me a disgruntled, irritated look and then collapses onto my couch. "If this is what dating you is like, I can't wait until we break up."

"We are not dating," I insist, racking my brain for some sort of solution. "We need to figure out a plan to get out of this mess."

I spend most of my days problem solving—coordinating a bus route to the senior living facility so that residents can come to class, figuring out when the toilet paper goes on sale at Costco Business Center and finding new places to store it (under my bed)—so surely I can figure this out.

But seconds tick into minutes, and when no brilliant idea comes to me, I give up and slump against the counter.

"I think we're already in the mess," he says, like it's a lost cause.

"We're so fucked," I grumble. I don't have the time to untangle myself from this disaster, and certainly not for Niko's sake. I have money to raise, a club to save. "You're going to have to learn how to play."

"What, like it's hard?" he cracks with a curl of his lips. He looks entirely too comfortable leaning against my ancient corduroy loveseat, hands clasped behind his head. It is almost as if he belongs there, like he's been missing this whole time, and I don't like the strange, sad feeling this gives me.

"Yeah, actually, it is," I say, righting my shoulders as I push myself forward to stand in front of him. "You're going to have to spend the next month practicing."

"I'm preparing for the qualifier," he says, like any of that is my concern.

"Too bad." I brush him off with a shrug. "Now you're also preparing for the Paddle Battle."

"Fine, Bex." He lets out an irritated sigh like I'm a mosquito that he keeps swatting at but can't quite kill.

"Are you seriously *Fine, Bex*-ing me like I'm annoying you?" I sit down next to him and grab his elbow with a shake. "You're the one who got us into this mess."

"Well, you really helped by making it worse," he hisses back.

"Worse?" I say. "Or better? Don't you think your partner also being your girlfriend makes you look even better?"

He shrugs. "I guess you have a point."

"If I do this for you, you have to help me with something, too. Something big."

"Name it," he says.

"We don't split the prize money," I tell him matter-of-factly. "I get it all."

"No way." He shuts me down immediately with a firm shake of his head.

"Okay," I tell him. "Then no tournament, or comments for the profile, or—"

"Goddamnit, Bex." He groans, dropping his head in his hands as he hunches over his knees. "Fine."

"Perfect!" I cheer with a clap of my hands. "That should be a fair deal for me making you look good in this profile. We commit to really becoming teammates, just until the tournament, and win."

"Oh, we're going to win," he says confidently. "Because I don't lose."

"You know there will be some seriously good pickleball players in the tournament, right? Some of these people play every single day. They'll be vicious. It's not going to be easy."

His eyes do this thing I've seen before, they widen, almost like they're taking me in, and then they narrow, as if they're fixated on a target of some kind. "Who said I like easy?"

I press my lips together, trying to contain the swell of giddy nerves his words set off.

"Fine," he agrees begrudgingly. "We will practice hard, and when we win, you get all the prize money."

"And you'll also pay me back by promoting the racquet club in this profile," I add, and suddenly I feel deviously, wonderfully brilliant. If I can't get out of this situation, I'm going to have to make it work to my advantage.

He stares at me, dumbfounded. "It's supposed to be about *me*."

"I'm not asking for you to make it about me. Just mention your doting girlfriend and her family's beloved but struggling racquet club, which is your favorite place on earth."

He thinks for a moment, running a hand through his hair.

"Come on," I push, before he can get a word in. "I'll help you rehab your image; you help me by winning this tournament. We'll send you off to that qualifier with lots of buzz and a brand-new break-up for all your doting fangirls and boys to gossip about."

"You are deeply infuriating," he grumbles. "You know that, right?"

"And how about when we made out, like, thirty minutes ago?" I ask, glaring at him. This man is testing my patience, and so far, I'm failing. "Was that also infuriating?"

"That seemed very mutually not infuriating to me."

"You should thank me for that kiss," I tease, as he rises to stand. "It just saved your ass."

"Oh yes, you have my infinite gratitude, Pickleball Princess," he says with a sigh, and then looks down at his watch. "I should go. Loretta says she doesn't care when I come home, but I know she's tracking my every move."

"Oh fuck," I whisper, as panicked realization hits. "Loretta."

Lying to a reporter I'd just met was one thing. But lying to the people I love, who know me so well? That feels harder than winning this goddamn tournament.

"She'll be thrilled that we're a couple," he says with a shrug. "It's literally her dream come true."

I chuckle at this because he's not wrong. I've picked up on the comments she makes about Niko being single and can see how much she wants him to find someone. I'd just always chalked that up to her being an attentive aunt and not her necessarily wanting Niko to be with *me*.

I make a mental note of this but try not to dwell on it or the warm, fuzzy way it makes me feel.

"I just told Deb this morning that I wouldn't touch you with a ten-foot pole, much less a paddle," I say, giving him a salty look. "She's going to think I've lost my mind."

"What makes you think she doesn't already?" he asks.

I leap up and walk over to the calendar hanging from my fridge, which, I'm not proud to say, I haven't flipped in a few months. It's still stuck in January, and it's now the middle of April.

"The tournament is in exactly five weeks." I unhook the calendar from its magnet holder and spread it across the kitchen counter, hoping Niko doesn't notice the dishes in the sink that I keep putting off washing. "We'll need to practice as much as possible and do it around my work schedule."

"I can do that." Niko nods. "And does practicing count as going on dates?"

"I said I was sorry about telling her that." I groan. "We can just tell people we're together. We don't need to go on actual, real *dates*."

"Oh, come on," he says, pressing his palm into the counter as he hovers just a little too close. "We need to at least get a coffee sometime."

"The most important thing is practicing and winning this tournament," I remind him, scratching a giant *X* through May 20. "If we're going to do this, we take it seriously."

"I take everything seriously," he replies, crossing his arms against his chest defensively.

"Oh really?" I counter. "Does that apply to pickleball?"

He dips his chin slightly but doesn't say a word, which I've learned is his way of admitting I'm right. "We practice daily," I demand.

"Deal," he says, but the aloof look on his face tells me he's not convinced that he's going to actually have to learn how to play pickleball.

"I mean it, Niko. If we're going to do this, we need to *do* it. Because I'm not just doing this to get publicity." My voice scrapes with desperation, and I can feel the fear of failing and letting everyone down press against my heart like a brick. "I need that prize money."

"And I am doing this because I need some good publicity," he says. His words, like his stony gaze, are cool, aloof. "If I'm ever going to have any sort of career, I need to do something to change people's opinions about me. So we'll do it. We'll win—get you the money, get me a nice headline, and walk away from this whole thing unscathed."

He reaches out his hand, and I press my lips together, considering all my options one more time before begrudgingly grabbing a hold of it. "Five weeks."

Niko nods, giving my hand a firm squeeze. His hand is warm and solid in mine, like a stone warmed on a beach, and the sensation turns my insides to goo. I curse the way his touch—even something formal and forced like a handshake—threatens to knock my knees out from under me. I tug my hand away quickly, not wanting to tempt myself further.

"I need to lock up and go lie down before my head explodes," I say, shooing him toward the door.

"I'll sign us up when I get home," he says. "And don't worry, I can cover the registration fee."

"Wow, how generous of you," I coo sarcastically.

"Good night, Princess," he says, as he teeters on the top step, his lips curling into a satisfied smile. "See you bright and early tomorrow for practice."

10

Sunday, April 16

NIKO IS, ONCE again, stretched out over the reception desk, eyes fixated on his phone. I watch him from the top of the stairs, admiring how his focus is always so linear and direct. My brain is always chasing a billion different thoughts, like a Choose Your Own Adventure book. Niko, on the other hand, seems like he does one thing at a time and doesn't move on until he's mastered it.

I wish this did not make me ponder what he'd be like in bed, but after Saturday's kiss, this has in fact been one of the main thoughts lurking in my head.

The other: how the hell to get through the next few weeks of pretending to be Niko's doubles partner and girlfriend. I decide to go with unabashed confidence and hope for the best.

"Hey." I give him a cheery wave as I descend the stairs. "You ready to do this?"

He looks up and gives me a slow, resigned nod. "I got the email saying we've been accepted into the tournament, so it's happening. We're official."

I attempt to steer my body away from the pull of him, willing some sort of Niko-repelling force field into place around me. But every organ, every muscle inside me, betrays this very smart plan, and my gaze immediately attaches to his face like a magnet when I hit the bottom step. His eyes shoot up, and if he's also a nervous wreck from last night, he's not letting on. I may wear all my emotions on my secondhand sleeves, but Niko keeps his sewn up and hidden from sight.

"Official," I repeat, as I move to stand in front of the computer, switching the screen on and opening up my email, even though I'm only doing it to distract myself from staring at him. "Not seeing other people then. How very old-fashioned of us."

"Wow, did we just have *the talk*?" Niko shifts on his feet, his eyes never leaving my face. "That took a lot less time than I imagined."

On paper, this morning should be just like any other. The desert sun hangs wide and bright through the smudged glass windows, and the smells of coffee and cleaning spray mix in the air. I make a mental note that I should water the succulents that dot the top of the towel shelves.

But everything is different, as the nerves churning around in my stomach remind me. In the span of a mere twelve hours, everything's changed.

Well, except the utter pleasure it brings me to verbally spar with him. That has stayed exactly the same.

"Wait, was that your first time having the talk? Am I... your first *real* relationship?" I tap deliberately on the keyboard, my voice so saccharine it could make even a sweet tooth gag. "Aw, Niko. How absolutely adorable."

"Trust me, Princess." His eyes narrow into daggers as he watches me. "If we were really dating, you'd know."

Jesus Christ, this man's arrogance extends far beyond the tennis court. And as much as I hate to admit it, occasionally it is earned. Even if we hadn't fallen into this ridiculous arrangement, my kiss with Niko alone would have sent things rocketing in a completely new direction. This man, whose mouth is usually reserved for frowning and snide comments, kissed me back, said *things* to me, the kind of words that aren't easily shoved aside, and I'm not sure how to process them—or the feelings that burn inside me like some sort of lusty indigestion.

"Let's see how you do during today's lesson," I say as I move around, grabbing the spray bottle off the counter and walking over to mist the plants like it's the most important job on the planet. "Then I'll decide if I'm ready for a committed relationship with you."

Niko has been nothing short of irritating since he dressed me down in Loretta's hospital room. He's abrasive and arrogant, practically humorless. And yet, I also want to rip his clothes off and ravage him right here on the floor. It makes no sense, but here I am, skin prickling, heart pounding at the sight of him.

My teammate.

My *boyfriend*.

The kissing can't happen again, not anymore. I want to

save the club more than I want to climb on top of him, and Niko is now my partner, a person I need to rely on if I want to take home that prize money. In just a few weeks, we have to be so in sync that we can seamlessly beat whoever or whatever this tournament throws at us.

In sync *on the court.*

Not, you know, with our lips.

God, I need to stop obsessing about our kiss for this to work.

And on top of all that, the arrogant Tennis Prince has to learn how to play pickleball.

Wait, scratch that. *I* have to teach him pickleball.

God, I'm so, so fucked.

Kissing him was a boneheaded move, period. Even if Angela Rakkas hadn't walked in and complicated things, I should have grabbed his face in my hands and pushed him far, far away from me. But since I can't take the kiss back, I have to start over, now.

"Was I supposed to wear colors?" Niko's voice cuts through the chatter in my head, and I swivel around to find the corners of his mouth perking up as if they were eagerly waiting for this moment. "Because if so, I left all my neon gear at home."

I don't need to look down at the poppy-orange crop top I'm wearing today to know what he's talking about, but I do anyway, out of habit. It already feels like he's winning this Battle of the Day After Our Kiss, and this, of course, irks the hell out of me.

"I'm pretty sure anything you put on your body immediately turns to white anyway," I sass back, pinching a corner of his pristine T-shirt and examining it. "You're like the opposite of one of those hypercolor sweatshirts from the eighties."

His face shifts into something more confused. "I have no idea what that is."

"It's vintage, Niko." I sigh, but my brain stops working when I search for more of a comeback. All I can think about is how, just hours ago, he had me pinned against the edge of the reception desk, encasing me with his arms, whispering "You have no idea what you do to me" in my ear before unleashing a kiss on me that was so wildly sexual that I'd practically orgasmed right there on the spot.

What *do* I do to him, exactly? Bug him, I'd always thought. But now there's more to it, and I desperately want to know the answer.

"I tend to think vintage means something that's out of style," he says. He seems so tall today that he takes up every inch of space in the entryway.

"You mean like tennis?" I taunt. I work through the nerves rattling around inside me and squeeze by him, avoiding those storm-cloud eyes. It's no use—my skin still prickles like I've just stuck my finger in an electrical socket.

"Come on!" I say before he can bust out a retort. I bounce toward the door with the enthusiasm of a high school cheerleader. "Let's do this before the regret consumes me."

He follows me outside wordlessly, hovering at the edge of the court as I fish a paddle out of my gear bag and hand it to him.

"We're going to start with the absolute basics," I explain, trying to dig up some patience as he crosses his arms in front of his chest, his eyes narrowing skeptically as I walk a few paces away from him. "Think fast."

I toss a lime-green ball at him, and he catches it effortlessly, like a Major League outfielder grabbing a pop fly.

Niko stares down at the plastic ball in his hand with a look of unbridled disgust. "It's a wiffle ball."

"It is not a wiffle ball." I will myself to stay calm and not let his usual grumpy asides get to me. Too much is on the line, and I need to keep my cool.

"Look at this, Bex." He steps closer and positions it in front of my face, ever the professor, annoyed like I'm a student who's just not getting it. "Plastic."

He points with the edge of his paddle. "Holes. Same weight, more or less. Wiffle ball."

"Yeah, but wiffle balls are white." I snort. "Your favorite color."

"You know, I'm only half as boring as you think I am," he says, the edges of his lips quirking up into a smile that is downright playful on him. I bite my tongue before any other comebacks slip out of my mouth because I have a hunch about what this is: a peace offering. It's going to be way harder to work together if we're constantly competing to see who can out-snark the other.

No more sarcastic comments, I promise to myself, not today anyway. I make a mental note to resume all biting remarks immediately after we've charmed Angela into writing a glowing piece and won the tournament, the prize check cashed in my bank account.

No shit-talk, and no kissing, either, I remind myself as I grab my own paddle.

Luckily, we both seem to have tacitly agreed to act like the Great Make-Out Session of the Century never actually happened. Niko and I, grabbing at each other like we hadn't eaten in weeks and were both made of Doritos? A figment of my imagination! A secret we'll both take to the grave.

But I can't forget those sounds he makes. And now I know he's a talker, too, with a filthy mouth. My eyes flit up to his lips, which look deceivingly soft, considering the strength of his kisses.

"I can't believe I'm about to play tennis with a fucking plastic ball," Niko says with a laugh. He tosses the ball in the air and whacks it hard across the court, where it hits the fence, far out of bounds.

I'm downright grateful for his obnoxious comment, because it helps me snap out of my lust haze before drool can collect at the corners of my mouth. God, this is Niko—a condescending, arrogant tennis snob with a closet full of pristine polo shirts the color of an ice cap. Besides, I don't need sex with some guy to save me. I can save myself—and the club—thank you very much.

"Well, that's your first mistake," I say, offering him a patronizing smile as I tuck my braid through my visor. "Pickleball is nothing like tennis."

He rolls his eyes like he doesn't believe me, and his refusal to give me even an inch of trust as his coach only irks me. Good. *Annoy me some more, Niko!* This is exactly the fuel I need to regain my focus.

"You know, you sound like every client I have that shows

up all cocky and arrogant because they can bang a tennis ball across the court," I reply.

"I'm not cocky and arrogant because I can bang a ball, Bex," he says, quirking his lips up at me as he twirls the paddle in his hand. "I'm cocky and arrogant because I'm really fucking good at tennis."

"I know you are," I admit, because there's no denying his level of skill. "But pickleball isn't all about offense and force. Pickleball is taking those people who come in and bang the ball around and *de-banging* them. If someone tries to win with speed, you slow down the ball, show them their mistake. Make them have to rethink their strategy about banging."

It's not until the words are out of my mouth that I catch the twinkle in his eye, the crook of his lips edging upward ever so slightly at what I've just said.

"What does banging have to do with pickleball, Bex?" he asks coyly.

"You know what I mean." I rush the words out nervously. "If your opponents are any good, they're going to figure out that all you do is slam the ball across the court, and they'll adjust accordingly. They'll de-bang you."

"No banging," he says, and then adds, "*The ball.* Got it."

"You can bang the ball occasionally," I correct, praying that my cheeks don't flush with my words. "But I'm going to need you to change your mindset for pickleball. Being strictly about power isn't going to work anymore. You need to think more defensively, no matter if you're on the serving team or not."

"What does the serve have to do with it?" he pushes back.

"Only the serving team can score," I explain. "Didn't you read the link I sent you last night?"

He's quiet, his eyes drifting off over my shoulder for a moment before looking back at me.

"I skimmed it," he says haughtily.

"Because you assumed you'd just be able to swoop in here and tennis your way onto the pickleball court," I counter.

"Fine, coach," he says, bowing toward me. "I promise, I'm listening."

I give him the rundown of the rules, all the stuff he should have read and known already. When I'm done, he shrugs like it's no big deal.

"Let's play," he says.

"No, first we work on your serve. It's underhand in pickleball, remember? Go on the opposite side."

I drag the ball basket over to the back line of the court, and once he's in position on the other side, I knock one over the net to show him how it's done.

"You want your serves deep," I yell, batting a second ball over. "Keep the opposing team as far back as possible, try to prevent them from getting up to the kitchen."

He rolls his eyes at *kitchen*, the word he so fervently despises, and then grabs a ball off the ground. He thwacks it at me, almost like he's trying to punish it, and it once again bounces off the fence behind me with a loud *clink!* and lands way out of the lines.

"Go slow," I say, keeping my voice patient. "You want it to be slow and deep."

He pauses mid-swing as I say this, his eyes grazing over me hungrily, scowling, before he knocks the ball across the court, landing directly behind me. My stomach hollows like it's on its own private roller coaster. I've said all of these things before to countless students, but in Niko's presence, every word sounds downright sinful, like I'm suggesting he throw me down on the court and strip my skirt off right here.

"Patience is key here." I recalibrate, steadying the pounding in my head as I toss the ball back to him.

He averts his eyes from the ball for the moment, locking them with mine. "I'm patient—about most things."

His arm cuts back through the air and sends the ball hurling across the court before my mind can obsess over his words.

This time, it actually lands in bounds, right where it's supposed to be. "That was great!" I exclaim, unable to contain the excitement in my voice. "It was a nearly perfect serve."

He cocks his brow at me, and I can tell he's trying to suppress a smile.

"See?" I give him a thumbs-up. "You don't need to be gentle. Just don't pound it."

Shit. Heat creeps into my cheeks, and his lips twitch ever so slightly, his eyes staying on my face longer than they need to.

"Do it again," I say quickly, before he can get a word in, but even that sounds dirty now.

He hits the ball, but this time, he's back to using too much force, and it drops out of bounds, just over the line.

"Don't—"

"Pound it, I know," he interrupts, his face stern, unreadable. "I can't help it. I like pounding things."

I want to give him the benefit of the doubt and assume that he's not purposefully tormenting me with these deliberate word choices. But there's another part of me that very much wants to read into everything he's saying right now, to escape into the possibility of flirtation. As ridiculous as this whole scheme is, the last twenty-four hours have also been a relief, a distraction from the heavy stress permeating the other parts of my life.

Of course I don't *like* Niko. But I do like the off-ramp from reality he's currently providing.

"Holy shit, that was perfect!" I yell as the ball he sends hurtling through the air lands just at my feet. His serve—the curve of the ball, the power with which it flies just over the net and lands with a drop—is better than that of anyone I've ever seen play at the club. Including, I admit begrudgingly to myself, mine.

Niko cups a hand around his mouth and shouts, "So what do you say, then, Bex? Are you ready to commit to me now?"

I nod my head slowly. "I guess we're official."

"You're stuck with me, Princess." He tugs a ball out of his pocket and taps it directly at me. I duck as it whizzes by my shoulder and then give him a murderous look, but he just smirks and walks backward toward the end of the court, hands in the air, celebratory. "I'm all yours."

11

Wednesday, April 19

I WAKE UP to a text from Niko. Come with me to take Loretta to the doctor today, it reads. We can tell her the good news.

I roll over in my bed and groan. I hate lying, and doing it to Loretta feels downright sacrilegious.

But it's for a good cause, I argue with myself. A cause that could possibly save the club she loves so much.

Fine, I write back. Deb gets here to run the front desk at nine. What time?

Great, he replies. We can tell Deb too. 9:15 a.m. See you soon, princess.

Niko is punctual down to the second, and he strides into the club with a determined look on his face just as Deb's setting herself up at the front desk. Even though he's chauffeuring Loretta around, he's dressed like he's about to walk into Wimbledon: crisp white shorts, a white T-shirt, socks yanked midway up his calves, and sneakers blindingly clean.

"Hey," I say, and suddenly I am unsure about what to do with my hands, my body, my face as he gets closer.

"Hello," he replies, stopping to stand directly in front of me. He leans in, just a few inches from my face, and tucks a loose strand of hair behind my ear before giving me a soft peck on the cheek. "You look beautiful today."

Deb watches all of this with the attention of a rapt toddler in front of the TV and practically chokes on her coffee at his words.

His voice has just the touch of a growl to it, like there's an honest layer of want behind what he says. His assertiveness is unnerving. Normally, I'm the chipper one in the morning, but the reality of our situation has thrown me off my game.

"Hey, you," I mumble again, heart racing. Am I nervous to see him or nervous to lie about our relationship? Maybe both?

Deb dabs the corner of her mouth with a tissue and looks back and forth between the two of us, shock plastered across her face.

"Bex asked me out," Niko explains to her with a shrug. "We're dating."

"After you asked me to play in a tournament with you!" I say, regaining my footing. "Get this, Deb—he's crazy about pickleball. Obsessed with it."

"Aw, not as obsessed as I am with you," he coos, affectionately tapping my nose with his index finger.

"You're so sweet." I am hamming it up now, nuzzling against him as his hand curls against my cheek.

Deb focuses all her attention on me, still looking utterly perplexed. "Didn't you just tell me that you'd—"

She's thinking back to our conversation from the other day when I swore to her that I'd never pair up with Niko in any situation. I knew she was too smart to be fooled by this.

"We're just seeing where it goes," I say, hoping this sounds plausible. Niko runs a hand down my arm, lacing our fingers together. It's a comforting gesture, one that I like more than I want to admit to myself. "Maybe it won't go anywhere."

"Let's give it a month or so to see," he says, giving my hand a squeeze.

"Yes, that sounds good," I say back, beaming up at him with an absurdly huge smile. "And then if we still want to be together, we'll have to do long distance once you leave."

"My goodness" is all Deb says. "Does Loretta know?"

"She's about to. Bex is going to take her to her doctor's appointment with me, so we better run," Niko says. "Come on, love."

He pulls me toward the entrance of the club, and once we're outside, I yank my hand away.

"Love?" I say, giving him a look. It's not that I don't like it, but it feels odd coming out of his mouth. And maybe, I realize, I've come to enjoy him calling me princess.

"Think she bought it?" he asks hopefully.

"I don't know. Boomers are pretty good at sniffing out bullshit," I say. "Which means Loretta is going to be on to us immediately."

I move to open the car door, but Niko's hand is there

before mine, and he blocks me with the length of his arm. "One more thing," he says, quieter now, as if Loretta might hear. "Starlight's hosting a cocktail party on Saturday night, and everyone registered for the tournament is invited. Pick you up at seven?"

"Seriously?" I say, and it comes out like a nervous whine. I should have thought harder about what it would mean to pretend to be dating someone. A cocktail party was the perfect place to slip up, revealing our secret plan by accident.

"What, do you have some other hot plans?" he asks. "Bingo night? Walking to Target?"

"Okay, thanks a lot for somehow insulting both my social life and my shitty car in one fell swoop, you ass." I step closer to the door, and this time he slides his entire body in front of it as he places his hands on my shoulders.

"I'm sorry," he says. "It was a dumb joke. Let me try this again. Angela will be there to interview me, and it would be a big help if you came. Also I'm driving, and Loretta and Deb are tagging along. It might even be...How do I say this?" He scrunches his face in thought, like he can't come up with the word he wants to say. "Fun?"

I let out a laugh at his performance. "Fine," I agree. "Will you just let me in the car please?"

Niko pulls open the door, and I slide into the back seat. The second Loretta twists around to greet me, I feel the bubble of bile lighting up my stomach. I know Loretta; she's hawkish and observant and doesn't miss a beat. There is no way we're going to pull this off.

"This is a nice surprise," Loretta says when she sees me,

eyes flitting across my face, already in detective mode. "I thought he was just stopping by to pick something up."

"I was," Niko says as he hops into the driver's seat. "Picking up my girlfriend."

For a moment, Loretta looks like she's about to call our bluff, and then something in her face shifts, and she begins to cry.

"Oh, thank you, Lord," she says, pressing the fingertips of her working hand to the corners of her eyes.

"Oh, Loretta," I mumble awkwardly, reaching over the armrest to give her a loving squeeze. "It's still very new."

Her excitement is so palpable that it only makes the guilt I already feel for lying that much worse, and I try to push it aside by remembering what I stand to gain if we pull this off.

"Bex is going to teach me pickleball," he explains as he drapes an arm over her headrest and reverses out of the parking spot. It's hard not to admire how every movement of his body ripples with muscular strength. Maybe I don't hate all that conditioning he does after all.

"Goodness." Loretta's staring at Niko, mouth agape. "Is hell freezing over? A girlfriend, and *pickleball*? Are you sure you're my nephew?"

Niko chuckles as Loretta reaches over and cups his cheek. "I'm not sure which makes me happier."

"Hey now," I gasp with exaggerated offense. I react to her words without thinking, like I really am dating her nephew and what we're telling her is actually real.

"Oh, don't worry, dear," she says. "I'm most happy about the pickleball."

She lets out a cackle, and I know she's ribbing me.

When we finally pull into the hospital parking garage, a familiar sinking feeling hits me. When I'd shown up a couple of weeks ago to see Loretta, my adrenaline had numbed the anxiety I get from being here, but today it is overpowering.

We walk toward the front door, and I stall once we're through the entrance, a moment so brief I assume Niko won't even pick up on it. But of course he does. He's eyeing me the way he does the ball machine on the court, like he's five steps ahead and ready to pounce at any second.

"What is it?" he asks as Loretta shuffles along ahead of us.

"Nothing," I lie. "I think I'm just going to hang out here for a bit."

"Okay," he says, giving me one more concerned look. But he doesn't push it, and he says goodbye with a shrug of his shoulders and a tilt of his head. I watch him move down the hallway, athleticism evident in his every step. He's going to grasp pickleball instantly, I think, as I study his stride. Something about this fills me with pride, but I brush the feeling off before I can obsess over it.

I circle the lobby for thirty minutes, staring at social media blankly on my phone until Niko appears, arms crossed in front of his chest.

That chest. That mouth. The things he said to me just a few nights ago. A shudder ripples through me as I relive it all again.

"Hey." I give him a feeble wave and look back down at my phone.

He stops a few feet in front of me. "The doctor just sent

Loretta in for an MRI to see how the scar tissue is doing. They're trying to bump her to the front of the line."

"Wow, you really get the royal treatment when you're over seventy, huh," I joke awkwardly.

"Well, brittle bones and all that," he says plainly. "You wanna come sit in the doctor's office waiting room? It's going to take a little bit of time."

I nervously flutter a sigh through my lips and begin twisting the end of my hair into a loose braid.

"I hate this place," I confess, before I even consider who it is I'm confessing to. "This is where my mom came when she had her first seizure, where they found her cancer, all of it. This hospital is just like a giant trigger for all my trauma from the last couple of years."

The creases that line his brow soften, and he reaches a hand out as if to comfort me and then pulls back quickly, like he isn't quite sure what to do when no one else is around. Already the lines of our intimacy are blurred. That kiss sure as hell was real, but our new relationship is anything but.

How exactly do you comfort someone you're newly pretending to be dating?

Niko is quiet for a moment, his eyes shifting over my shoulder before landing back on me. "You know, every time I'm in a hospital I think about fucking up my knee," he says gently. "The way my career, my entire life, literally ended in a second."

There's a hurt edge to his voice, a prick of sadness mixed with something I suspect is anger. It is the most he's ever said to me about his injury, and I keep my mouth shut, hoping he'll continue.

"I know that doesn't even begin to compare with what you went through, losing your mom," he adds hastily. "I'm just saying, I hate it here too. It brings up a lot of stuff I don't like to think about."

"I really get that," I say softly, genuinely touched by his words. "Thanks."

"I think that's why I was a bit of an asshole when I first met you here, when Loretta broke her wrist," he says with a hint of sheepishness.

"A bit?" I tease, and he shoots me a chuffed look. "I'm just joking!"

"I know," he says. "What I'm saying is, hospitals bring up so much stuff for me. And I'm sorry if I took it out on you that day."

"Wow, Niko. Is this"—I lean closer to him, smiling, feeling a bit lighter—"an apology?"

"Shocking, I know," he replies, and I can almost feel him unwind and settle into himself, shoulders relaxing, face at ease. "I'm also saying, I'm sorry for bringing you here. I should have thought about what it's like for you to come back here. I can drive you home if you want and swing back and pick up Loretta."

It's such a kind and simple gesture that my heart swells.

"Nah, that's okay." I wave him off. "I can handle it for a bit. But thank you. I really appreciate you being nice about it."

"See, I'm not a total asshole," he says, smirking at me.

"Eh, that remains to be seen."

Niko laughs at this. "Well, just don't tell Angela."

He says it like a joke, but I sense a hint of something

sincere behind it. He wanders over to one of the beat-up purple plastic armchairs and sits down, patting the one next to him with his hand, trying to get me to join him. So I do, perching next to him as we sit in the quiet. Then I finally ask the question that's been lurking in my mind since the night we concocted this plan.

"I need to know why this interview is so important to you that you lied—without my permission—to that reporter about us playing in this pickleball tournament." I pick at my cuticle before looking at him. "It seems completely...I don't know, random? Out of the blue? Unnecessary?"

Arms crossed in front of his chest, he stares into the distance, looking straight ahead without meeting my eyes.

"I think," he says, slowly, "that when you lose everything that makes you *you*, it can be really hard to know even who you are anymore. Do you know what I mean?"

"Kind of," I say softly.

"There's just nothing else to me without tennis," he says, and there's something so sad about this that I physically wince at his words. "If I don't have tennis, Niko Karras is just... nobody. Maybe I was just trying to sound more interesting. I'm sorry for dragging you into this."

I shrug. "It's okay. I dragged myself into it, I guess."

He gives me a half smile. "We're like two opposite sides of the same coin."

"Like pickleball and tennis?" I say, raising a brow.

"God, no," he huffs. "Don't get confused. Pickleball could never be on a coin with tennis. Ping-Pong, maybe."

"Right, right," I say, rolling my eyes at him. "So what

I'm hearing then is you're still a total asshole when it comes to pickleball."

"Sure, if that's what you want to think, Princess." He gives me a sly smile as he kicks those long legs out in front of him, crossing them at the ankle. "But I'm pretty sure you're starting to like me."

12

Friday, April 21

I'M EXPERIMENTING AT my dining room table, and I can't stop laughing at the words I've plastered across the front of a faded yellow T-shirt. Only a few hours earlier, I practically crawled up the stairs to my apartment, exhausted from a day that started with an hour of practicing against Niko's power shot, followed by back-to-back lessons until dinnertime. Once upstairs, I reheated some lasagna rolls, turned on Bravo for background noise, and starting playing around with the transfer paper I'd dug up in my craft drawer the other day.

I relish the feeling of getting immediately sucked into a project, the way it both soothes and invigorates me. And even though I'd done a ton of sewing with my mom's old machine over the last couple of years, I've never tried to print anything until tonight. I'm teetering on the edge of delirious, but I am also obsessed with this new idea, especially when I imagined all my seventy-plus-year-old friends wearing these shirts and asking me what the slogan means.

Except Deb. Deb will know, obviously. If she is already familiar with the inner workings of polyamory, thanks to TikTok, she is definitely going to be up on this.

There is another thing coursing through me like caffeine, spurring me on despite the fact that I have to be up at the ass crack of dawn tomorrow morning to practice with Niko. It is hope, and it has been bubbling up over the course of the past few days, since Niko and I stumbled into this plan and decided to go for it.

Maybe it's the fact that he's been instantly amazing at pickleball or that I enjoy our sweaty practice sessions together way more than I thought I would. But winning the tournament—and more important, the money—feels like less of a long shot than it did a week ago, and a steady, determined calm has settled into my body where restless anxiety was previously squatting.

Once I have two shirts printed—one for me and one for Niko to wear to the cocktail party tomorrow—I crack open a window to let in the cool night air. Outside, the sliver of moon is hazy behind cloud cover, but the stars are full and bright, hanging over the shadowed edge of the mountains. Despite being exhausted, my mind is still churning, and so I opt for a quick walk outside to try to sooth my amped-up nervous system. Sliding on my sneakers, I leave my phone on the kitchen counter and head down into the silent sanctuary that is the club's reception area at night.

I'm about to turn toward the front door when I catch a

glimpse of the south court lights still blazing, an oasis of neon yellow in the otherwise vast darkness. Of course, it's possible I forgot to turn them off. But it's also possible Niko is out there, preparing to slam his tennis racquet around.

I can't help it. I'm curious.

I can take a quick detour to the courts to shut the lights off, I reason. *Wouldn't want to waste electricity. Our bill is sky-high already.*

I push through the swinging glass doors and walk toward the closest court. I'm barely on the edge of the green asphalt when a person seems to come out of nowhere, like they'd materialized from the shadows just to scare the life out of me.

I know immediately that it's Niko, because who else could it be? But I still let out a shriek, my hands instinctively reaching for my face.

"Jesus Christ, Bex," he chuckles as he slowly comes into focus in the sharp brightness of the overhead lights. "I know I'm terrifying, but I didn't realize I could make you scream like that."

My brain short-circuits, the fear and adrenaline of being surprised mixing with the rush of seeing him standing here, lit up like an angel, shirtless.

"I thought I told you to tell me if you're going to stay late to play after the club closes." My voice pitches a few octaves too high, sounding like I've just inhaled helium.

His body shimmers, covered in a sheen of sweat, and he squirts a shot of water into his mouth before turning the bottle upside down and spraying it onto his hair. He runs a hand through the messy dark strands and shakes the drops free with a quick twist of his head. They scatter across his shoulders and chest, and my tongue feels like it's swelling up inside my mouth. I'm having an allergic reaction to how unfairly attractive he is. Niko looks downright pornographic, like Mr. Darcy emerging from the pond in the BBC version of *Pride and Prejudice* that my mom and I once watched together in fits of swooning giggles.

"I wasn't playing tennis," he says, lifting his hand up with a smile. Wrapped in his fingers is the pickleball paddle I gave him the other day.

I swallow back my surprise. "Wow. I didn't expect you to be so committed."

Niko shrugs, dragging a hand across the back of his neck. Every muscle in his body flexes as he moves, visible thanks to his lack of any sort of body fat. He is built like a machine, and I can't forget the way it felt to touch him, rock solid.

"Let's have a little scrimmage," he says, quirking his brows up in invitation.

"I was going out for a walk," I counter, and he brushes me off with a dismissive smirk.

"Come on, Princess, let me try to beat you," he teases, and the hint of flirtation in his voice sends fresh adrenaline flooding into my veins. "Don't make me beg."

Sorry, nervous system, I think to myself. *Change of plans.*

"Well, when you frame it that way." I flip him the middle finger and jog over to the lost and found bin by the benches at the edge of the court, grabbing one of the nicer paddles left behind. "I'd say that for every point, the loser has to take off an article of clothing, but you'd be naked in, like, two seconds."

"If we're playing strip pickleball, then I'll definitely win," he says, and the look on his face is scorching. Why do I keep walking right up to the line with him? *Rein it in, Bex.*

"How about instead of an actual game, if you win a point, you get to ask the other person anything—and the loser has to answer," I offer, my curiosity about Niko getting the best of me.

"Deal," he says as he reaches over for a fist bump before jogging off to his side of the court. I make my way across from him, taking a couple of practice swings as I bounce on my toes. I have a vague memory of being tired just a few minutes earlier, but I'm reinvigorated and feel like I could play pickleball all night.

"Okay, Tennis Prince!" I shout, egging him on. "Let's see that ATP ranking in action."

To his credit, Niko doesn't acknowledge my taunts. Instead his focus is solely on the ball, which he bounces once, twice, and then—boom. His serve is textbook perfect, so good, in fact, that I almost let it whiz by me as I marvel at his skill. Thankfully, I jolt to life just as it bounces a couple of feet in front of me and make it in time to return his serve.

Niko plays a long game with each swing, trying to keep the ball far back on my side of the court so I can't move up to the net, which is where players ideally want to be. No matter what I do to try to thwart him, his returns land far and deep in the corners of the court, and soon I'm sprinting back and forth trying to make each shot.

I finally lob the ball over his head, and he swings with determination, just barely missing it. "Goddamnit!" he huffs as he slices his paddle through the air like an ax, almost like he wants to split the court in half. It's just a scrimmage, a silly practice game, but it dawns on me that he approaches every task with the same level of intensity, no matter the gravity or importance.

Which makes it all the more fun to torment him for losing a point to me.

"Wooooo!" I pump both arms in the air. He saunters up to the net with his usual swagger, unsmiling and serious, his arms wide, as if he's inviting whatever questions I throw his way. And there's one I've been dying to ask over the last few days that feels unanswered.

"Well?" he says once I'm directly across from him, still catching my breath.

I study Niko for a moment—and not just to ogle the shape of his body, which is, undeniably, mouthwateringly perfect. I'm noticing for the first time that the defensiveness I always sense in him—the slightly protective arch of his shoulders, the touch of a scowl always lingering in the lines of his brow—is starting to seem less and less angry and more about self-preservation. With all his bravado, he reminds me of a wounded animal at times, even when he's trying his best to hide it.

"Why me?" I ask finally, looking directly up at him. His eyes shift as he tries to figure out what I am asking.

"As your partner," I add. "For this tournament. You could have asked Deb. She's almost as good as Loretta. You could have found some old tennis pro friend, or someone way better at pickleball than me. So why did you ask me?"

I can see a current of something vulnerable ripple across

his face, but it's there for barely a millisecond before disappearing. "I just needed someone who could keep up," he says cooly. "And you're here all the time. It's not like I'd have to chase you down to practice."

"Mm." My lips flatten into an irritated line, and the exhaustion is back, refilling my bones. Maybe he is just an angry, bitter jerk after all. "How flattering. You really do have a way with words."

"It's all part of my charm," he replies, his stare severe. "My turn."

"I'll give you one free question," I tell him, "but I'm done playing for tonight." I plop down on the ground, right in the kitchen. Niko comes to sit directly across from me, legs crossed, his knees close to touching mine even though he's sitting right on the other side of the net.

"Fine," he agrees. "One question."

He stares at me for a moment, and I can't tell if he's hesitating or figuring out what to say. But then he opens his mouth. "Why'd you say yes?"

I've never met anyone with eyes like his, that seem to penetrate my skin and bones and see directly into my brain. His muscles may be the thing that carry him on the court, his athletic skill and dedication keeping him afloat, but his eyes are the true secret weapon, what he inflicts on all his competitors to make them stumble and second-guess themselves.

"Do you mean aside from the fact that you told that reporter I was your partner?" I say, giving him an incredulous look. "It's not like I had a choice."

"Bex, I've seen you in action," he says, his voice softening just a smidge. "You're not someone who's afraid of saying no. If you had wanted to back out, you would have."

I pick at a flaky piece of the court and let out a sigh. "Sometimes it feels like the club is actually crumbling around me. And I don't know how to put it back together."

He leans in a bit closer, peering at me curiously through the woven nylon net.

"Money," I say finally, and I can hear the desperation reverberate in my voice just as much as I feel it in the tight ache of my shoulders. "I need that prize money to pay for all the repairs we have to do on the courts."

"Oof" is all he says.

"Yeah, *oof* just about sums it up." I give him what feels like a pathetic smile. I'm stuck back in a pit of stress; maybe that hopeful feeling from earlier was just a mirage.

"The club is my whole life. I don't have anything if I don't have this place. The thought of losing it terrifies me because it's like I'd lose myself and everything that makes me me."

"I don't know if that's true," he starts, but I shake my head at him.

"Think about all the pressure you've put on yourself over the years," I tell him. "And now imagine that, but bigger. At first, I thought I was just doing all of this to honor my mom and her legacy here, but it's been hitting me how much bigger it all is than her, or me."

"Which is..." he says.

"I can't let the members down," I say as I rest my elbows on my knees. "This is their home. And it's my home. So there you go. That's why I said yes."

Niko is quiet for a moment and then reaches his hand under the net and slides it over my calf. The weight of it is warm and reassuring, even if his face is still stony.

"I'm sorry I gave you a hard time about the condition of the courts when we first met. I didn't know how much Loretta loved it here."

"Okay, now you're just sweet-talking me because you're my pretend boyfriend," I joke. I consider reaching for his hand, but he pulls it away before I can do so.

"No, I'm serious. I overreacted. I was afraid..." His voice shorts, and he's quiet for a moment. "I know how hard it is to bounce back from an injury, but especially when you're her age. I was worried about her. It wasn't the best way to handle things."

"Thanks," I say, meeting his eyes and giving him a small smile. "I appreciate that."

"So let's just focus on winning the tournament, then," he says with a confident tilt of his chin. "We'll put on a good show for the interview tomorrow at the cocktail party, we'll keep practicing, and we'll do whatever it takes to win."

"Whatever it takes?" I reply. "That sounds serious."

He doesn't mention anything about the dating part of this plan, and I don't ask.

"If it's pickleball, it's all fair," he says.

"Deal," I agree. "We play to win."

And we leave it at that.

For now.

13

Saturday, April 22

"ABSOLUTELY NOT." NIKO flings the T-shirt over his shoulder, tossing it at me in the back seat of his car like I've just handed him a scorpion. Whatever hints of playfulness I've seen in him over the last week have been replaced tonight by his usual hardheaded dickishness, and now I'm trapped with him and his handsome face for the entire night.

He parks in front of Deb's house, and I use this pause to unbuckle my seat belt and slide into the gap between the front seats. I prop my elbows on the center console and lean as close as I can to him. I'm near enough to deduce from one inhale—and a quick glance at his still-damp hair—that he's freshly showered, and a zing of desire pulses up my spine.

"It's a prototype of the new T-shirt I designed. I wanted you to have the first one, *honey*."

I dangle it in front of his face and then drape it on top of his head. Yes, the shirt is ridiculous. That is the whole damn point: grab attention with the slogan and then draw people in to the more important message directly underneath that reads SAVE SUNSET SPRINGS RACQUET CLUB.

I'm wearing a cropped version of the same shirt, looking like some sort of nineties raver Tweedledee to his uptight Tweedledum. Obviously, I'm no marketing executive, and I get that some people might find the shirt a little, shall we say, lowbrow. But I trust my creative instincts enough to know that it might also be maybe sorta brilliant, the kind of thing I'm confident I could convince both old-timers who love the club and cool Gen Z hipsters who hoard weird vintage stuff to buy. Repairing the courts is a short-term solution to a much longer-term problem: The club needs a ton of work, and even if we win this single tournament, I'll still need a lot more funds to make it happen. Saving this iconic, aging landmark is something I hope to make universally cool and maybe, if I'm lucky with selling T-shirts, lucrative.

"I don't think it's exactly my style," he grumbles as he yanks it off, ruffling his hair in the process. Loretta grabs it and unfolds it in front of her, letting out an approving "Ooooooh!"

"What do you mean? Lime green is your color." I muster up the most obnoxious smile and send it beaming in his direction, even though he's staring directly ahead, probably willing Deb with silent prayers to come out of her house and end this conversation.

"And," I add, tapping him on the shoulder, "Angela will get to see what a supportive partner you are."

"I would wear it if my teammate told me to!" Loretta chirps. "Especially if my teammate was also my girlfriend."

"She's—" Niko says and then quickly stops himself. He lets out an exasperated sigh and whips his head around to give me a scolding look, and I shoot one right back at him. Clearly, in all his childish irritation, he almost spoiled our ruse over something as minuscule as a freaking T-shirt, and as we discussed last night, we need to come together if we want this ridiculous plan to actually work.

Deb opens the door opposite me and slowly slides into the back, and I scoot out of the middle and into my seat. She's especially bejeweled today—giant, chunky turquoise necklace and round purple glasses with lenses the size of dinner plates—with her phone attached to a small tripod she holds in her hand, a square light clipped onto the front.

"Good evening, kids!" she says as she scans the scene with her screen. Niko grunts a hello to her and continues his speech about the shirt I've made him.

"Theia, it says *Big Dink Energy*." His voice is unfailingly patient with Loretta, always, and it makes me melt a little, even when he's being so prickly with me. "Do you even know what that refers to?"

"I've known about it long before some young person coined the term," she says pointedly, and I let out a chuckle at her spicy defensiveness. "Don't assume that just because I'm old, I'm clueless."

"And she knows me," Deb says, smiling broadly from behind her phone. "So of course she knows what it means."

I clasp a hand to my heart, letting my mouth drop open as if I'm wildly insulted by her words. "Oh, come on, Deb. We all know who has the BDE in this car. I'm right here."

"I'm sorry, but there is no way in hell I am putting that on." Niko lets out an irritated huff of a sigh as he reverses out of Deb and Maureen's driveway. "Much less in public at a freaking cocktail party with a dress code."

"But it's our team name!" I say, and I can't help but enjoy the fact that this, of all things, is irking him. Also, I'm genuinely curious about what he might look like in some color.

"It is absolutely not our team name," he snaps back, white-knuckling the steering wheel.

"Hear me out." I'm not backing down. Even though I knew the shirt would drive him nuts, I'm serious about him wearing it. "We need something that will help get us attention. Something that says, 'Holy shit, former tennis stud Niko Karras is playing pickleball now! And at the very cool and very old and rundown and in need of financial support Sunset Springs Racquet Club!'"

I assumed this shirt would be a hard sell, but after last night, I thought he might give in more easily. But I am learning that Niko isn't an especially easy read; he can fluctuate between hot and cold just like Sunset Springs in January.

"I never agreed to be on a team named Big Dink Energy," he says, his voice back to icy calm.

And I never agreed to be on a team with you! I want to shout, but I bite my tongue. I'm antsy and anxious about making a good impression at tonight's party and being trailed by Angela. When it's just Niko and me, it's easy to fall into a comfortable back-and-forth and not worry about maintaining this façade of coupledom. But we're about to spend the entire evening with a reporter documenting our every move, and it feels like we're starting the night off on the wrong foot, sniping at each other.

And then there's the other realization that's been plaguing me since I woke up earlier today and felt instantly excited to see Niko. There is a genuine part of me that enjoys spending time with him, whether it's watching his competitive side flourish when we're on the court together or bantering about stupid stuff. I delight in earning his discerning, hard-to-get approval, and deep down, I want him to like this shirt.

"Also," he continues, "since when do doubles partners even have a team name? That's not *a thing*." He twists the fingers of his right hand into quotation marks as he keeps his other hand on the wheel in front of him.

"That doesn't mean we can't make it a thing," I say, and then lean back in my seat, crossing my arms across my chest. "It's pickleball. We can do whatever we want."

I am talking about the T-shirt, of course, but I think I'm also talking about everything else that keeps bubbling up between us.

Never mind that he somehow looks extra tan, extra muscular, extra handsome, and extra *everything* tonight. I'm here to make Niko look good, so he'll make the club look good, but all I can think about is that there is a six-pack lurking underneath that white polo shirt, and if he changes into the T-shirt I made him, I just might catch a glimpse of it.

I'm determined not to let the memory of his lips against my skin draw me back into more poor decision-making. As much as I crave the distraction, I also know it's not the time to be focused on anything but digging the club out of this financial hole. But that doesn't mean I haven't been constantly replaying that one incredibly sexy moment over in my mind every free chance I have.

Imagining the rough gravelliness of his voice when he said "You have no idea what you do to me" has been at the core of every masturbation fantasy I've had since I first dragged my fingers across the sharp line of his jaw.

And I've had a lot.

Niko shifts up front, like his legs are suddenly too long for the car and he can't seem to get comfortable. It pleases me on some sinister level to see him squirm.

"Fine." I take the shirt back from Loretta and scrunch it into the tote bag at my feet. "Wear your stupid white polo shirt tonight. But don't come crying to me when all the cool pickleball kids on the playground tease you for your outfit."

"Bex, I could give two shits about what anyone at this pickleball thing thinks about me," he scoffs.

"Fine, but you should care what I think," I mutter, and that gets his attention.

He whips his head around for a split second, but it's long enough for me to catch that his dark eyes are somehow blazing with color.

"When have I ever given you the impression that I don't?" He keeps his voice low, steady, but there's a hint of something vulnerable there that I latch on to and turn over in my head.

"Whew, it's steamy in here!" Deb says as she breaks down her little filming setup and tucks her phone and tools back in her purse. "You two must really be having some fun in the bedroom, bickering like that and then ripping each other's clothes off."

"Deb!" I exclaim, and I blush with embarrassment, even though we haven't ripped anything off each other. Yet.

"Oh, please. What, do you think just because I'm on two different types of cholesterol medication that I don't know what sex is? Or still have it? Tell them, Retta."

"You can be sexually active long into old age," Loretta lectures, and now Niko is downright writhing in his seat with discomfort. "In fact, some might argue that it helps keep you young."

"Theia, please don't," he groans.

"It's like a crossword puzzle but for your libido," Deb adds matter-of-factly, and I choke out a laugh.

"Okay, I really don't know how we got on this topic, but can we please get off of it?" Niko says, and I hide my face in my hands, laughing. I'm both loving this conversation and slightly mortified by it, but not nearly as mortified by it as Niko, who seems to be cringing at every word. It's fascinating to see him like this, almost shy about sex, when he was so raw and verbal and dominant when we kissed.

"Your uncle was a real devil before he died, you know," Loretta says, her voice deliberately innocent. She isn't one to back down, and I now see where Niko gets his relentless determination from. Genetics are a powerful thing. "Insatiable, even."

Deb lets out a howl of a laugh as if we couldn't already tell how much she was enjoying this. "Sounds like someone had a bit of that BD—"

"Okay, time for music!" Niko cuts her off loudly as he reaches for the radio, putting on some godawful eighties station. But I can tell from where I sit, angled just off to the side of him, that there is a smile hiding behind the sharp line of his lips, and I smile back, even though he can't see me.

14

DEB GRIPS MY shoulders, twisting me closer to Niko until my back is flush against his chest. I shuffle back a step and bump directly into his groin, causing my entire face to sizzle with heat. Niko clears his throat, which tells me he's just as uncomfortable. But Deb is oblivious, clucking as she instructs him to place a hand at my waist, just barely touching my exposed skin at the edge of my shirt.

Some poor soul had painstakingly hung hundreds of different-colored pickleballs with clear fishing line from the ceiling of the covered entryway, and Deb shooed away the professional photographer the second we got close enough so she could stage her own photo shoot. She's trying to pose us "correctly"—her words—in front of the official photo spot at the entrance to the party, but it's hard for me to focus when all my thoughts are rushing to the small spot, just above my hip, where our bodies are connected without any sort of barrier between them.

"I need you two to focus so we can get this shot," she chides as she maneuvers our bodies like we're mannequins, until she finally has us exactly where she wants us. "Perfect. Don't move."

I freeze in place as she starts snapping away, but my eyes wander, taking in our surroundings as much as possible without turning my head.

Under an awning of twinkly lights, we were offered drinks immediately upon arrival. A pathway of flickering lanterns leads partygoers toward the entrance of the building, which is flanked by two gurgling koi ponds. Even I have to begrudgingly admit that Starlight is stunning tonight, completely transformed from tennis club to nightclub.

Together, Niko and I look like something a kindergartner would have at their school desk. I'm dressed like a box of crayons in my cropped pink T-shirt and tangerine ankle pants, accented with my favorite secondhand sea-blue platform heels. He's a piece of plain white construction paper.

We're shockingly oppositional, but there's also something about us that fits together. Perhaps I could add a little bit of color to him. Maybe he could help me stay in the lines.

"Come on, you two, can you cuddle or something?" Deb cajoles as she steps forward to tweak the edge of Niko's collar, tugging it until it falls just so. "Look alive! Look happy!"

I decide to change position and turn sideways, nuzzling my cheek against his shoulder and bringing my palm flat on his chest. He's stiff against me, and I give him a little squeeze, trying to signal that I also feel awkward and exposed doing this. It's nothing like when we're alone, kissing or not.

"Eyes up, please, Bex!" Deb instructs, as Loretta stands next to her, studying us with her uninjured hand resting on her chin. "Niko, look here, please."

We're frozen in position, balls bobbing around our heads, when I catch the shape of a man in my peripheral vision, stopping just off behind Loretta.

"Niko?" The voice that belongs to the stranger is deep, British, and undeniably sexy, and I turn my head to get a closer look.

"Bex!" Deb scolds, because I've ruined her photo. But I'm a red-blooded American woman, and a British accent is our kryptonite. And damn, am I glad I looked. The guy lurking there with bright, curious blue eyes is the closest thing I've ever seen to a cartoon prince come to life. He has one of those exquisitely proportioned faces; every feature is symmetrically aligned as if sculpted, chiseled, and placed just so by an artist. His blond hair is the color of perfectly ripe corn in August, and my mouth almost waters at the sight of him, just on instinct alone.

But he's not looking at me. All his attention rests on Niko, whose expression lingers somewhere between surprise and irritation.

"Hey, man!" the absurdly handsome creature says as he takes a couple steps forward. "I thought that was you."

Deb gives up on her photo and moves to the side with a disgruntled sigh as the stranger leans into Niko, offering him a half hug, half back-slap of an embrace. I'm still half attached to Niko's arm, and so the mystery man also half hugs me by default. It's all very awkward.

"Freddie," Niko replies as he pulls away from both of us, his voice as cool and hard as his gaze, a stone floating at the bottom of a roaring river. "It's been a while."

"Deb Curran." My friend reaches for the stranger's hand, beaming. "I'm a massive fan."

Unfazed, his smile turns on like a spotlight, and he flashes it back at her. "A pleasure," he purrs.

All at once, I realize exactly who this is: Freddie Alwin, former pro tennis player and one of the highest-ranked pickleball stars playing professionally right now. Staring at this famous face, I'm both giddy and confused. Freddie is a big deal and currently rising to the top tier of the pickleball world. There's no way Niko doesn't know this, so how the hell has he not mentioned that they are friends?

Loretta tugs Deb toward the entrance of the club and Freddie turns back to Niko.

"Yeah, mate," he says, casually tucking his hands into his pockets. "I made the switch over, and I haven't looked back. I'm sponsored by Reebok now."

"For *pickleball*?" Niko asks, tilting his head like a confused dog hearing a strange sound for the first time. A quick scan of Freddie's outfit—lightweight athletic tee in a silvery blue, sporty black slacks, just out-of-the-box sneakers—reveals that he is, indeed, sponsored from head to toe.

"Oh yeah, it's incredible. I bloody love it. Have you played?"

"Actually, I just entered my first tournament," Niko says curtly. "We're training now."

"Wow," Freddie exclaims enthusiastically, and when he

claps his hands, I notice the glimmer of the giant gold watch on his wrist. "Look at us. I'm so glad to hear you're getting back out there, you know?"

Niko nods, signaling that he does, indeed, *know*, but I feel left in the dark, like they're having some other conversation behind the one I'm hearing. I keep a pleasant smile on my face as I watch the two of them. But inside, I'm like a chain-smoking detective yanking their hair out trying to solve a complex case after pulling an all-nighter and chugging a pot of burned coffee. There is a bulletin board in my mind with photos of Niko and Freddie tacked up on it, and I'm about to pin up a red string that connects the two of them.

Before I can piece it together, Freddie turns all his attention on me, and good lord, his gleaming smile is as blinding and overpowering as his obvious confidence.

"And you're the beautiful woman he pays to put up with him, then?" he asks, brow cocked curiously, clearly expecting me to melt like a marshmallow over a flame in his presence.

"I'm actually the beautiful owner of the Sunset Springs Racquet Club. You should come check us out sometime," I say, offering up a big smile and strong handshake. "Bex Martin."

"You don't say?" His face lights up, like every word I'm saying is the most interesting thing in the world. "I've heard that place is special. Very authentic Sunset Springs. I'd love to visit."

"It's one of the original midcentury modern buildings in the area, from the 1960s. I want to try to get it designated as a historical building." I talk about the club like it's my child, and frankly, I feel as proud as I imagine parents do, watching their kids take their first steps or graduate from high school.

"Bex and I are playing the Paddle Battle here together," Niko says. "She's got a monster serve."

I do? I mean, I *do*, but this is the first time I've heard him compliment my pickleball game, and I shoot him a skeptical look.

"Ah!" Freddie says, slapping his hands together enthusiastically. "Fantastic. I'll be there. I've been training at Starlight for the last few months, but I'm technically the celebrity guest that day."

He gives us a sheepish shrug, but the modesty feels forced. Freddie is hot shit, and he knows it better than anyone.

I can feel Niko prickle a little next to me, and I give him a quick look, trying to ascertain why. All he says is a flat "Great."

Freddie tilts his chin back in my direction, the high beam of his eyes once again on me, leaving me feeling exposed.

"Bex." He repeats my name back with a nod. "Smashing outfit, Bex. That shirt is perfection."

"Oh, thanks. I made it," I tell him, feeling a self-conscious flush of pride.

"Wait, seriously?" Freddie replies. "You made that?" He gestures down at my BIG DINK ENERGY tee, the same shirt Niko had so unceremoniously refused to match with me. "I love it."

"I do it for fun, mostly. It's not a big deal," I say, and I'm immediately annoyed with myself that my initial instinct is to downplay my creative projects. "I'm going to be fundraising for the club, though, so I thought I'd try my hand at T-shirts."

"Well, it's fantastic," he gushes. "Can I buy one? I love to support local spots."

"No!" I say, and then shake my head, trying to clear out the nervous jitters. I'm used to talking about the club, but I rarely discuss my fashion creations with anyone outside of Sunset Springs. "I mean no, you can't buy one. But I'd love to make you one, on me. I'd just need to get your size and print it up for you. I could have it ready in a day or two. Just having you wear it around would be massively helpful."

"Wonderful," he says, and he seems genuinely enthused. "Can I put my number in your phone?"

"Yeah, of course." I dig my cracked iPhone out of my bag and hand it over to him.

Freddie flashes one of those wickedly handsome smiles as he taps his number in and passes it back to me. I study his perfectly white, even teeth; either he's one of those genetically blessed dental anomalies, or he's coughed up thousands for veneers. Either way, his mouth, like everything else about him, is movie-star caliber.

"I sent myself a text message from your number," he says with a flirtatious quirk of his brows. "Let's connect."

"That would be great," I say, beaming back at him.

"Well." He leans in to do that half hug thing again, grasping Niko's biceps affectionately. "I guess I'll see you soon then, eh?"

"I can't wait," Niko replies flatly.

"Bex, lovely to meet you." Freddie gives me a firm shake of his hand. "I'll wear that shirt with pride."

"Amazing! Thank you." A light thrill passes through me.

Freddie Alwin was a massive deal. If I could get him in one of my T-shirts, who knows who else would see it or, better yet, want one.

Freddie saunters off with a wave, and the second he's engulfed in the crowd I smack Niko on the arm.

"Why didn't you tell me that you knew Freddie Alwin? I don't appreciate my *boyfriend* and teammate keeping secrets from me."

"It's public knowledge." Niko gives me a peeved look. "You seem to know everything, so I just assumed you knew that too."

"How the hell would I know that?" I ask, already defensive. No matter how many times I tell myself that he is strictly my on-court partner, I still always feel like I am on high alert around him. Our kiss has triggered every fight-or-flight response in my body, and I can't shut it off. I prepare for his retort, readying myself for something salty about how I'd denied we were a couple, a failed execution of our shared plan.

"Well, I specifically recall you making fun of how I hurt my knee when we met." His eyes narrow as he moves closer to me, and the look on his face is both menacing and playful, like a cat delighted with the mouse it's just cornered. "So shouldn't you also know that I was playing Freddie Alwin when that happened?"

"Okay, first of all…" I take a step back, offended by his assessment of me. "I didn't *make fun of you*."

"I have a very good memory, and I'm pretty sure the word you used was *tantrum*." Niko gives the glass in his hand a small circular shake, jostling the ice.

"Well, what would you call it?" I retort. "That's sure what I remember it looking like."

He purses his lips together, clearly annoyed, but doesn't offer up an alternative.

"You still could have said something!" I throw up my hands. "He's a huge deal in professional pickleball. I literally would have been begging you to put me in touch with him had I known you were friends."

"We are not friends," Niko hisses, like it's the most offensive thing anyone's ever said about him.

"So you hate the guy because he just happened to be there when you hurt yourself," I say.

"I didn't just *hurt* myself, Bex. I ended my entire career. My life."

There's nothing I can say back. I can't comprehend what it's like to have your body not cooperate with your brain, though it dawns on me, as I stare at him, face clouded with rage, that I've seen it happen before, recently. It just didn't end my mom's career, her passion. It ended everything.

"I'm sorry," I say. "I didn't mean—"

"It is fucking humiliating to lose," he says, cutting me off. "Especially to an opportunistic asshole like Freddie Alwin. The guy's a prick."

"He seemed perfectly nice to me," I protest, thinking back to how eager he was for his own BIG DINK ENERGY T-shirt.

"Trust me, spend five years living with him on the road. He'll become very obnoxious very quickly."

"That still doesn't explain why you seem to hate him so

much," I say as I take a step closer to him. Everything about Niko is severe—the pitch-black of his irises, the sharp widow's peak in the center of his hairline, and the way his muscles cut lines through his skin in directions to all the parts of his body I still desperately want to run my hands across.

He's quiet for a minute and then takes another step closer. "Because he was there. Because he was part of what happened, whether he caused it or not, and now he's always going to be linked to that loss, to that terrible, shitty day when my entire life changed. It doesn't make sense, and I don't care if it makes sense to anyone but me. He's a part of it."

He slowly blinks once, then twice, like he's sending me Morse code with his eyes.

"Also he's a fucking dick," Niko says again, breaking the silence.

I can't help it. I laugh, a loud guffaw that cuts through the quiet of the night. For all his moody, brooding shit, Niko somehow has the timing of a stand-up comic. He's genuinely funny when he wants to be, though I have no idea if he realizes it.

"Well, I'm still going to give him a T-shirt," I say diplomatically.

"Which you called 'not a big deal,'" he says, and it takes me a second to realize he's quoting my words from the conversation just moments ago.

"Yeah," I reply, annoyed at how random this inquisition is. "So what?"

His eyes drift upward as if it should be obvious why this is irking him. But it's not.

"You shouldn't talk about the stuff you make like that."

He pauses in thought for a moment, like he's staring in front of two roads and deciding which one to take.

"Okay." I look down at my outfit, perplexed, because I'm not quite sure what point he's trying to make.

"Your clothes are special," he says finally.

I register the kindness of his words, the way his eyes soften into something almost sweet as he stares at me. But this brief moment of affection for him is pushed aside by a lingering grievance from earlier.

"Says the guy who flat-out rejected the T-shirt I made for him!"

I throw up my hands in annoyance. Kissing or not, he constantly makes my head spin in intoxicating, infuriating twisters of frustration.

Niko glances off in the distance and then looks back at me. "It doesn't mean I don't like it," he says quietly.

This still sounds like bullshit to me, and I quirk my face into a skeptical scowl to let him know.

He raises his hands defensively. "Look, I'm not as confident as you are with things like fashion."

I blink, stunned, and almost shout *Uh, that's impossible*, because, well, it is. This is a person who flaunts his arrogance like a three-piece suit. But instead I wait for a second and watch him, and the unsure look on his face tells me that maybe there's some truth to this admission.

It takes me a beat to realize that this is Niko's version of a confession. It's something he doesn't let just anyone know about him. But of all people, he told me.

"Okay, well..." My frown lines soften into something

close to a smile. "Thanks, I guess. But it would have been nice if you'd worn it."

"As if a shirt that says 'Big Dink Energy' will convince anyone that Freddie actually has it," Niko scoffs, a devilish smile slowly spreading across his face.

"Well, you couldn't pull off that shirt, even if you did wear it."

"Oh, come on, Bex." His lips curl into a smile that sends my stomach burning. "You don't need a T-shirt to know what I have."

We're trapped in an awkward silence until Wilson comes sashaying up to us, a tumbler of brown liquor in hand. "And here I thought I was going to have to convince you to come tonight," he says to me, planting a kiss on my check. He reeks of self-tanner and cologne, and it makes my stomach turn with nausea.

"Hi, Wilson." The best I can muster is a tight-lipped smile.

"You got my email, I assume?" he asks, cocking his brow at me.

"Yeah, I did, but I didn't look at it," I lie. "Considering it's dead on arrival." I burn with the desire to put this man in his place, and I can't wait to walk away with his prize money and use it to make sure he never asks about buying the racquet club again.

Wilson ignores my retort and turns to Niko with open arms.

"I almost did a double take when I saw your name on the registration." He says everything too loudly, like he wants the whole party to hear it. "We're going to have to give you a hero's welcome."

Niko nods politely. "It's nice to meet you..."

"Wilson." His voice booms. "Big fan. I thought you were done playing, so it's pretty exciting to have your return be here at Starlight."

"Thank you. I'm looking forward to it," Niko says, and seeing him like this, all manners, makes me want to laugh. I much prefer his saltier, ornery side, as much as it also drives me nuts. "But it's not actually my return. It's just pickleball."

"That's what they all say," Wilson cracks, and I can tell it gets under Niko's skin.

"Listen," Wilson continues, "I was going to try to track down your number, but while I have you, I'm just going to lay it out now, man to man." His energy is used-car salesman, all showy and smooth, as he positions himself directly in front of Niko. "I love that you entered the tournament, but an exhibition match between you and Freddie would be an even bigger draw. Especially with you both playing pickleball. Best of two out of three games. And obviously, I'll pay you."

Wilson pauses, like he's planned how this conversation was going to go and this is where he decided to take a breath.

"Freddie's all for it," Wilson continues. "I've already run it by him. The chance to be his partner is part of the silent auction we're running leading up to the tournament. It's all going live online tomorrow. But playing with him, and *against you*? It will be an even bigger draw for people bidding on the chance to be in the game. And the press will love it. Or maybe you and Freddie could pair up, and—"

Niko cuts him off. "Bex is my partner. If I'm going up against Freddie, it's with her."

"Fair enough." Wilson lifts his hands defensively, his drink sloshing. "How about this. I'll match the tournament prize money for an exhibition, if that helps to entice you. And if you win, you get double that. We'll make it interesting."

This is when my eyes practically roll out of my head and fall into the champagne flute I'm clutching to my chest.

"You don't have to tell me now," Wilson says, leveling a look at Niko. And then with a jab to his forearm, he adds, "Just tell me tonight, before you leave."

"We'll do it!" I interject, practically throwing my body in the middle of the two of them. "We're in."

15

AFTER WILSON HAS walked away, satisfied with our plan, I drag Niko over to a high-top table set up on one of the tennis courts, next to two women gushing about the new line of pickleball bags they're designing.

"Shouldn't we have discussed this first?" Niko says, his voice clipped. He weaves his arms tightly in front of his chest, clearly exasperated with the entire situation.

"Oh, you mean like how we thoroughly weighed the pros and cons of this plan before deciding to become doubles partners who are dating?" I ask, giving him an incredulous look. "Come on, Niko. This is basically how you and I make decisions as a team."

He presses his eyes closed a beat too long, brow clenched in quiet thought. It's the face someone makes before they're about to say no to something, and so I decide not to give him the chance.

"Did you hear how much money he's offering, Niko?"

I'm as close as I can get to yelling while also trying not to draw attention to ourselves. "If we can win the tournament *and* the exhibition match, that could cover the cost of court repairs, easily. And maybe other stuff."

This is my meal ticket, my escape from this hole I can't seem to crawl out of.

"Please," I beg, reaching up and grabbing onto his forearms. His muscles, like the look on his face, are unmoving, firm. "I need this. The club needs this. Think about how much Loretta loves the place."

His jaw relaxes a bit. "See, now you're just trying to manipulate me, Princess."

"I am," I agree as he inches just a little bit closer to me. "For a good cause. And you can show the world how incredible you are at your favorite game. Isn't that your dream?"

I'm trying to butter him up, but it's also the truth. Niko had effortlessly grasped pickleball in a matter of days.

His lips part into something that barely resembles a smile, but for Niko it might as well be a grin. "Okay," he relents. "I'm in. But—"

Before he can finish his sentence, his phone buzzes in his pocket and we break apart.

"It's Angela," he says, glancing down at the screen. He paces as he types out a reply, distracted as he walks along the edge of the table. When he finishes he moves closer, and wraps an arm around my shoulder, fake-boyfriend mode activated. "She'll be here in a couple of minutes. Can we discuss this later?"

He feels solid behind me, like I could fall back and trust that he'd catch me. I spin around to face him, and all I can see are the geometric angles of his face. He looks like he's cut from ice, cheekbones razorblade sharp.

"No, we can't," I tell him, poking him in the chest with my index finger. "If I'm going to have to sit here and lie to Angela, you can do this exhibition match with me."

"I watched you lie to Angela the other night with flying colors," he says as his lips curl into a sly smile. "You're very good at it." He's leaning close to me, and every now and then, I can catch waves of his scent. It's crisp and minty, like a chilled mojito on a blisteringly hot day.

"I was panicking then," I say, suddenly flustered. "We had just..."

I swallow, the weight of his gaze causing me to perspire. Why does everything he does have to be so intense? He couldn't even have a conversation casually. "You know."

Niko chuckles, his eyes searching through the crowd and then landing directly back on me. "You don't have to lie about anything. Have you felt like you've been lying to Deb or Loretta?"

He has a point. Something about this has started to feel natural, shifting without me entirely realizing it. "Not really," I admit.

"Just be your regular charming self, Bex. You're very hard to dislike."

I stare up at him, waiting for him to follow this up with some sort of snark, but instead he looks at me expectantly, and so I let out a nervous sigh. "I'll try my best."

"Princess, we both know we're in way too deep for you to blow this up now," he says, giving my wrist a squeeze.

I hate that he's right, and I hate that I lace my hand through his and play along when Angela arrives a moment later, clutching two phones against her chest. "One's for recording," she explains off the bat, like she gets the question a lot. "Should we grab something to eat first?"

"Sounds great," Niko says with a relaxed, cool look on his face. "Bex and I are excited to chat with you."

He tucks an arm around me as we meander over to one of the tables covered in platters of sliced cheeses and mounds of grapes and berries, and we make mindless chitchat as we pile paper plates with food. We scoop up some napkins, and each of us grabs a drink from the bar before finding a table to crowd around.

Angela slides a phone in between our plates, and she and Niko fall into an easy conversation about his time at UCLA and that iconic moment he arrived at the US Open as a nobody and left a star. He's downright animated as he retells the story of growing up playing tennis against his father, who coached him through high school, and qualifying for the US Open as an unknown college player. There's a lightness to his voice that's new to me, a spark of joy that seems both completely foreign to the Niko I know but intrinsically a part of him and who he is. I'm in the middle of wondering how I've completely missed this side of him when I see it shift away in an instant.

"Does Freddie Alwin's rise in professional pickleball have anything to do with your new interest in playing?" Angela inquires. "Surely you've been following the way he's exploded onto the scene?"

His jaw clenches the tiniest bit before he takes a small sip of his beer. "You know, I've been so focused on my own recovery since my injury that I haven't had time to give anyone else's career much thought," he says diplomatically. "But I'm happy to know that my old friend is doing so well in his new sport."

"Old friend?" Angela pushes. "You two were rivals for quite some time. He was your opponent during your last match at the French Open."

"Ah, well, I tried to leave all that behind on the court. And I hope to keep it that way in pickleball too." Niko's face doesn't change as he speaks, but there is an edge to his voice, and it's all right there for me to see. There is way more to their connection, and I have a feeling it played a bigger part in the reason he'd roped me into being his partner than I realized.

"And besides," he continues smoothly, "I try to never hold on to the past. I'm more interested in the future. Like what Bex is doing to try to save the racquet club."

He's giving me an opening, and I push my suspicions about Niko's motives aside for now to put on a good show for Angela.

"Yeah, my parents were looking to start their own club but couldn't afford anything on the market," I say, finding my voice. "Then they stumbled onto this place in foreclosure and took it on. When my dad died twenty-two years ago, my mom did it all herself. She was the first person to bring pickleball out to Sunset Springs. She was amazing, and now I'm just trying to live up to, like, a fraction of her legacy."

Niko and I may be pretending to be partners, but there is

nothing even remotely fake about my love for the club and its storied past. I speak directly from my heart, and by the time I'm done, describing my mom in her hospital bed, computer on her lap as she ran through the ins and outs of the club just days before she died, Angela appears to be on the verge of tears, and Niko's face is hard and focused only on me. I've rarely shared these intimate moments with anyone outside of my core circle of friends. They've long been too raw to even mention. But now they feel vital and important, a crucial part of my story and the club's.

"I know most people don't think a twenty-six-year-old with no business experience can handle taking over a family business, much less one that requires you to operate on all cylinders all the time," I say, "which is why I want to prove them wrong. But first I need to save the place from falling down."

A lump has formed in my throat. I'm choked up with emotion, but strangely, it's not grief. I blink as it settles in. I'm proud. Confident. I don't just want to do this. I really, truly believe that I can. For the first time in days, thirty thousand dollars feels like a hurdle I can actually leap over.

Angela leans forward and taps the red button on her iPhone screen, ending her recording. She looks between the two of us and then shakes her head in a way that tells me we did a good job, giving her exactly what she needs for her story. Relief rushes through me, just like it did when I was a kid and got a decent grade on a test, knowing I didn't let my teacher down.

"Both of you have such incredible stories," she marvels.

"In many ways, Niko, your path as an underdog mirrors exactly what Bex is going through right now."

He nods, though I can tell by the way he squints his eyes in thought that he's not totally sure what she's getting at, which is a relief, because I'm not either.

"Look." She glances between the two of us eagerly. "I need to get my editor to sign off on this, but after talking to you both today, I think the only way to do this story is to make it about the two of you, together."

"What?" Niko says, as I blurt out a loud "Huh?"

Angela slowly shakes her head with determined purpose. "Two people, both trying to salvage their past by forging into the future," she says, her vision taking shape as she talks. "And you're not just a couple but also partners on the court as well? It's too good not to tell as one connected story. We can have our photographer come out, shoot the two of you playing at the club, and then we'll document the tournament as well."

"Well, things have kind of changed," Niko starts.

"We just agreed to a one-off exhibition match, too," I tell Angela. "We're playing against Freddie and whoever bids the most to be his partner."

"Well, hell, if you win *that*?" A pleased smile creeps across Angela's face. "It'll make the story even better."

16

Monday, April 24

WHEN I WALK up to court 4 two days later, Niko is already leaning against the chain-link fence, arms crossed, looking bored. He's the only person here, and I swear I see a twitch of excitement at the corner of his eyes when I stop in front of him.

"You're late" is all he says, but there's a smile creeping up at the edge of his lips.

"No, you're just weirdly early," I tease. Every interaction with this man waffles between ice-cold and scorching hot, and it seems to permanently raise my heart rate to its maximum level and torment my nervous system.

But even with that weighing on me, the past week has felt oddly like a relief, the first time in ages my thoughts haven't been totally tainted by the shadow of grief or the stress of keeping the club running. Even this morning feels sunnier, like the light is streaming in just a bit more.

And there's something else cranking the joy on inside me today. Dragging Niko here today—to play against some of the club's longest-running members—has triggered a forgotten, dust-covered truth about myself: I love playing pickleball.

I haven't given myself a chance to simply play for fun or let myself enjoy it in so long. But the pure pleasure of it, the playfulness that's at the heart of the game, and my fierce competitiveness have come rushing back since pairing up with Niko, and my entire being feels slightly more buoyant than it did just a few weeks ago.

"Well, look what the cat dragged in," Randall rasps in his familiar scratchy drawl as he saddles up to the court. His scraggly gray hair is swept back in a faded red bandana, and the tank top that hangs off his lean runner's body looks like it has been in his closet since the sixties. Unlike most of the residents of Sunset Springs, Randall is a lifelong local and a total desert rat. He was one of my mom's first tennis clients, and I went to elementary school with his son, which is why he still calls me "kid" even though I'm inching closer and closer to thirty.

"Randall!" I crack a cocky smile in his direction as I weave my hair back into a braid. "What are you doing here? Did you escape the nursing home again?"

Before Mom got sick, I used to roll in here on the weekends with a dozen donuts from Krispy Kreme and a penchant for kicking boomer ass. But now running the club comes first, and I haven't made it to the long-standing meet-up, nicknamed the Six AM Club, in months. This crew has been gathering to play for years—Randall is one of the other few members who has a key to the courts—and the shit-talk and teasing is as important to the Six AM Club as the game play, if not more.

Randall envelops me in a warm hug, and when I pull away, I push him over toward Niko.

"Randall, this is Niko. Niko, Randall."

A flicker of recognition passes across Randall's face. "You're the tennis player I see on court one all day long, right? Going apeshit on the ball machine?"

Niko nods.

"You're a monster out there," Randall says, still sizing him up. "Do you coach clinics?"

"Only a little. I just did one at UCLA a few weeks ago," Niko says.

"Well, give me your number. I have a whole crew I still play with, and we'd kill for a coach. We're getting rusty." Randall glances around, lowering his voice. "Just don't tell anyone here today that I'm still playing tennis."

"I heard that!" I quip, teasing him back. But I clock his words on a serious level, too. No one has taught tennis at the club since Mom passed, and hiring a new pro has been on my to-do list forever. I've been putting it off because I haven't been able to square it with our budget, or at least that's what I've been telling myself. But I know there's a deeper reason I've been avoiding filling that spot, one that is intertwined with the complex feelings of replacing her with someone new, even though it feels sort of absurd. I'm not hiring a new mother, just someone to coach a few tennis lessons. And yet, I can't bring myself to do it.

"She always does," Randall says as he reaches in and

grasps Niko's hand in a firm handshake. "Has she served your ass to you on a platter yet?"

Randall points in my direction, and Niko lets out a loud laugh.

"She's definitely tried," he says, and I can already see the two of them forming some sort of alliance. "Even though we're supposed to be partners."

"Niko and I are playing in our first tournament in a couple of weeks," I explain. "We've gotta toughen him up and help him lose the bombastic tennis swing."

"Ooooh, a project." Randall claps his hands together eagerly. "I'm excited already."

Then he steps a little closer to me, giving my shoulder a kind squeeze. "It's good to see you back here."

"It's good to be here," I say. "It's been so busy."

"Well, you two can get first game then," he says courteously with a little bow, as the rest of the regulars start to gather nearby, unpacking their equipment bags and spraying copious amounts of sunscreen on their bodies.

When the group is fully gathered, I introduce Niko and then give him the rundown.

"Norma—former prosecutor and a vicious serve," I say, pointing my paddle at the tall, glamorous woman across from me, her platinum hair secured in a perfectly coiffed bun at the nape of her neck.

"Guilty as charged," she says, her pun eliciting groans from the rest of the crew.

"Vikram's a snowbird from Minneapolis," I continue with a smile, because it's a jab I know will get under his skin.

"Oh, come on, Bex, I've been here full-time for twenty years," Vikram scolds me with a shake of his head.

"Doesn't count!" I tease back, before moving on. "And this is Derek. He likes to forget that he's not still playing tennis, so you two will definitely get along."

Derek, an older Black man with a shock of gray-white hair, lets out a snort at this accusation.

"Is she always this tough on tennis players?" Niko asks him, and Derek nods yes with a roll of his eyes.

"And here come the vultures," Randall murmurs, pointing at the trio of women who just stepped out from the lobby, all with short grandmotherly hairdos of various colors. "We call them that because they'll tear you apart until you're just a pile of bones and skin left to rot on the court."

"Jesus Christ," Niko mutters under his breath, as he readjusts his sweat band.

"Randall used to write screenplays," I explain. "He's got a flair for the dramatic. And his net game is sick."

"So what now, we play?" Niko asks.

"Yeah," I say, nodding. "And win."

Niko's swagger is in full force as we saunter onto the court to warm up for our first game. He plops down on the bench, legs man-spread so wide there's barely room for me to slide in next to him.

"Is it really necessary to take up three-quarters of the bench just to air out your crotch?"

"Jesus, Bex." He crosses his legs in front of him self-consciously. "I'm just tall."

"I know a lot of tall women, and none of them need

to spread out like that," I say, squirting a shot of Gatorade into my mouth as I sit down next to him, shifting into coach mode. "Listen, just because you're an amazing tennis player doesn't mean we're automatically going to win every game."

He nods like he agrees with me, but everything in his face screams arrogant skepticism.

"Niko, I mean it," I say firmly. "You need to actually try to play pickleball today, and not just the glorified tennis crap you've been giving me in practice."

"Bex." He folds his hands behind his head and leans back against the metal bars. "I want to remind you that you're asking me to take playing a game named after a pickled cucumber seriously."

"No, I'm asking you to take *me* seriously."

This shuts him up for a moment, and he swivels around to look at me. "I do" is all he says.

"Then you better remember everything we've gone over so far. Because again, you're not going to be able to just rely on strength and dominance alone."

"I can be soft, Bex," he says, and I immediately feel like my entire body is blushing. His voice is so cool sometimes that it's hard to know when he's trying to torment me with his words and when he's just, well, talking. Constantly being on edge around Niko frays my nerves, my heart never slowing down from its persistent, amped-up beat.

"Promise me, you will take this game seriously," I say, desperate for some assurance that he understands what I'm saying.

"I promise," he replies, and he sounds so steady and sure of himself that I let myself believe him.

Two of the vultures do indeed kick our asses in our first game. We lose eleven to three, but not before Niko lets out a loud "Fucking shit" when his serve goes out of bounds for the fifth time.

"You're still thinking like a tennis player," I say softly, as he downs a Gatorade in one giant gulp. I trail a glance over his Adam's apple and then remind myself to focus. "I know it seems counterintuitive, but you need to do less."

He runs the back of his hand across his mouth, his tongue darting out against his lips. I blink extra hard and try to stifle the thumping in my chest. He has taken up residency under my skin, and I try not to let on.

"That goes against everything I normally do on the court," he says finally, and he seems to actually be pondering my advice.

"Pickleball is a different beast," I remind him. "I'm your teammate. You have to rely on me now. And technically, I'm also your coach. I want you to be successful here. You should trust me on this."

He gives me a surprised look. "You don't think I trust you?"

"I don't think you trust anyone, at least not on the court." The words spill out of my mouth before I even realize what I'm saying. "Besides yourself."

Niko considers my words for a moment and then nods in agreement. "Fine, Bex," he says. "I trust you. Let's go win this next one."

We take our positions on the court across from Randall and Vikram. Vikram hollers out the starting score. "Zero-zero-two!"

There's a whole catalog of things that could distract me this morning, everything from my growing list of club repairs to the way Niko bites his bottom lip when he's concentrating in a game. But a few deep breaths clear everything out of my head, and the second Vikram raises his paddle, my brain settles on one simple thing: returning the ball.

This was one of the first things my mom taught me about pickleball, all those years ago: Just worry about getting the ball back over the net. That's how you stay alive in this game.

And so I channel all my focus into that one act, blocking out everything else—my grief, my worry, the way the tag of my shirt keeps irritating a spot at the back of my neck. It all falls to the back of my mind as I keep my eyes laser-focused on the ball, following its every move as it connects with Vikram's paddle with a loud, satisfying tap and shoots over the net, fast and low, landing just in front of me.

I knock it back with a powerful return, keeping my opponents far on their end of the court before dashing up to the net beside Niko. Randall lobs a perfect third-shot drop back at us, soft and low in the kitchen, but Niko's there with a quick return down the centerline.

They volley back at us, but we keep the ball in play and go back and forth with ease, despite their best attempts to thwart our returns. They switch up the speed of the ball, and even try to knock a shot behind us toward the end of the court, but I never take my eye off the ball, even as sweat starts to pool on the bridge of my nose, my breath now clipped and short.

Finally, after it feels like they're never going to back down, I knock the ball right into the left corner of the kitchen. Randall's backhand is no match for the placement of my shot, and he hits it right into the net.

"Yes!" I shout, pumping my paddle into the air. I feel downright euphoric, as if this is the only thing that matters in the world because, right now, it is. This is the magic of pickleball, and I'd forgotten the high that comes from finally shutting down your opposing team. It feels fucking amazing.

"Shit, Princess." Niko sounds downright impressed as he smacks a sweaty palm on my shoulder. "You're vicious out there."

"I know." I puff up my shoulders proudly, jogging backward toward the edge of the court to take my first serve.

Thirty minutes later, Randall and Vikram are slapping their paddles against ours, congratulating us on our win. "Good game, new guy," Randall says to a clearly proud Niko, before turning to me. "And you, kiddo. Damn. You played that one like you had something to prove."

"I did," I reply, and I can't contain the grin on my face. It's not the win that's sending me; it's how damn good it feels to just have fun doing it.

"I like watching you win," Niko says as he pops open the lid on his water bottle, and the look on his face is both victorious and smug. Suddenly I'm overheating just from the sight of him, remembering how it felt to entangle his body with mine.

"Don't get too cocky," I say, steadying my resolve as I poke him in the shoulder with the edge of my paddle. "Maybe we just got lucky that round."

But we win our next game, and the one after that, and by the time we're walking back to the lobby, we're both beaming, triumphant.

I slide onto the stool behind the front desk, and he leans his elbows on the edge, like he always does, bending to get a little bit closer.

"Aren't you going to congratulate me on winning?" he teases, one dark brow raised suggestively. "I was really good out there."

I make a big show of ignoring him as I fire up my computer, drumming my fingers on the desk. I hear him release an exasperated sigh, and instead of glancing up at him, I pull open the desk drawer and dig through the messy array of dried-up Sharpies and dull scissors until I pull out a ballpoint pen, holding it up with awe like I've just discovered gold in a pile of dirt.

Finally, I tilt my head a half an inch to see if he's watching my performance. A wave of pleasure washes over me when I discover him focused on my face, a smile lurking just beneath the surface of my lips.

I toss the pen at him, expecting him to duck from my attack. Instead he catches it effortlessly and leans across the counter, tucking it behind my ear. My throat practically collapses in on itself, but I recover quickly. "You're a pain in the ass, you know that?"

Niko nods. "Of course I do. I learned it from my coach."

We're both grinning now. "She must give good advice," I say, as I tug the pen from its resting place and bring it to my lips, puffing on it like a cigar.

"She does," he agrees, eyes still following my every move. "I might even trust her, a little bit."

"She'll keep that in mind."

And I do, for the rest of the day.

17

Thursday, May 4

"ALL I KNOW is that when I went to pick up my blood pressure meds at the pharmacy the other day, he wouldn't stop flirting with me. He even asked me if I needed him to go over the medication. I've been on it for years!"

Maureen gives the rest of us a knowing look. Our book club pick for the month, a meaty thriller with a creepy, blood-dripping cover, sits on the coffee table in front of her, untouched.

"But Thad is well aware that we're a couple! We always go in there together to pick up prescriptions," Deb exclaims, before chomping down on a carrot stick. She chews for a second and then gasps. "Maybe he's interested in both of us. Do we think he's poly?"

"Oh my god, not this again." I groan, but it's followed by a giggle. I love these book club conversations and the way they always seem to veer into Deb wondering about the sexual proclivities of everyone in Sunset Springs.

It only took a few minutes of my first book club meeting with Loretta, Deb, and Maureen for me to realize the truth: This book club isn't about books. Not one bit.

Oh sure, we talk about all sorts of things, like the latest house to sell for way over asking price despite its lackluster curb appeal or whether or not Costco has put their holiday items out for sale way too early (a unanimous yes). And we trade cross-generational information. I broke down my personal rankings of the Housewives franchises, and Loretta pontificated on the universal sex appeal of Bruce Springsteen.

Sure, I tried to read the books we picked, especially if I got lucky with a library request coming in on time. But I knew each month when I set foot in Loretta's living room with our selection tucked under my arm that I wouldn't crack it open to discuss a scene, much less even mention the main character's name.

But the dating status of the recently widowed pharmacist in town? We could spend an hour on it, easily.

"You need to get hip with the kids, Bex," Deb jokes. "Everyone's dating multiple people at once these days, even us boomers."

"Bruce Springsteen isn't," Loretta adds from her perch on the couch. She always found a way to bring the conversation back around to the Boss. "He and Patti have been together for something like thirty years. Did you know when I went to his concert a couple of years ago, it was almost three hours long?"

"You know what that means," Maureen cracks as she tosses back a handful of marcona almonds. "Stamina."

"I bet Patti knows all about it," Loretta says, causing the rest of us to erupt in a fit of cackling laughter.

"Deb, you should make this into a video for your TikTok," I say as I start clearing plates off the coffee table, carrying them into the kitchen. "I think the teens would love this horny group dissecting the prowess of Bruce Springsteen. You'd go viral."

She considers it for a moment as she sips her peppermint tea. "It's not half bad. I'll add it to my list."

I bring the dishes to the sink and flip on the water as Maureen pipes up with another idea for her wife's blooming internet presence. The sound of their banter blends in with the steady stream of the faucet, forming a sort of soothing lullaby of sound. I settle into my task, rinsing one dish after the other as my eyes focus on the giant window in front of me, just over the small pots of succulents that line the inside sill.

Directly in front of me, a few yards away, is Loretta's small carriage house, where Niko has been living. One square of window shines with light, which I take to mean he's home, just steps away from me. A million different scenarios flood my mind, snapshots of his life contained inside those walls. Niko puttering around the kitchen in pajamas, chopping vegetables for a salad, or wandering out of the bathroom, still wet from the shower with a towel slung around his waist.

There are so many parts of his life I know nothing about, and I can't help myself: I'm instantly curious.

How many pillows does he sleep with? Does he use a special face wash, or just whatever bar of soap Loretta has next to the sink?

Get a hold of yourself, Bex, I think, shutting off the water. I reach for the fuchsia towel hanging off a hook on the wall and begin drying the wineglasses resting on the dish rack, taking my time to slowly clean out the hollow of each cup.

Anything to distract myself.

Maybe he's one of those people who doesn't sleep with any pillows at all.

Clearly, it isn't working. Trying not to think about Niko in there is as impossible as ignoring the urge to scratch a fresh mosquito bite. A different plan is needed.

"Hey, Retta, do you think it would be okay if I stopped by and said hi to Niko?"

All three of them pause, mid-conversation, and look up at me. I can tell that they are collectively biting their tongues, holding back whatever witty comments they are surely dying to make about our "relationship." And frankly, I don't blame them. It's been just over two weeks since he and I announced our newfound love affair out of the blue, and they've been shockingly restrained.

"Of course, dear," Loretta replies with a nod. "I'm sure he'd love to see you."

I wait, dragging the cloth along the lip of the glass as I watch the three of them, anticipating the one-liners I'm sure they've been dying to say. Still, nothing.

"Oh, come on," I say finally. "Not one of you is going to make a joke about the two of us? Did you all sign some pact agreeing not to joke about Niko and me?"

Deb shakes her head. "No jokes here. We're all happy for you."

Maureen nods. "I think we all agree that a little romance might be good for you."

"So you've all been talking about us?" I ask, and the three of them straight-up beam.

"We're excited for you," Loretta says, and then adds, "both of you."

A full-body flush sweeps over me, the burn of self-consciousness from knowing we'd been a topic of conversation. Even though our relationship is a façade, the giddy sheepishness I feel anytime Niko's name comes up is genuine.

"I was just going to bring him some of the cookies I brought," I say as an excuse, even though the idea popped into my head seconds before the words left my mouth.

"You deserve some love in your life, Bex," says Deb, and the others nod in agreement. I can't take the weight of their gaze, their genuine happiness for me. It's hard enough to recognize how badly they want this for me. But it's another thing altogether to sit with an even more uncomfortable truth: It's something I want for myself too.

Not with a pretend boyfriend whose time in Sunset Springs has a very real end date. And not now, when I can barely keep the club afloat, much less anything else. But someday. Soon.

I run the dishrag over the countertop and then grab the half-full plastic container of oatmeal raisin cookies. "I'm just going to say a quick hi," I explain. "Don't leave without me."

"Take your time," Deb says, shooing me out the door with a wave. "We've still got a lot to discuss in here. You know, you're not the only one with a hot romance to gossip about."

She shoots Loretta a look, and Loretta raises her brows in response but says nothing.

"Oh my god, you three and that pharmacist," I joke as I head toward the back door. "Have fun."

● ● ●

Loretta's backyard is overflowing with native desert plants, cacti towering like skyscrapers over the small rectangular pool. My footsteps crunch through the gravel as I make my way toward the apartment out back, pausing at the door. The front window is still lit up, but I'm suddenly frozen with uncertainty. Niko's not expecting me, and it feels oddly intimate to just show up, unannounced. I barely call people on the phone out of the blue anymore, much less stop by their actual homes. I weigh this worry against the urge I have to see him, to say hi, to see how he's doing, even though we played together just this morning. The desire gnaws at me; it's more hunger than curiosity. Curiosity can be sated in other ways. This feels like I have no other choice but to bang on his door.

I'm about to knock when self-doubt stops me, and I turn to head back inside Loretta's house. And that's when I hear a click behind me, a bright light flashing on overhead.

"Bex?"

I spin on the balls of my feet, an awkward pirouette of sorts. "Hey!" I thrust the box of cookies toward him, and the plastic crackles under my nervous grip. "We're wrapping up our book club, and we had some extra food left over."

He grabs the container out of my hands. "Trader Joe's?"

I shrug. "Only the best for book club."

He breathes out a laugh and pops the lid open. He tears a

giant bite out of a cookie and stares at me as he chews. "Not bad," he says when he finishes.

"Well, that's all." I feel painfully awkward, like I've never talked to Niko before in my life, much less another human being.

"Do you wanna come in for a sec?" he asks, waving toward the open door behind him.

"Sure," I say, and follow him inside.

The kitchen and living room are one room, and it is decorated exactly like Loretta's house with brown wicker furniture covered in colorful floral prints. It looks more like a vacation rental on Maui than a house in the California desert, and I let out a little laugh at how very un-Niko it all is.

"Where do you even live, when you're not here?" I ask him, knowing only that he'd been training in Florida with one of his old coaches.

"I've been crashing at my parents' condo in Miami for a few years," he says as he places the box on the tiny kitchen island. "They live outside Athens full-time now, and so they very kindly let me stay there rent-free as long as I take care of the place. I'm supposed to help them sell it eventually."

"And go where?" I ask, as he pulls a glass off a shelf. I use this split second to admire the way his shoulder muscles shift under his shirt as his arm lifts overhead.

He turns to face me and gives a casual shrug. "No idea. You want some water?"

I nod, though his answer hasn't satisfied my curiosity. "Sure."

Niko shuffles toward the fridge, and it's only when he's not facing me that I notice he's dressed in a white T-shirt and navy-blue sweats, feet bare on the tile floor. I'd wondered how he'd look in a moment like this, and I like what I've discovered. He is especially handsome like this, casual and slightly disheveled. He is so rarely caught off guard that this feels like a glimpse into what that looks like.

"Let me guess, you wish there was *more* color in this house," I tease, sliding onto a woven rattan stool with a cushion covered in a print with bright-pink hibiscus flowers.

"Oh, yes." He matches the sarcasm in my voice, doubles it even. "Every day, I wake up and think, 'The one thing this place needs is more loud, clashing patterns.'"

"I bet you'll miss it when you leave," I say as he pivots around, pushing the glass across the counter until it's in front of me. "Are you excited to go back to Florida?"

"God no," he replies quickly, and he sounds so offended by the suggestion that I let out a laugh.

"That bad, huh," I say, and he catches himself.

"I mean, Florida's fine," Niko clarifies as he grabs another glass for himself. "I just associate it more with work than home. I was home schooled in high school because of tennis. Then my parents moved when my dad retired as my coach, and I was at UCLA. Now I go to Greece to visit them for the holidays. If I wasn't still training there, I don't know if it's where I'd want to be, necessarily. I just haven't ever had roots anywhere else, other than LA during college, and..."

He trails off, and I swallow. I can hear the word on his lips, even if he doesn't say it. *Here.* My skin bristles, hair raising along my arms. The chill of the air-conditioning probably, but I change the subject anyway, just to be safe.

"What are you up to tonight?" I ask, and then gulp back my entire glass of water in one long, nervous motion.

"Actually, I was just meditating," he says nonchalantly. My bottom lip drops open just a bit, unable to hide my surprise. Of all the things I expected Niko to be doing in here—one-armed push-ups, or practicing his scowl in the mirror—the last thing I thought I'd hear was that.

"Oh," I say. "That's cool."

"Day four hundred and twenty-four," he replies.

"Wow." I'm genuinely impressed. "I can barely make it one day meditating. Where did you learn to do that?"

"My therapist," he says, and he must sense my surprise. "What, you thought my training was all physical stuff?"

He's got me there. "Yeah, I guess I did," I tell him.

"So much of this shit is mental," he says. "Especially *my* shit."

He swallows back a sip of water, and his neck pulses in the most wildly seductive way.

"What *is* your shit, exactly?" I ask, not able to hold back the question. I am dying to know the cobwebs that linger on the edges of this man's psyche.

Niko thinks for a moment, pushing his hair off his forehead. "I'll tell you mine if you tell me yours."

I shrug in agreement, playing it cool even though I feel anything but right now. "Sure."

"Okay." He leans both elbows on the counter, fingers wrapping around the edge of his glass. "Let's see. Self-absorbed. I can't express my feelings, and I don't like that about myself. I want to have a relationship with my dad, but it feels like he only cares about me when I'm excelling at tennis."

He pauses, eyes on me as I digest this giant chunk of information. "How's that for shit?"

"Sounds like some hard shit," I reply.

"Constipation galore," he snarks, and I let out a laugh. "Your turn."

"Dead mom who I miss terribly," I tell him, pointing a finger at my chest. "Dead dad who I didn't ever really know, which is a whole other thing."

"I'm sorry," he says, wincing. "That sounds hard."

"Mommy *and* Daddy issues?" I joke. "Oh, it's great. Just a bounty of stuff to choose from."

Niko chuckles at this in a way that lets me know he empathizes, and it feels nice to be seen like this.

"Um, what else?" I drum my fingers on the counter as I rack my brain.

"That seems like plenty to me," he says. "It's nice knowing I'm in good company."

"Oh, wait, I thought of one more!" I sit up straighter. "I hate asking for help. I want to do everything myself, but because of that, I can't get a single thing done, and that drives me bonkers."

"Well, cheers to both of our shit." He raises his glass, and I clink it, even though mine's already empty.

"What does your dad think about you playing pickleball, then?" I ask. He's mentioned his father a few times in passing, and it seems like their relationship is tense, strained, more coach and student than father and son.

"I haven't told him," Niko admits. "Because he'd disown me."

It's a joke, I know, but there's a hardness to his face, his lips pressed together, that tells me there's a drop of truth to it.

"Though if I told him it involved me kicking Freddie's ass," he continues, "he'd probably approve, at least for one match."

"Oh my god," I say as realization hits me, scenes from the last few weeks playing back in my mind. The way Niko urgently and abruptly changed his mind about pickleball, needing to enter the tournament. His vague, brush-off answers every time Angela mentions Freddie.

"You didn't just sign up for this tournament because you thought it would make you look good in some profile," I say. It's so obvious, so glaring, that I'm mortified I didn't put this together from the start. It's because I was distracted, not just by the club, but by him. I instantly feel like the world's biggest idiot. "You've known this whole time that Freddie's been playing pickleball and training at Starlight. Did you know he was going to be in the exhibition match at the tournament, too?"

His silence tells me everything, and the fact that he hasn't been completely honest with me stings sharply, like a needle prick directly to the heart. "So, what, you're trying to steal his thunder?" I ask.

Niko nods. "That's part of it, yes."

"How big of a part?" I ask, body tensing as my hands grip the edge of the counter.

He swallows, avoiding my eyes. "The whole part," he says finally.

"Jesus Christ, Niko!" My body needs to shake off this

furious feeling, and I pop off the stool, pacing by him. "You could have at least mentioned this in passing over the last couple of weeks. Have you not heard me say communication is the most important part of playing pickleball?"

"I thought the most important part was patience." He attempts a smile, but I shut him down immediately with a frustrated shake of my head.

"Don't," I huff, pausing to look at him, hands on my hips. "I can't believe you didn't tell me that's what this was really about. You made it sound like you agreed to do it to help your image."

To help *me*.

Niko stills, his face stony, and it's a familiar, determined look I've seen before. At his core, Niko is a competitor, a gladiator meant for the ring. There's nothing he hates more than losing.

"I didn't know Wilson was going to hand me this exhibition match against Freddie on a silver platter," he says finally. "But yes, I knew he'd be there. He's the whole reason my career ended. You know I was playing Freddie when I fell."

"But he didn't make you trip," I snap. "He didn't smash your knee with a crowbar. You're not Nancy Kerrigan."

"No, that part was all me," he says with a cold laugh. "But Freddie shit-talked me for weeks. Behind my back, to my face. He had just done it on the court, and I snapped."

"And what, you're now on a mission to outshine him in pickleball because you overreacted to some trash talk?" This all sounds so juvenile that I have to scoff. And *he's* the one who thinks pickleball is childish? The nerve of this man.

"I'm trying to show him that I can take him on still, and

on his home turf." Niko is being so matter-of-fact about this that it only irks me more. "The exhibition match just makes it that much easier."

"So he was an asshole, and now you're trying to out-asshole him," I say. "What kind of a plan is that?"

"I've never not been an asshole, Bex," he grumbles as he saunters around the kitchen island and comes to face me again, a bitter scowl creeping across his face. "At least I've always been honest about that."

"You roped me into this tournament because you said you wanted a good story for the profile. You should have been honest with me." The hurt in my voice is palpable, as is the humiliation. What's worse, I'm not even sure why I'm so upset. I went into this with my eyes open, with the sole intention of finding a quick way to save the club. And yet somehow, this feels like getting my heart stomped on. "Do you even care about helping me at all?"

"Of course I do," he says, but it's hard to believe him now. "But I also care about putting Freddie in his place. Knocking his ego down a peg or two."

"Well, you were right about being self-absorbed." I want so bad to hide the hurt I'm feeling, but I've never been someone who can mask their true feelings. My cheeks burn, and I know it's written all over my face. "I'll let you get back to working on that."

I walk out of Niko's place without looking back at him, and I make sure to let the door slam shut as I go.

18

Friday, May 5

NIKO AND I meet up again in the morning to practice and immediately get to work. There's no talk of Freddie, or meditating, or our parents. Instead we're solely focused on the game. All business.

Or at least I am. Last night, I'd been annoyed with Niko, pissed off that he'd withheld this huge thing from me. But today, it is driving me, a motivating force. We both have reasons to try to win this exhibition match; we both have something to prove. The flirting, our getting closer—it was only throwing me off course. It is time to refocus.

We've been volleying back and forth at the net for at least ten minutes when he finally thwacks a ball so far to the right of me that I miss the return completely and lose our scrimmage by a point.

"Fuck," I spit, as I flop over my knees, soaked in morning sweat and completely out of breath. We've been practicing daily for an hour every morning and then sometimes again once the last members leave the club, and I've never seen anyone skyrocket in skill the way Niko has. He's already infinitely better than me, not that I'd ever tell him.

"You told me to look for your weak spots!" he shouts from the other side of the net, where he's watching me with utter satisfaction. "Which is obviously your backhand."

"Okay, Mr. Pickleball Expert." I sit down on the court and scowl back at him, but the triumphant smile on his face lets me know he doesn't buy my dagger eyes. I give up being annoyed with him and smile back.

"It's not my fault that all your good coaching advice just so happens to work against you, too." Niko walks over to the bench where we've left our bags, picking up his giant water bottle off the ground. "Changing the pace, observing when my opponent gets too comfortable..." He trails off as he pauses to take a sip, and I can't help it—I let my eyes linger. We've been so focused on playing, most of our conversations now about all the technical details of the game, that the thought of his mouth against mine feels like a fever dream and not real life, even though we are still very much in a real fake relationship.

Which is as it should be. I don't need an actual boyfriend, and I don't need a distraction. I need to concentrate completely on turning around the future of the racquet club, everything else be damned.

"People pay big money for this expertise, you know," I say, dragging the hem of my tank up to my face to swipe the pooling sweat from the corners of my eyes.

"Trust me, I know. My theia won't stop going on and on about you," he says, and he keeps his eyes on me for just a second too long. His words feel dangerously intimate, like a verbal caress, and I blink hard, forcing any possible tender thought about Niko out of my mind. *He was dishonest about why he wanted to play in this tournament*, I remind myself. *You're mad at him.*

"About how much she misses her lessons," he clarifies, taking another swig of water as the moment slips right past us.

"She's going to lose it over how good your serve is," I say, steering the conversation back on track to the game, and only the game. "Just wait until her cast is off and she can play you."

"She'll probably let me win," he says, the sincere affection for his aunt evident in the way every part of him softens when he talks about her, and it's undeniably endearing. "She's too nice to me."

You're mad, I try to remind myself, but it's no use. I'm not mad anymore.

"Speaking of being too nice," I tell him before blowing a bubble with my now flavorless gum, "I'm shocked that you haven't complained once today about the grating sound of pickleball driving you crazy."

My legs still feel slightly like noodles, but I push myself up to stand and stretch. Deb should be arriving soon for her shift, and I don't teach any lessons for a couple of hours. Still, there's a full backlog of bills to go through and invoices to log.

"I still hate the sound. I've just learned how to tune it out thanks to the constant sound of you popping bubbles and yelling at me to relax my swing." Niko swaggers closer to where I'm standing, and I let out a loud gasp as I study him mid-stretch.

"No way." I furrow my brow, letting my jaw drop open to give him the most shocked face I can muster. Even though I'm still sore about last night, I can't help but tease him, just a little bit.

"No way what?" he asks. The way he positions himself—with his hands on his hips, one leg bent just so—gives him the look of a statue of some brash, confident explorer who's about to galivant off into the wilderness.

"I think you've started to"—I gulp and glance back and forth in shock, as if I don't quite believe what I am seeing—"*like* pickleball."

I am giving him the performance of a lifetime, the hammiest, hackiest acting job ever seen. I've gotten good at detecting when something amuses him, even when he tries not to let on. He may be a powerhouse on the court, but his tells are all in his movements, the two lines that crease down from his eyes, the way the corners of his mouth tug upward just a little. They're subtle, the tiniest hints of something, like that one flower that blooms a little too early in March but signals that spring is indeed on the horizon.

"Don't mistake my love of competing with a love of pickleball, Bex," he says, as he twirls his paddle in his hand. "Or you're going to be sorely disappointed."

I rib him about it as we walk toward the lobby, and to his credit, he chimes in and plays along, like the intensity of the game has relaxed him. For all the back-and-forth we've had about the virtues of tennis versus pickleball, I've never once asked him what he actually loves about his chosen game, and now something in me is curious.

"Hey," I say as I pull the door open to the reception area. "How did you get into tennis anyway?"

Just as he's about to reply, Deb pops her head over the edge of the desk. "Karl had to cancel his lesson at the last minute today," she says. "Food poisoning."

"Oh no," I say, glancing down at my watch. That gives me a free two hours, which I can fill with all the crap I didn't get done last night.

"Let's go get a coffee," Niko says before I have a chance to reply to Deb. "My treat." He cocks a brow at me. "*Princess,*" he adds, and I know he's doing it because Deb's standing right there, ogling us, her eyes even larger thanks to the magnifying power of her glasses.

"All right, Tennis Prince," I say, grabbing hold of his hand. If he's going to perform this little sham relationship for our audience of one, then I'm going to commit and go all in. I just wish the sensation of his fingers sliding around mine didn't feel so genuinely nice. He gives me a reassuring squeeze, probably to confirm that we're pulling off this fake couple routine well, but it softens the heavy weight of stress that is housed all across the tight muscles of my back, the gnawing anxiety of the business that I carry with me always. I haven't ever done this with the support of anyone but myself, and something about the simple gesture sends a wave of sadness rippling through me. It's not longing for my mom as much as it is longing to have someone else to lean on. I wish I had it, and I hate that faking it feels so close to what I imagine the real thing is like.

I settle into Niko's car, and the energy between us is calmer than the last time I was here. That pack of Trident is tucked into the compartment under the control screen, and I reach for it and open it up to discover it's completely full.

"I think you got this to troll me," I say when he catches me tugging out a piece. "You were plotting to get me in here and then see this pack of gum, which I know you hate when I chew."

Niko just stares straight ahead at the road, turning the car down the main street of Sunset Springs toward my favorite local spot, the Caffeinated Cactus. "Or maybe I just like having a little reminder of you wherever I go," he says.

"Yeah, right." I cough out a laugh, but then I flash back to that squeeze of his hand just minutes earlier, and I begin to question everything.

"I guess you'll never know," he says, shrugging his shoulders as he rotates on the front seat to look out for the car behind him as he parallel parks. He does this even though his rental car is brand-new and comes with a fancy back-up camera that's offering a zoomed-in close-up of the pavement and the car behind us. I wonder why he doesn't use it. There's something about Niko that seems to always choose the harder option, never taking the easy way out.

"So," I say as he shifts into park, "tennis. You. The Life Story of Nikolaus Karras. Let's hear it."

He shuts the car off and pauses, his hands still on the steering wheel. "Honestly, I only started playing because tennis was the one thing my dad loved, and I just wanted his attention when I was little."

He says this matter-of-factly, but his words strike me as so sad that I fight the urge to wrap my arms around him in a bear hug. Instead I follow his lead and open my door, meeting him out on the sidewalk.

"Did it work?" I ask as he swipes his credit card into the parking meter.

"Oh, hell yeah, it worked," Niko says with a bitter laugh. "If I was interested in tennis, he was interested in me."

The meter beeps its approval, and our eyes meet. "Daddy issues," he says, calling back last night's conversation, and I nod in agreement.

"We've all got 'em."

Niko's hand brushes up against the curve of my back for a split second as we walk toward the café, and I relish the sensation.

"And then," he continues, "I fell in love with it, and soon it was the only way for him to get my attention."

"That kind of breaks my heart," I tell him honestly.

"Eh, it's not that sad," he says as we make our way down Sunset Springs' main drag. "It's kind of—what do they call it, a love language?—between the two of us. And he was a great coach."

I think about how I spent my formative years toddling around after my mother around the club, riding my bike with training wheels around the courts on quiet days after school or helping her to fold towels before she unlocked the front doors to welcome people in on the weekends. I'd never thought about how so much of our bond was built through our time at the club, and only recently had I begun to dig into what she must have felt, losing a husband young and having to shoulder the responsibility of a kid and a business all on her own.

"That actually sounds a lot like my mom and me," I say. Niko jogs a couple steps ahead and gets to the Caffeinated Cactus first, pulling the door open. It hits me that, aside from that first time at the hospital, he's always done this, making a point to grab every door. I'd let that one moment sour my opinion of him for weeks when, really, maybe this person here now, the one who speaks plainly about vulnerable things and always grabs for the door handle first, is not the asshole I had originally thought he was.

I'm about to tell him so when he reaches out and grabs my shoulder to stop me, bumping his chest into my back. I turn to look at him, and he's staring at the first table tucked just inside the tiny, cramped coffee shop, and I follow his gaze only to discover Ed and Loretta, locked deep in an intense conversation, his hands clasped around her uninjured one. They look comfortable, more like lovers than friends, and the realization hits me like a belly flop into the rec center pool: They don't just *look* like lovers; they are lovers.

"Hi!" I say in an unnaturally high-pitched voice.

The way their eyes practically pop out of their heads tells me that they'd never considered what might happen if they were found out, even though they're sitting knee to knee at the coffee shop everyone at the club visits on the regular.

"Oh, hello there, you two," Ed says, shoving his hands in his lap. He is always the epitome of casual—threadbare old T-shirts and Birkenstocks that look like they were purchased during Reagan's presidency—but I notice he's made what looks like an effort, dressing in a rumpled, collared shirt. He's flushed, like a teenager who's been caught making out with their date, and Loretta's beaming so brightly that it almost hurts my eyes to look at her. They both look so damn happy, and the sight of them, swept up in the joy of each other, makes me match their giddy, happy energy.

"Hey!" I say enthusiastically, as Niko hovers just behind me. "What are you up to?"

I know damn well what they're up to, but there's something so cute about seeing the two of them squirm a little that I feign ignorance.

"Just grabbing some coffee," Loretta says, eyes twinkling. "You all seem awfully cozy this morning."

We do? I think, just as I feel the weight of Niko's arm loose around my waist. It's been there since we stepped over to say hi, but I am only now registering it and how comfortable and natural it feels for us to stand like this.

"We just won a bunch of games," Niko says playfully, as he presses his fingers against my body with just the slightest hint of pressure. "So Bex is in a good mood."

"I'm in a good mood because you are finally showing some promise as a pickleball player," I joke, grinning up at him.

His body moves as he laughs, and it feels like a gentle morning wave in the ocean against me. "You mean I'm way better than you?"

I swat at him playfully. "Okay, rude."

It takes a second to realize we've just been bantering back and forth as Ed and Loretta stare up at us.

"Well," Loretta says, watching the two of us with an amused look on her face, "we were just finishing up here."

Ed clears his throat and begins picking up their cups and napkins from their table.

"All right, well, see you at home," Niko says to Loretta, before steering me toward the register, arm still draped around my waist.

"They're adorable," I say as we wait in line to order. "They looked like two teenagers caught sneaking out of the house in a 1950s sitcom or something."

"Loretta hasn't even mentioned anything going on between the two of them," he says, cocking his head as he takes one more quick peek in their direction. "I wonder how new it is."

"Well, can't be more new than this," I joke, gesturing between the two of us. Niko chuckles.

"Yes, our relationship is definitely still the talk of the over-sixty crowd," he says. "I think they're buying it."

I nod in agreement. With the way we're laughing and standing just a little too close, I can almost see how someone might confuse this for the real thing.

19

IT'S EARLY ENOUGH that the heat has yet to reach oppressive territory, and so we grab a table outside in the shade.

We are both nursing iced coffees with whole milk, and Niko's dumped a pound of sugar in his, which surprises me. Niko has such a bitter, biting edge to him that I just assumed that was how he liked his coffee, too. But he grabbed the container immediately and dumped it right into his cup, swirling the white crystals around with his straw until they faded into the liquid.

"So is this how you woo all your pretend girlfriends?" I tease, though if I'm being honest, I'm trying to dig around for information. Niko has been a mostly closed book since he arrived here, and everything available about him on the internet is, frankly, boring. I don't care what his stats were in the 2018–2019 ATP season. What I am dying to know is how many people he has slept with, whether he has ever lived with a partner, and what his kinks are. Hell, I'd even settle for knowing boxers or briefs (though I am hoping the answer is boxer briefs).

"Yes, there's nothing I love more than bringing dates to the same coffee shop as my aunt," he joked, scooting his chair in just a little bit closer to the table. "It's a real aphrodisiac."

Niko is more self-deprecating than I initially gave him credit for, and I decide that I like this about him. He's secretly got a sense of humor about himself, and the more I get to know him, the more he lets it out.

"Well, now that we've gone over that," I say with a loud sip of my coffee, "let's cover our bases."

"Bases, Bex?" He crosses a leg over his knee and relaxes into his chair, eyes on me.

"Just the basic stuff: favorite color, dead person you'd have lunch with, credit score, any secret kinks I should definitely mention to Angela next time."

I'm poking at him to see if I can get a rise out of him, but he just gives me a sultry half smile, his eyes narrowing in a way that tells me he actually might have a secret kink or two.

Goddamnit.

"Okay," he drawls, still watching me. It's the same look I've seen him give me during pickleball practices, like I'm a rabbit scurrying across some rocky terrain, and he's a coyote, trailing just behind, waiting for the perfect moment to pounce.

"Blue, though I know you were dying for me to say white," he says.

"You are one hundred percent correct," I admit.

"I like to wear white," he clarifies. "It's just an old habit. But blue is calm. Soothing. I prefer it."

"So then not lime green?" I ask, and he shudders.

"Definitely not," he says adamantly with a shake of his head.

"I'll keep that in mind," I say.

"Lunch date would be Arthur Ashe," he says, "obviously."

"He was my dad's favorite too." I perk up as I say this, recalling one of the many facts about my father I'd heard from my mom over and over again when I was a kid. She wove my dad into everything, making tidbits about him a part of our everyday conversations, and even though I don't remember him, something about sharing this with Niko fires up a buzzing warmth in my chest that I know isn't just the caffeine hitting my bloodstream.

"Credit score—high seven hundreds, thanks to a credit card I forgot to pay off a couple of years ago. I used to crack eight hundred, easily."

"Still very impressive," I say, giving him an admiring look.

"And my kink I've already told you." He says this while making direct eye contact with me from across the table. "But in case you don't remember, it's that mouth of yours."

The words sound downright dirty, and I don't know what else to do but pick up my cup and take a giant sip, and then another. Niko, on the other hand, is still unfazed, giving me his best poker face, hands clasped on the table. "Your turn. Though I assume favorite color is going to be hard for you?"

"Very funny, Mr. Tennis Whites," I crack.

"I thought you called me Tennis Prince?" he says, and that hooked half smile is back, searing my insides.

"Depends on my mood," I say with a bratty look. "Okay, so, my favorite color is that mix of orange and pink at sunset, right where the two meet. I don't know if it has a name, but the closest I've ever come to finding it is a burnt sienna crayon."

"You would know the actual names of crayon colors." He says this as if it's something he likes about me.

"Well, then remember that when Angela's asking about our magical storybook romance. I'm sure she'll love that detail."

He drags his hand across his chin in thought.

"How's this? On our first date, I showed up to the front door of the racquet club with a bouquet of crayons," he says, his face lighting up as he describes this made-up scenario. I chuckle along, but the image of it is sweeter than I want to admit.

"Credit score has been a journey," I say. "But I just crossed seven hundred this year."

"Wait, you forgot dead person you're taking to lunch." He says this like it's urgent information he can't miss.

"I know the right answer would be to say my mom, but honestly, I think I'd pick Jim Henson."

"The Muppets guy?" Niko is incredulous.

"He's an icon!" I say, on defense. "Tell me you've seen *Fraggle Rock*."

I give him a pleading look, but he shakes his head. "Clearly I've missed out on something."

"Only, like, my entire childhood," I reply. "My mom

never could afford to send me to camp during the summer. So I'd hang out at the club while she worked and watch old episodes of *The Muppet Show*. It was my childhood dream to be on that show."

He looks down and types something into his phone. "Wow." He glances up at me and then back down at the screen. "Now I get why you love to wear color so much."

He flips his phone around so I can see the video he's pulled up on his screen. A puppet with bright blue skin bounces on shamrock green felt legs, as hair the color of a cherry slushy bounces around their head. "I think you might be related," he says with a teasing grin.

I ball up my paper straw wrapper and toss it at him, but I can't stop laughing.

When our laughter quiets, I realize I have one more question to answer. Why the hell did I think it would be a good idea to joke about kinks? The truth is, I've had a fair amount of time to fantasize about different scenarios over the last couple of years and not a ton of time to act upon any of them. The list, dare I say, is sort of long.

"You can't laugh," I say, prefacing my confession with a warning.

He holds up three fingers and presses his other hand against his heart as he gives me a solemn nod. "I swear on that Fraggle's life."

"Niko!" I scold. "Puppets can't die. Or at least, not Muppets."

"Don't change the subject, Bex," he warns. "Just tell me. I promise not to yuck your yum."

"Okay." I take a deep, anxious breath. "I think it would be like, outside, or sort of in public, where someone might find us? There's just something that seems so freeing about that."

He lowers his hands to his lap and, to his credit, doesn't tease me at all. Instead he just mutters a quick "Noted" and goes back to drinking his iced coffee.

"So," I say, feeling way more awkward than I did when we sat down, "do we know each other now? Or at least, do we know each other enough to convince Angela that we're some sort of dynamic power couple?"

"I'm still stuck on those Fraggles," he says with a sly smile.

"Okay, fine. Then here's a question." I tuck my hands under my thighs, pressing my palms into the worn, faded metal bars of my chair. "What do you like about pickleball?"

He lets out a scoff of a laugh but doesn't answer right away, and I can tell he's thinking about my question. He dips his head, takes a pull of coffee from his straw, and then stares directly at me.

"I like that it's actually challenging," he says finally. "You were right that it's not the same as tennis, and because of that, it feels new, like a puzzle my brain has to solve. I'm less in my head than I am on the tennis court."

"Good answer," I say enthusiastically.

"And," he says, his voice a little quieter, "my partner's not half bad either."

After that, I don't ask any more questions for the rest of our coffee date.

20

Friday, May 12

THIS LAST WEEK has felt too easy, too comfortable, and the second Angela walks into the club for her follow-up interview with both of us, photographer in tow, I'm immediately reminded of what's at stake here. It doesn't help that I'd been up since four in the morning, dealing with a plumbing issue that started in my kitchen upstairs and has now impacted the entire club. I got the water turned off an hour ago, but the plumber can't come back until tomorrow morning, and there's a chance I'll have to close down the club for the weekend if it's not an easy fix. Numbers race through my head as I try to pay attention to what Niko is saying, quick hurried calculations of the money I'd lose without a couple of days of pickleball lessons and court rentals.

He's pontificating about finding his footing on the court and off, as a partner. I smile and nod along, reminding myself that I need to be *on* throughout this whole conversation and the practice game we are about to play, to give Angela something to write about. I've pigtailed my hair today, inspired by the 1980s tennis skirt that called to me this morning, and secretly, I was hoping Niko might be into it. Pairing the skirt with a dusty pink polo shirt and knee-high socks was definitely a choice; I look like a cross between a country club maven and a scrappy Little League pinch hitter.

Normally, I love playing up a style choice. Something about it makes me feel more confident, mentally sharp, even. But today, I don't feel put together. I've been dashing around for hours, splitting my time between hounding the plumber to get over here and teaching my morning pickleball lessons. Switching between the two roles —owner and coach—makes my brain ache. I'm pretty sure that if I could take a picture of my mind today, it would look like the aftermath of someone trying to juggle a dozen eggs.

"Should we go play?" I hear Niko say, and even though it registers that I am supposed to reply, it takes me a second.

"Yes!" I say, once my instinct clicks on. Everything else will have to wait. It is late afternoon, and I want to get this done so I can maybe find time to eat something other than the bag of stale pretzel rods I devoured around breakfast time.

"I'm so excited to show you the club," I tell Angela and her photographer, Dennis, as I wave them out toward the courts. As we walk, Angela peppers us with questions.

"What happened first, pickleball or romance?"

"Romance," I blurt out with confidence just as Niko says, "pickleball."

I wince in horror. We are total amateurs when it comes

to executing this scheme. How have we been at this for several weeks and never actually discussed the logistics for lying about our relationship?

"I'll let Niko tell it," I say, rushing to play defense as I lead our group.

"Well, I guess it is a mix of both," he says, never missing a beat. "I met Bex the first day I arrived in Sunset Springs. She came to the hospital because my aunt Loretta fell and broke her wrist, and Bex is her pickleball coach."

"This is all true," I say, relaxing a bit as we round the corner.

"I was worried about Loretta, and I might have come across as a bit of a jerk to Bex."

That is also true! I almost reply but censor myself, dropping a cool "Water under the bridge" instead.

"But she charmed me with her passion for pickleball," he continues, "and I immediately had a little bit of a crush. So I guess you could say it was both."

He's looking at Angela as he speaks, which is a good thing because I feel unnerved by his words, stripped raw in a way that feels brand-new. Even though we're supposed to be pretending, this feels genuine.

The photographer hovers off to the side, quietly observing our back-and-forth. Every now and then, he brings the camera up to his face, lens extended, and then stares down at the screen intently to study his work. I try not to let it rattle me, but every time his lens is trained on the court, I feel a shot of anticipation run through me.

I want this to work. It *has* to work.

I start the game off with the first serve. This is essentially just like our practice games because we're showing off for the journalist and her camera, not truly playing to win. But I know it's practically impossible for Niko to turn off his competitive side, and this makes me want to have a little fun with him, pushing his buttons just a bit. And so I add a little extra oomph to my serve and return the ball to him with more force than he's used to from me.

He lets out a little grunt as he knocks the ball back onto my side, attempting to force me up to the net. It's one of his many noises that send my heart racing, and I try not to get distracted by it. Instead I channel all my focus into scoring the next point. When I finally break through his wall of defense and he misses a low shot down the middle, I let out a yell of excitement just as my stomach grumbles, reminding me that I did, indeed, forget to eat lunch today.

Soon I'm leading three-zero. He finally gets a chance to serve and digs into my lead, tying it up before losing the point. We keep going like this, one person pulling ahead, then the other, the game stretching on longer than normal. He may be a tennis pro, but I have years of pickleball on him, and if there's one thing my mom taught me as my coach, it was how to sniff out my opponent's go-to moves and then break them out of their habit. And today I'm determined to break Niko, point by point.

Thirty minutes pass, according to my watch, though it feels like hours. Finally, I'm up ten to eight and readying my serve, angling to shut this down with the winning point at eleven. "Ten, eight, one!" I holler, calling out the score. I give the ball one small bounce, like I always do, and then focus my eyes directly on it, left arm pulling back to hit what I trust will be the winning serve of the game.

And then everything goes dark.

Not pitch-black, exactly; it's more like the world comes in and out, and I'm straddling the line somewhere between awake and asleep. My head feels like it's floating away from the rest of my body, and my arms move like they know they need to do something, reaching out in front of me as my knees buckle. There's stinging pain in my shins as they hit the court, but then everything in me relaxes, and finally, I can rest.

Except I don't sleep, not for long. It's a breath of quiet, and then I crack open my eyes and find Niko above me. He's fanning my face with one hand and gently cupping the back of my neck with the other.

"Hey," he says hovering directly over me. I flit my eyes, trying to catch up with what's going on, but all they can focus on is the depth of his chocolate-brown irises. Staring into them feels like meditating; they calm me with their steady resolve. "You fainted, but you're okay."

Fainted? I immediately try to scramble up to sit, palms pushing against the hard court below me. But Niko's hand shoots to my chest, giving me the gentlest press, holding me in place. "Bex, seriously, do not try to sit up right now."

"But the game," I mumble, as someone hands Niko an ice-cold washcloth that he then brings directly to my forehead. I wonder for a brief second how they got it this wet with the water shut off at the club, but then a dull ache in my head pushes the thought away.

"Thank you," he says to the owner of the hand—it's

the photographer, I realize—as he holds it in place while also softly stroking the pad of his thumb along my eyebrow, smoothing out the fine hair there.

"You won the game," he assures me, a small, sweet smile cracking across his face. "You competitive monster."

"Takes one to know one," I croak, my voice hoarse, as a wave of nausea ripples through me. "Oh man," I moan, trying to shift over on my side in the fetal position. "I feel like I'm going to barf."

Angela's face appears behind Niko, and she hunches next to him, obviously concerned. "It was all I could find," she says, as she passes him a handful of what looks like oyster crackers in a plastic bag, the kind of thing you get with a cup of soup at a restaurant. He shifts onto the ground next to me, crossing his legs, and then removes his hand from my forehead and tears open the packet of crackers, pulling one out and tucking it into my fingertips.

"I want you to sit up slowly," he says, and then wraps both hands around my shoulders, guiding me upward. One slides down my back and holds me in place like a steady, solid plank of wood.

"Have a sip of this." He passes me a cup of lemon-lime Gatorade. Raising it to my lips, I take a small sip, pause, and then slurp the rest down. My stomach settles immediately, and when I've polished off the drink, I bring a cracker to my mouth, taking a tiny, tentative nibble.

"Oh god, I'm starving," I realize as the delicious hit of salt zings on my tongue. My body feels leaden, empty, like I haven't eaten in days.

"What have you eaten today?" he asks, and even though I'm confident he knows the answer, nothing about his face is judgmental. He gives me another once-over and, when he appears satisfied that I'm not going to tip over, hands me the packet of crackers so I can feed myself.

"Cold brew," I admit, popping more into my mouth.

"And?" he asks, hand still firm and comforting against my back.

"More cold brew," I say. "And some pretzels." I crunch the rest of the crackers and watch him, expecting to see some sort of stern reaction on his face, but instead there is a glimmer of pure affection. It's like someone looking at a puppy who's just chewed up an entire living room but can't help but be adorable. This is happening more and more when I'm around him, and it's an unfamiliar and off-putting sensation that feels both terrifying and addictive.

"Well, let's stay here as long as you need," he says. "And then we'll go get you something to eat."

"But the interview," I protest, still not understanding how we can just stop everything to sit here.

"Oh, I think we got everything we need today," Angela says kindly, though I see that her phone is clutched in her hand, a voice recorder running.

"Oh good," I say, greedily taking another cracker pack out of Niko's hand and tearing into it. "I feel fine now."

"Nope," he says, somehow even more ornery as a caregiver than he is in everyday life. "You need to wait a little bit longer before trying to stand."

"Are you just mad because I beat you in front of a reporter?"

I say. "Angela, I hope you got that the owner of the Sunset Springs Racquet Club beat Mr. Famous Tennis Pro here."

Angela attempts a serious nod but the way she presses her lips into a line tells me she's trying not to laugh.

"Jesus, you're relentless." Niko chuckles.

"No, I'm just really good at pickleball," I say matter-of-factly, the food and Gatorade finally kicking in. "Isn't that why you asked me to be your partner?"

"I asked you to be my partner just so I could keep you around and bug you," he jokes back. "And boss you around." He looks down at his watch. "You need to stay here for at least ten more minutes."

I roll my eyes at this, but secretly, I like that he cares.

"I'm setting a timer," he says, tapping his watch. "And...go."

When he finally helps me up, we're the only two people left at the club. Angela and her photographer said rushed, awkward goodbyes as soon as it became clear I was fine. Niko insists on walking me upstairs to my apartment, and once I'm settled on the couch, he rushes back downstairs for a couple of minutes, returning with a giant bag of takeout food in hand.

"Dinner," he says, unpacking two giant turkey subs onto the coffee table alongside bags of salt-and-vinegar potato chips and two glass bottles of Coke.

"Plates?" he asks, and I point him to the cabinet above the sink before turning to admire the spread in front of me.

"Oh," I moan with pleasure as I eye the soda. "You got real Cokes. You're my hero."

"It's Mexican Coke or nothing," he agrees, twisting off the top of a frosty-cold bottle and passing it over to me.

"Amen," I say, and clink the lip of my Coke to his before taking a long, slow sip. I swear I can feel my body come alive as the caffeine and sugar hit my bloodstream. I don't know if I've ever tasted anything so refreshing in my entire life.

We eat in silence, and I chew my sandwich slowly, enjoying every bite, the tangy mustard, the sharp bite of cheddar, the crunch of iceberg lettuce. Once we're finished, he walks our plates back over to the kitchen sink, twisting the handle of the faucet to give them a rinse.

"No water," I remind him. "The whole club is shut off until the plumber can get here tomorrow."

"Right, shit," he says, stacking them on the counter. "Then you can't stay here."

"I'm fine," I insist. "I have a Brita that's full in the fridge and plenty of back-up water because I'm a well-stocked earthquake prepper who will be very hydrated during the end of the world."

"Bex," he says, now looking over at me with his hands on his hips, "just come stay at my place."

"It's just water, Niko," I reply. "And I need to meet the plumber tomorrow morning before the club opens."

"And you fainted out there today," he replies. "So it makes even more sense for you to not be alone tonight. I can drive you back in the morning."

I flutter out a sigh. He's not wrong. And washing my face with warm water sounds very nice right now.

"How do we explain it to Loretta if I show up to stay at your house?" I ask.

He laughs, as if the answer is obvious. "Bex, we're supposed to be dating. Frankly, it would be weird if you didn't."

21

I HAVE A whole speech planned for when we run into Loretta and must explain that I'm spending the night with Niko, but her car is absent from the driveway when we pull up in front of the house. Niko opens the car door for me and ushers me toward the side gate, and I follow him along the stone path through the backyard, his arms full of my stuff.

He unlocks the door, ushering me inside before hustling ahead of me, disappearing into what I assume is the bedroom. I linger in the foyer, suddenly buoyant with nerves. We're alone, together, and even though I was here just last week, it suddenly feels more intimate. I channel all my nervous energy into admiring a glass bowl filled with scented pine cones, and when he returns I'm still studying it like it's a newly discovered specimen from another planet.

"Hey." He glances down at his watch. It's dark outside now, so it must be close to nine, I'd guess. "Are you tired?" he asks, but I shake my head no.

"Could I shower?" I ask. I hadn't been able to take one this morning, and right now, water seems soothing, comforting, something that could wash this antsy feeling right off me.

"Of course." He jumps up and steers me toward the small bathroom I spotted when we walked in the front door.

He flips on the lights to reveal a hot-pink-tiled sink and bathtub.

"Holy crap, I am obsessed with this," I gush, running my hand over the perfectly maintained vintage countertops. "This all must be original from when the house was built."

"I had a feeling you'd love it," he says with a soft smile. "Let me grab you a towel."

When he returns, he's got a bathrobe draped over his arm. "Loretta bought this for me when I got here, but I've never used it."

He passes it to me, and the turquoise terrycloth is buttery soft in my hand.

"Thanks," I say. "I'll be quick."

"No rush." He waves me off and shuts the door behind him, and I can't help but notice how polite he's being. It's almost like he's nervous about having me here, and it's a thought that tickles me.

I carry these feelings with me into the shower, picking apart the way he cared for me earlier today as I scrub soap on every part of my body and shampoo my hair twice, just to give myself an excuse to stay in the warm, steamy bathroom a bit longer. Finally, when there isn't an inch left of skin that hasn't been polished and cleaned, I begrudgingly shut off the water and slide into the warm embrace of the bathrobe.

It hangs off me. I look like a small child playing dress-up in a wizard's cloak. The towel I wrap my hair in is enormous too, and I feel utterly cozy, if not a little ridiculous.

I shuffle back out into the living room and discover Niko bent over the couch—still in his clothes from earlier today—tucking a sheet into the cracks of the sofa.

"Is this my spot?" I ask, watching him.

He quickly spins to look at me, his forehead creased with worry. "You okay?"

"Yeah, why?"

He's quiet as he paces for a moment in front of the TV before plopping down in the cushy armchair in the corner of the room. "That was just a long shower. I was worried maybe you fainted again, that's all."

He sounds exhausted with concern, and it reminds me of the Niko I first met in Loretta's hospital room, scowling and stressed.

"I am still in one piece, thank you very much." I stick out my hand, giving him a pointed thumbs-up. "All good, Doc! Ready to party."

"Bex, you should take it easy." He rises to stand and walks down the hall. "You're taking my bed."

"Niko, I am fine on the couch," I say as I follow him.

"Will you please just trust me on this? I've had the same thing happen before from being exhausted and dehydrated. You should get some good rest." He switches on the lamp on the bedside table and gestures at the queen-size bed, which is covered in a poppy-orange comforter.

"You don't need to take care of me," I say forcefully, standing in the doorway.

But I'm not sure why I'm protesting because, deep down, I'd liked it when he'd cared for me today. The soft, feather-light touch of his palm against my forehead. The gentle but firm tone of his voice as he instructed me not to move.

Now I know that there is a tenderness that lurks just behind every frown on this man's face. I am beginning to see it not as anger or scorn but deep, careful concern.

He shakes his head, chuckling like he's sharing an inside joke with himself. "I know I don't, Bex. You of all people don't need anyone to help you do anything."

"Thank you, I think," I say, though I'm oddly disappointed by this assessment.

"I want to take care of you," he continues, and our eyes lock. "I want you to let me take care of you."

There's a funny edge to his voice, and the massive towel on top of my head seems like it weighs a hundred pounds. I suddenly feel ten feet tall and also the size of an ant under his gaze.

"Will you let me take care of you?" he asks quietly, his voice a hoarse whisper, and I think I know what he's asking. I want to scream yes, but I stop myself out of habit, and then immediately feel frustrated by that choice.

"I'm not sure I know how," I admit finally, the words spilling out of me. It's a small confession of something more, something bigger, a larger piece of who I am, something I am finally seeing clearly for the first time. I have programmed myself to help others, to care for my mom, to tend to clients, to save the club. I make lists, and then lists of my lists, to keep myself on track, self-sufficient, on top of things.

But it's more than not knowing how to ask for help. Even when it's right in front of me, I'm not sure I know how to allow myself to accept it.

Niko walks toward me until his face is just a few inches away from mine, and up close, I can see that his eyes burn with desire even though he looks weary. I inhale the musk of him, sweat and sun and darkness and the absolute force that comes along with someone who spends their life always trying to win. It's the scent of exertion, of drive, of a person who gives one hundred and ten percent to every small thing in their world. It's heady and delectable, and my tongue drives out against my bottom lip, desperate to taste it.

I want him to ravage me. I remember the way he kissed me, like a thirsting man lost in the desert, stumbling upon water for the first time in days. But this version of Niko isn't ravenous or desperately crawling out of his skin. Instead he reaches a hand to my face, brushing the back of his palm delicately against my cheek like I'm made of glass. He traces a finger along the bridge of my nose, following along the bow of my upper lip, and then across my jaw until his hand reaches the nape of my neck. His fingertips softly cradle the back of my head as he runs the pads of his thumbs along the arch of my eyebrows. It's reminiscent of his touch earlier, the way he so gingerly held me, and I exhale, shoulders relaxing, trusting that I can actually let go, just a little.

He brings his hands to the twisted part of the towel and tugs, unfolding the creased cloth until my damp hair unravels, falling down my back. Then he tosses the towel onto the chair behind him and leisurely brushes my hair out with his fingers. It's such a simple act, so kind and loving, and this, of all things, causes my lip to part on instinct, a faint sigh escaping my lips.

Niko smiles as he watches me slowly come undone, one achingly tender caress at a time.

"You know," I say, heart thumping beneath that terrycloth robe, "it dawned on me recently that I've never asked you about any of your other doubles partners. Anyone I'd have heard of? Did you win a lot?"

I feel every inch of my five-foot-two frame as he towers above me, hands still stroking my hair.

"I never really liked playing doubles," he says, dipping his head next to my ear, his breath spiking a shiver that starts at my neck and runs down the entire length of my spine. "I've always been happier being out on the court by myself."

"So then why rope me into being your partner?" I press. It's a question I've already asked him just a few weeks ago, but now I'm beginning to doubt his original answer. "They do have singles pickleball too, you know."

"Why do you think, Bex?" He shifts even closer, so his body is flush with mine as he pulls back to look directly into my eyes. He's holding my face in his hands, demanding an answer.

"Because you finally realized that pickleball is arguably cooler than tennis?" I'm trying to avoid what I really think with humor, and he lets out a low grunt of a laugh, which flips on every switch in my body.

"Guess again." There's a demanding, bossy edge to his voice that I find incredibly sexy.

"Because it's good exposure for you." I whisper the words slowly because I can barely form them when he's this near. "Or maybe you're lonely. Or you've realized you need someone else to save your ass on the court."

"Close." He says this with a growl, eyeing me like he has the power to tear my clothes off with his eyes and just needs me to give the final go-ahead before he does it.

"You're missing the biggest reason," he says. And I know what this is, what he's giving me—it's an opening. And just like the other night when I pulled him in for a kiss, I feel emboldened, reckless, ready to jump into the raging water without a life jacket on.

"Because you want me," I say, sliding my palms up the expanse of his arms. It's like grabbing on to two live wires that zing and spark under my touch. "You can't stop thinking about our kiss, and being around me all the time and not being able to touch me is making you crawl out of your skin."

I'm not just speaking for him. It's what I've been feeling too, and each day it has ramped up and up, and now it feels dangerously close to tipping over. His head drops, resting against mine, and I don't know if it's a sign of defeat or relief, but it fills me with pure, heavy desire.

"Because you don't know *why* you want me," I continue, almost breathless, and now I'm the bossy one. My need for him fuels unbridled confidence, and I urge him closer with my touch, rasping my words against his chest. "But you do."

Niko pulls away from me, and his eyes have never looked more intense than they do right this very second. "You're wrong. I know exactly why I want you, Bex."

He glides his hands down my back to my waist, with a squeeze, like he wants me to know that I belong to him. It's possessive, and if it was anyone but Niko, it would bug the crap out of me. But I'm drunk on carnal need, and I love it. There is something in me that completely releases under his touch, as if my subconscious knows it can truly relax as long as he's holding me. I'm not sure how it's possible when I also feel like I am on high alert every time I'm in his airspace. But this is the heady mess he makes of me. "Tell me," I urge him on.

"Because, Bex," he says with a pained laugh, "I haven't been able to stop thinking about you since the moment I laid eyes on you in the hospital. Every day, I show up at the club, and I can't wait to see what amazing outfit you've concocted. Also because I roped you into doing this tournament with me and you said yes, even though you've got plenty of shit on your plate already. Because you kissed me first, when I'd wanted to do that for two weeks but was too chickenshit to try. Because you constantly flip your hair over your shoulder in this way that drives me utterly, fucking insane."

I reach up and twist my damp hair, letting it fall over my shoulder.

"Like that," he purrs and leans closer. "I've never seen anything so sexy as you, pissed off at me, flipping your hair around."

"So you only wanted to play with me because you like how I flip my hair," I say, trying to make a joke as I repeat his words back to him, but my voice comes out raspy and pleading.

"At first, yes," he admits, picking up a wavy lock and

rolling it between his fingers. "But I'm beginning to think now it's because I've always thought I was happier on the court alone, and you're the first person who's ever made me question if that's really true."

I swallow hard, processing the words coming out of his mouth.

"Will you let me take care of you, Bex?" Niko asks again, and this time, I give in to the temptation to say yes.

"I'll try."

My entire body aches with anticipation. He strokes a tendril off my forehead, runs his thumb across my bottom lip, tugging it down ever so slightly. "So you'll let me take the couch? And sleep in the bed?"

"As long as you're not about to tell me to go sleep," I say. "Because I feel fine, and I need you to trust me to make decisions for myself."

He nods slowly.

"Lie down," he says, and I blink a couple of times as I process the demand. Did he not hear what I just said?

"I told you, Niko I'm not going to—"

"Sleep, I know." His voice is direct and hard. "That's not why I want you to lie down."

"Oh," I manage to squeak out.

"What I want is to make you come." He doesn't take his eyes off me, and for a second, I'm frozen. Not out of fear or apprehension, but anticipation. This is exactly what I want, to be cared for, to be selfish and just take for a little bit. I just need to give myself permission that it's okay to do exactly this.

I nod yes as my senses click on again, and I stumble

backward until my legs hit the edge of the bed. He prowls closer, running his hand from the top of the robe's collar all the way to the belt tied loosely at my waist. I follow his gaze down to where it rests at my stomach as he gives it a tug, twisting his fingers through the knot and loosening it. We're both watching him undress me, and I'm hypnotized by the unhurried, steady movement of his fingers as they pull on the belt and spread the robe open. I shiver, and my heart is racing, blood pumping through every vein at a mile a minute. He tugs the robe down over my shoulders, and it drops to the floor so that I'm standing there in front of him, absolutely naked.

He lets out a pleased groan at the sight of me. "Are you fucking serious, Princess?" he says, lips parting. "If at any time you want me to stop, just tell me."

"Like a safe word?" I let out a nervous giggle. "Can it be something pickleball related. What about 'dink'?"

"That works." He laughs low and breathily against my ear and runs a hand over the round curve of my stomach, teasing his index finger along my belly button. "You are so fucking gorgeous, Bex. Now will you please, for the love of god, lie down on the bed?"

This time, I don't protest. Instead I fall back onto the mattress, and he slowly climbs over me, fully clothed, his lips meeting mine with the softest, slowest kiss. His calloused palms on my skin are just the slightest bit rough, and the sensation is ecstasy. Niko takes his time, gently stroking the curves of my hips, down over my ass, and then up the slope of my spine, until he's back at my neck. I like this patient side of him, and he braces his palms on the side of my face and leans in, kissing me reverently, like the entire existence of the universe hinges on this very moment. His lips travel down my body slowly; they press against my collarbone and taste every inch of my breasts. Then his tongue swirls along my belly button, and I reach down and catch his chin in the palm of my hand. He nips at my fingers, kissing the tip of my thumb.

I open my eyes briefly and watch as he lifts my hips slightly, sliding a pillow underneath me. He looks wild and untamed but different from the beast I see on the court. It's almost like he's drugged, and his eyes roll back in his head as his shoulders nudge my legs apart, his tongue circling a freckle on the inside of my thigh. I love that this turns him on. Sometimes it's so hard to get a reaction out of Niko that to see him completely unravel like this is maybe the most erotic thing I've ever seen in my life.

There are words I want to say trapped somewhere, things like, "I like you more than I should," and "I haven't felt this alive in so long," but they don't make it to my mouth. Instead I stroke the soft curls on his head as he plants kisses closer and closer to the tuft of hair between my legs. A shiver ripples through me, and my body jerks, and Niko clearly loves this, letting out a laugh as he drags his tongue down and grazes my clit with the lightest touch. He blows softly, giving me another barely there kiss, and I tangle my fingers in the hair at the nape of his neck, urging him closer. He senses my desperation, and his cocky chuckle is hot pleasure on my damp skin.

"Niko, please," I beg, scooting up to look at him.

"Lie down and let me take care of you," he says more firmly.

I drop my head onto the soft pile of down pillows, one hand wrapping around the metal bed frame. Niko glances up as I tug on it, holding it tight like a lifesaver.

"Oh god, that's so hot, Princess," he groans, and I roll my hips at the nickname, which has now definitely become a thing between us. "I want you to stay just like that. Don't take your eyes off of me."

Little does he know it's impossible not to stare at him because he's the most frustratingly beautiful man I've ever seen. His words send a wave of warmth rippling through me, and he meets the moment with a firm push of his tongue like he could sense I was already letting go.

Wrapping both of his hands around my ass, he lifts me closer to him as he pushes inside me with strong, tender strokes of his tongue. Then he slides his tongue back up to my clit, circling it slowly as I writhe under him.

"Look at you, so desperate to come on my mouth," he laughs, nibbling me gently with his teeth. "Don't you know how patient I am, Bex? I could keep you here all night like this, right on the edge, and I'd love every minute of it."

"Of course you would, you sadist," I choke out. "You love to torment me."

"It's the only way you'll let me hang out with you," he says, and for a moment, I wonder if he's serious. Does Niko go back and forth with me because it's the only way I let him in? Before the thought can haunt me, he shifts and slides one hand out from underneath me, tracing my entrance with his finger.

"Do you want to come, Bex?" he teases, slowly pushing one finger inside me.

"Yes," I squeak out, bucking my hips and grabbing frantically at his hair.

"Not yet," he says, and grabs a hold of my hand, pushing it back toward the bed frame. "Hold on with this one, too."

I begrudgingly oblige and wrap both of my hands behind me just above my head. It's erotic and submissive, and I feel both wildly free and completely safe like this.

Niko places a soft kiss on the inside of my thigh as he slowly glides his finger in and out of me. He adds a second, and my body clenches at this extra bit of friction. "I know how badly you want to come," he says quietly. "But you have no idea how badly I don't want this to end."

I don't know if he's talking about me, spread out in front of him, or this night, or whatever this whole thing is crashing down between us.

But I can't ask him because my brain is too scrambled. My breath is rapid, faster and faster. I'm too raw and undone by his lips sucking softly on my clit, his hand moving at a snail's pace inside me. He pulls all the way out, and I gasp; without him inside me everything aches. But then he's pushing back again slowly, stretching me as his lips gently tug and suck, tug and suck. In that moment, the world ends, or maybe it begins again. My eyes clench shut, and the blackness gives way to stars, sparkling in every direction. He senses my every move, pushing faster and harder inside me. It's only then that I realize he's matching the pace of my moaning, which is coming out of me like a chant. "Yes, yes, yes," I'm saying, as he thrusts in time with me, as I come undone on his mouth, on his hand, on this magical thing blooming between us.

I don't know how long we stay with Niko's head on my stomach, his palm flat on my hip bone, with my hand mindlessly stroking his hair away from his forehead. When my pulse finally settles and the adrenaline surge resides, the room comes back into focus.

I literally cannot move. Not because of my fainting spell earlier or because Niko is lying half on top of me, but because he's drained me of every working muscle, bone, fiber.

If I had any energy left, I'd drag his face to mine, flip him onto his back, and see if I could make him moan my name. But all I can do is tap the side of his head with my index finger and mumble.

"Niko," I whisper.

"Mm-hmm?" He lifts his eyes, planting a kiss on my hipbone as he watches me.

"Thank you," I say. "For taking care of me today."

His lips curl into a mischievous smile. "If I had known that playing pickleball would mean I'd get to end up with you in my bed, I'd have started a lot earlier."

"Only when I beat you," I tease.

"Fine with me," he says with a shrug, snuggling back down against my stomach. "You can beat me every day then."

We're both quiet for a moment, and I run my fingers through his hair, scratching my nails gently against his scalp. "Seriously though," I finally say, "I appreciate it. I'm normally the one looking out for everyone."

"Well..." He flips over onto his back, scooting up next to me until he's flush at my side, his arm gliding over my waist as he pulls me snug against him. "I'm normally only ever looking out for myself. It's nice to get to do things for you. Thank you for letting me."

There's a raw vulnerability to his voice, like he's just figured this out about himself and he's still contemplating it.

"So what you're saying is," I say, running a hand down his forearm until our fingers meet and intertwine, "that we make a good team."

"No," he says, and my heart drops just a little. Maybe I've misread the energy between us, assuming intimacy when this is simply just a fun time for him.

But then Niko gives my hand a squeeze. "I think we make an *amazing* team."

22

Saturday, May 13

NIKO DOESN'T SLEEP on the couch after all. He wakes me up with coffee and scrambled eggs, and the sincerity of the gesture made every bite taste utterly delicious. I keep waiting for some sort of awkwardness to kick in between us, like we'll both realize we took things too far last night and immediately clam up or start acting weird. But if anything, our interactions feel even more relaxed, instinctive, like second nature.

Now, back at the club, my "boyfriend" leans in and gives me a kiss on the cheek as he drops me off at the front desk to wait for the plumber, before heading out to the court to meet Randall for their first lesson together.

After last night, I'm bubbling over with a sensation that feels foreign and familiar all at once. It's an uncontainable excitement with nerves that fizz up through my body like a freshly poured soda. I am the human version of last night's bottle of Coke, and I can't focus on anything in front of me, no matter how hard I stare at the computer screen.

A few hours later, I've just bid the plumber farewell with a hug—she's an old friend of my mom's and knocked twenty percent off her invoice, thank goodness—when Freddie Alwin struts in through the glass door. It's like someone flipped on the high beams on a backcountry road. He has an undeniable je ne sais quoi. Maybe this just comes with being absurdly attractive or well-known and worshipped. Whatever it is, it's working for him. It's obvious just from the way he moves that he's long been used to the way people react to him, almost like he is anticipating it.

It's funny to compare him to Niko, who is just as handsome, if not more so, but carries himself defensively, like he's ready to challenge anyone at any time. Freddie, on the other hand, bounds through the world like a golden retriever puppy who knows you won't be able to resist petting him.

I'm not immune to his charm, obviously. He is universally desirable; a wooden log would jolt alive in this guy's presence. But the sight of him doesn't send my pulse skyrocketing like it does when Niko storms into the room. Instead it's more of an intellectual understanding that I'm *supposed* to find this man irresistible, and so I guess I do.

Still, I try to feign nonchalance and lean back casually, as if gorgeous pickleball pros waltz in here on the regular and I'm not plotting a way to use his celebrity to help save the club.

"Hey, Freddie," I say, trying to find the right balance of friendly greeting and playing it cool. "This is unexpected."

"I figured why text about grabbing a T-shirt when I could just swing by and check the club out for myself?" His voice is just like his looks—ice-cold martini smooth. Everything about Freddie Alwin goes down easy, except when I remember the way Niko seethed as he told me about their past.

"Well, welcome to Sunset Springs Racquet Club," I say with a broad sweep of my hand. As I do, I notice that his eyes trace down my body—to my old Van Halen T-shirt that's been cut into a tank top and Lululemon black leggings that were an amazing thrift store score.

"Wow, is this the official club tour?" he says with a chuckle. It's warm and inviting—the kind of laugh that nudges at the corners of your mouth to join in. "I was hoping you'd show me around."

"Yeah, of course!" I'm supposed to be handling the front desk, but it isn't every day that Freddie Alwin just strolls in off the street. I'd scanned his social media after the party at Starlight, and having him see how special this place is—and sharing that with his gajillions of followers—could be a massive help. And besides, he isn't the only one who can crank the charm up to a ten. I give him a wide grin and bound around the desk. "You're going to love this place. It's special."

"I can't imagine why," he says suggestively, studying me through hooded eyes. Then he has the audacity to wink at me, the gesture so outrageously forward that my cheeks feel like someone's lit a match directly on them.

"Well," I reply, fighting to keep my voice steady as I sidestep him. "Shall we?"

Freddie moves through the club like he's walking onto Centre Court at Wimbledon. No wonder he's been under Niko's skin for years. They both exude unbridled confidence, but they carry themselves completely differently. Niko broods, whereas Freddie seems to float above it all.

I usher him out to where Deb and Maureen are finishing up a game with some friends and wave them over.

"Freddie Alwin!" Deb calls out, her voice slicing through the air. They met briefly at the cocktail party, and I assume there's no way he remembers her. But Freddie shocks me by firing up that power plant of a grin and strolling right over to her, planting a kiss on her cheek. It's a move that would seem over-the-top from anyone else, but this guy pulls it off easily.

"Deb, darling," Freddie purrs in that British accent of his as he clasps her hand, a move so smooth you'd think they were old dance partners. The whole thing is borderline cartoonish—like he's imitating what he thinks Americans want British men to be. But at the same time, he's so attractive that it feels impossible not to swoon. "I take it you're the fiercest competitor here?"

"Flattery will get you everywhere," she chuckles, but judging from her beaming face, it's working. "This is my wife, Maureen."

"Lovely to meet you," Freddie says, grabbing Maureen's hand with a flourish.

Maureen's silver hair bobs as she nods appreciatively at Freddie. "I read about your championship win earlier this year," she says, her tone suggesting she knows every statistic since the inception of the sport.

"Ah well, it was a tough match. I was lucky to pull it off." Freddie's aw-shucks smile is disarming, like he's just a guy who happens to be good at pickleball and not one of the top-seeded players in the country.

Just as I think Freddie's charm offensive has reached its peak, Niko strides through the reception area doors and out toward court 1, his mirrored sunglasses catching a glint of sunlight so that he almost appears to have actual stars in his eyes. His head turns and fixates directly on Freddie, and there's an electric crackle in the air—a storm brewing on the horizon even though the sky above us is perfectly clear, a robin's-egg blue.

"Alwin," Niko greets him with a thin line of a smile, tennis racquet in hand.

"Karras," Freddie responds, glancing down with an amused look on his face. "Leaving us so soon? I thought we'd convinced you to join our cult."

"Just for the tournament and exhibition," Niko replies, his tone light but edged with steel. His eyes dart over to me briefly before landing right back on Freddie. "Besides, I'm not sure there's room for both of us on the pickleball circuit. If I played, I might just have to beat you all the time."

"Well," Freddie says, his smile never breaking, "that depends on if your pickleball game is anything like your tennis game was when you quit."

I analyze the corners of Niko's eyes, trying to pick up any hints of meaning behind this odd back-and-forth, but there's nothing there but his usual steady gaze.

"So, Bex." Freddie turns to me, face still totally at ease. "Sounds like you might need a new partner sometime soon. You should give me a call. I'd love to apply for the job."

"Thanks for the offer," I say, suddenly feeling a deep sense of irritation at the idiotic, straight-male peacocking taking place in front of me. "Should we continue the tour?"

But Niko's eyes are locked on Freddie, unflinching, and there's a flicker of amusement dancing there. "You could probably beat him, Bex."

"Well, that would make one of you," Freddie shoots back, matching Niko's cool composure with the ease of someone who's faced down worse banter.

"I could beat both of you, easily," I snap at them, and Deb lets out a slow whistle next to me.

"Isn't that the truth," Niko says, flashing me a grin that's all mischief and no malice.

"I believe it," Freddie agrees, drawing out the word as he claps a hand on Niko's shoulder, a subtle reminder that he's not backing down. "Lucky for us, you'll have a chance to do just that soon."

"See you at the Paddle Battle." Niko dismisses both of us with a sneer as I steer Freddie away from our circle.

"The two of you have some history, huh," I say once we're out of earshot.

"Ah, it's all water under the bridge, really," Freddie says, giving me that easy smile. "Eventually he'll get over it."

I don't pry more about what happened between the two of them, but if there's one thing I suspect about Niko, it's that he never gets over anything, especially when it has to do with his tennis career.

● ● ●

Thirty minutes later, I'm back in the reception area, sending Freddie off with one of my newly printed BIG DINK ENERGY shirts, when Niko walks in, throwing me a look that's part *You okay?* and part *Is this guy for real?*

I brush him off with a roll of my eyes. Whatever beef he has with Freddie has nothing to do with me.

"I love it," Freddie says, holding the lime-green shirt up to his chest. "It's going all over my social media."

"I appreciate that," I say. "I need all the help I can get raising awareness about this place."

"Consider it done," he says kindly.

"Maybe we could also chat sometime?" I ask. "I'd love to pick your brain about how I could fix the club up, enhance it for members."

"Of course," he replies. "Anytime. Or maybe even next week? I'm traveling after the Paddle Battle."

"Great!" I can't hide it—I'm thrilled. "I'll shoot you a message."

Freddie throws up a hand to Niko. "Karras," he says, before heading out through the front door.

Niko waves back and then turns to me with a sour look on his face the second it swings closed behind him.

"Please don't fall for his bullshit," Niko says brusquely, and it feels vaguely like a critique of sorts.

"I get that he's a lot, but he seems utterly harmless." I narrow my eyes into a sharp glare, conveying my annoyance at his words. That bubbly feeling I'd had earlier has gone flat. "And he has a huge following online. He's going to post about the club across his social media. That could be huge for me."

"Yeah, I'm sure he just came over here out of the goodness

of his heart." Niko crosses his arms in front of his chest, a gesture that only irks me more.

I ignore him and make my way around to the computer, flicking it on with a sigh.

"Okay, fine," I say, not letting it go. "Let's say he did come over here for some devious reason. What would that be?"

Niko pauses, running his hands up his biceps as he thinks. Then he shrugs. "I don't know."

"You know what?" I stack my elbows on the counter and lean toward him. "I think you're jealous. You can't stand that your former rival is now an actual pickleball star who wants to help me out."

Niko scoffs at this. "Bex, I seriously do not care about that."

"Then what is it?" I press. I can tell there's more to it, but I can't figure out what.

Niko's normally confident face flickers with something that looks vaguely like self-doubt. "He knows we're dating, and he still came here and flirted with you, in front of me," he says finally.

"We aren't actually dating, though," I retort, accentuating every syllable. Except that ever since last night, I've been wondering if maybe we are. The once-clear boundaries of our plan have blurred, and I'm not sure I want to go back to what they were before.

Niko flinches, shooting me a look that I assume is meant to remind me that someone outside might hear us.

"He doesn't know that, though," he says finally, his voice low. "Doesn't that prove what kind of person he is?"

"So you're jealous that a hot pickleball star might be interested in me, your fake girlfriend," I say, drumming my fingers on the counter.

"I don't know, Bex. Maybe I am!" Niko sounds more agitated than I've ever heard him, and he throws up his hands, pacing back and forth in the small space.

"Well, this isn't all about you, remember?" I say this calmly, trying to act like everything between us is business as usual. But my thoughts are still back in Niko's bedroom, remembering the feel of his cheek, warm against my inner thigh, his lips all over me. "I agreed to do this to help the club, not be in the middle of some pissing contest with you and some old rival."

"Well, we're in this mess because you told Angela we were dating," he says, and the words crush me. He sounds so peeved that it's enough to make me think last night was a fluke, a brief moment of delusion.

"No, we're in *this mess* because you lied and said I was your partner," I clarify with a tight smile, trying not to let any of the hurt I'm feeling inside become visible.

"Well, I didn't want the girlfriend part," he snaps, and then regret washes over his face. "I'm sorry. That wasn't..." Niko trails off, a pained look on his face.

"I guess this is the first real fight of our fake relationship," I say, my voice clipped and cool even as his words sting me all over. "You should probably go."

He winces. "Yeah, okay. You're right."

"I really am sorry," he says, and then walks out without another look back. I sink back into the chair, exhausted by whatever the hell that just was.

Twenty minutes later, my phone pings with a new text message.

I'd like to take my fake girlfriend on a real date it says, and I can't help it—I instantly smile. The buzz is back.

I wait a couple of minutes, making him sweat a little, and then type back: She'd be into that.

Tomorrow night? he replies after a moment, and I send him a thumbs-up, trying to keep it casual. But I spend the rest of my shift tidying up the office and humming to myself, that sparkling, thrilling feeling reemerging, whirring inside me for the rest of the night.

23

Sunday, May 14

FOR A WHILE after my mom died, I was panicked about all the pieces of her I was starting to forget. I could feel her slipping away, the sound of her laugh became less clear in my mind, the once-strong scent of her Estée Lauder perfume now fading from the collars of her T-shirts that I've saved.

Recently, it's started to feel like she's become something bigger, too, something all-encompassing and intangible. That final orange sliver of the sunset or the stillness that settles on the courts when the last client leaves the club for the day. The longer she's gone, the more I feel her all around me. It's no replacement for the real thing, obviously, but it's a small comfort and something I cling to.

But tonight, as I lock up the club before my *real* date night with Niko, I'm reminded of how she's here in every dusty corner, every crack of this place. The pressure I feel to keep the racquet club up and running tangles with the overwhelming fear of losing it, and I bounce between the two worries in my head all day long. It all feels dangerously close to losing *her* all over again, and anxiety ripples through me, a familiar nervous feeling I haven't been able to shake since I realized how much money we've been bleeding over the last couple of years.

This is the unease that races through my thoughts most of the time, and tonight it's especially bad. We have less than a week until the tournament and exhibition match, and so far, winning and walking away with the prize money is the only solution I've come up with to turn things around. It's a shot in the dark and nothing even remotely close to an actual business plan. But right now, it is my best option for quick cash, even though it isn't guaranteed. *We should be practicing tonight*, I think to myself. *Doing everything we can to make sure we win. And not running around goofing off on a fake date.*

I'm so distracted by these thoughts as I press the buttons on the door lock pad that I don't notice Niko already there outside until I hear his voice behind me.

"Hey, you."

I spin around to find Niko leaning against his car, all casual elegance in a crisp white button-down shirt and dark gray pants. If we weren't in the middle of a landlocked desert, amid the rustle of scurrying lizards and fan palms, I could almost imagine him just stepping off a yacht somewhere. I watch as he saunters in my direction—okay, fine, I'm ogling him; I can't help it—until he's inches away from me, lips on my cheek with a quick kiss. "You look beautiful."

"Thank you." The sight of him makes my stomach

somersault, and I smooth down my vintage Dries Van Noten sundress—a hall-of-fame-worthy thrift store find—with jittery, clammy hands. His presence instantly washes away all my other, persistent worries. "I'm very impressed that half of you is dressed in something other than white."

"Lucky for you, I don't own white pants," he says as he slides a hand down to the small of my back, guiding me over to the passenger side door. "Yet."

"Don't threaten me with a good time, Niko," I say as he opens the door for me, and I slide into the seat. I glance up at him as I turn to grab the seat belt, and he's smiling down at me, elbow hooked on the edge of the open door. Just the sight of him is reassuring now—so different from how it used to be a few weeks ago—and it puts my pounding heart at ease.

"Well, now I know what I'm wearing on our second date," he says playfully.

"I'll make sure to bring the red wine then," I reply with a wink, before he shuts the door and jogs over to the other side of the car. This feels new but also intimately familiar, like our usual back-and-forth has gone through a makeover and come out on the other side, sparkling and bright.

We drive under a sky splattered with stars. It's the kind of darkness that makes you believe in UFOs or the possibility of something bigger than humankind. There is a magic that comes with nighttime in the desert. It's so vast and endless that sometimes you almost forget you're just two and a half hours from one of the largest cities in America.

If Niko is nervous, he masks it with an easy confidence, both hands draped casually on the wheel as he drives. I, on the other hand, am buzzing with that frenetic feeling that comes with being on a first date, something I haven't done in a long, long time.

Years, actually.

"So, where are we going?" I chatter nervously, watching street lights blur by outside the window. "Let me guess. Loretta's for game night? No, wait. In-N-Out? A secret pickleball practice?"

"Even better," he promises, the corners of his eyes crinkling with amusement. "Prepare to have your vintage clothing–loving mind blown."

We drive through the quiet streets—almost everything here shuts down by eight at night—and after about ten minutes, the car slows. He steers us into the parking lot in front of the Sunset Springs Design Museum, an architectural relic itself and an icon of fifties architecture with its long rectangular shape and clean lines.

There are only two other cars here, but sure enough, the museum appears to be open, its soft lights beckoning us inside. "Isn't this place closed at night?"

"I made some special arrangements," he says coyly. "Come on."

Outside, the air is heavy with the scent of blooming jasmine and crisp, clean eucalyptus, and they mingle together like some sort of potent aphrodisiac. Niko laces his fingers through mine, and everything about it feels just as intimate as two nights ago, if not more so. Together, we make our way up the steps of the museum. He releases me briefly to open the door before grabbing my hand again once we're inside.

The lobby is cavernous, and our footsteps click and echo on the marble floor. A woman in a black suit sits behind the information desk, and Niko nods a greeting in her direction, then leads me off into a room filled with bold, abstract paintings.

"So, what, you're secretly the mayor of Sunset Springs and never told me?" I ask, glancing back at the security guard as she resumes scanning her phone. "They're acting like you own the museum."

"I know people in high places" is all he says, his expression smug.

"How the hell did you manage to pull this off?" I ask as we walk slowly though the dimly lit hall. Being in a museum normally makes me feel like I have to whisper, but I can't contain the awe in my voice.

"Ed's on the board of trustees," he explains, giving me a mischievous wink. "I might have begged him for a favor. Or, you know, asked Loretta to beg him for a favor. He seems to do whatever she says."

"Are we the only people here right now?" I marvel, basking in the soothing stillness of it all. I've walked these halls before, many times over the years, but to be completely alone, surrounded by nothing but the spectacle of art, feels entirely different and downright magical.

"Yup." He shoots me a pleased look, tugging me a little closer to him with each step.

It's thrilling enough to simply be completely alone in a museum, but it's the next room that truly takes my breath away. It's an exhibit I've seen before, years ago, that documents the rise of mod-style fashion and architecture in the

1960s. Inside each glass case, mannequins dressed in striking vintage outfits pose next to large photographs of Sunset Springs architecture from the same decade, highlighting the symbiotic relationship between fashion and design.

Sunset Springs may currently look like a time capsule, but back in the day, it was a celebrity resort town, a warm, hedonistic escape from the chaos of Hollywood. This exhibit captures everything I treasure about my hometown, the vibrant colors and unusual shapes of the homes and buildings here contrasted against the rugged, raw beauty of the mountains and arid landscape. And of course, *the outfits.* I've admired them since I was little, and in an instant, I am a wind-up toy spinning with emotions, longing for sweet moments from my past, mixed with the pure, unadulterated pleasure that comes with being truly seen by another person.

I don't know how Niko found out about this place, but the fact that he has brought me here tears open a blocked-off room that lives just beyond my heart, and so many feelings spill out into me at once. This, it dawns on me, is what it means for someone to take care of you.

"Did you know this is my favorite room in this whole museum?" I ask, my voice breathy with surprise.

"I didn't, but I took a guess," he says, gesturing to a gorgeous Hawaiian-inspired muumuu styled next to a photo of one of the first tiki bars in the area. "I mean, it doesn't take a genius to know you'd love a room full of colorful old clothes."

He's looking at me like I'm both the sun and moon, wrapped into one. The sight of his eyes sparkling like this erases the pragmatic voice in the back of my head that just a few minutes ago was desperately trying to remind me that I have more pressing things to do than melt in the presence of this man.

We have a deal, a bargain, a plan that benefits both of us—not a relationship. Nothing about this is real, and in a few weeks, Niko won't even be here.

I'm trying so hard to stay laser-focused on us winning the tournament so I can keep the club afloat. And yet, I don't want to worry about those things right now. I want to bask in the glow of this night, to relax and enjoy myself. I can get back to worrying tomorrow.

"How did you even know about this place?" I ask as we wander slowly around the room. His hand is a comforting presence in mine.

"It gets kind of lonely living with your seventy-year-old aunt," he says as we stop in front of a black sequined A-line gown positioned next to a photo of the long-gone Sunset Springs Steakhouse with its infamous bright green awning and giant neon road sign. "I've tried to do some touristy things in Sunset Springs in my downtime."

"Weird. I thought you quite literally only played tennis all day long," I say, giving him a playful nudge with my elbow as we move on to the next section. "This movie theater is now a Sephora," I say with a wistful sigh, pointing at the photo of the wonderfully angular building, complete with a sea-blue Cadillac parked in front of it.

"I can see you in this," Niko replies, pointing at the minidress and pillbox hat on the mannequin in front of us, in a floral pattern the same color as the car in the picture. "Behind the desk of the racquet club."

"Telling you to wrap up on the court?" I suggest, imagining some of our snippy conversations from the past month.

"Putting me in my place, probably," he replies, "which I'm sure I deserve in this imaginary scenario."

We slowly make our way around the room until Niko tugs me toward one of the images we haven't looked at yet. "Apparently, this one is new," he says, pointing at the photo displayed on a wooden easel.

This mannequin is bare, no outfit on it yet, and so I turn to look at the photograph positioned next to it. The image is of a gray stone building buttressed by overflowing succulents and towering cacti in front of it. It's an older photo, but the tall sign in front of the building is the same, and a small gasp escapes my lips as I fully process what I'm looking at.

It's a photo of the racquet club.

"The picture is from 1968, when the club first opened," Niko explains. "I asked the museum if they had any of the club, and it turns out, they have a lot. I told them you might have an outfit you could lend to go with it. If you want to do that, of course."

I'm flustered by his thoughtfulness, so overwhelmed that it takes me a second to figure out what I even want to say to him. This is the same man who growled at me across Loretta's hospital bed, but the more I get to know him, the clearer it is that he is all softness behind a prickly exterior. And the truth is, I like both sides of him, whether it's his death-laser focus and the way he always plays to win or planning something extraordinary and sentimental for this fake real date.

"Niko, this is..." I clasp his hand to my heart, pulling

him into me as I stumble over my words. "This is the best date I've ever been on."

He clears his throat. "Would you like to go get something to eat? Drinks? I made us a reservation at—"

I bring my free hand up, pressing my index finger against his lips, which break into a small smile.

"I want you to take me home."

I give him the most serious look I can muster, trying to project with my mind just exactly what I mean with this command. His eyes widen, and then squint, and widen again, as he figures out exactly what I have in mind.

"Oh," he says, finally getting it.

"Take me home, Niko," I repeat. "Right now."

24

WE DRIVE TO the club in silence, Niko going ten miles over the speed limit. I watch his hands clench the steering wheel and suspect this is him being restrained.

We are out of his car in seconds, and he grabs my hand as we stumble toward the front door of the club. I move like I'm on fire, twisting the lock open and tapping the alarm off before shutting the door behind us.

I dash toward the stairs, but he grabs my hand before I can take another step and swings me around until I'm pressed between him and the wall across from the reception desk.

"Niko," I say, and each syllable of his name lands heavy with want. My hands fly up to his chest, and I trace the edges of his shirt collar, grasping it tightly and tugging him closer to me. I'm desperate to kiss him, to bring his lips to mine, but he twists his head slightly, hands coming up to my hair, as he runs his lips down my neck.

"Do you know how hard it is for me to walk in here every

day and see you sitting behind that desk?" He's savoring me in a slow, deliberate way that I feel with every sense I possess. "How much I want you?"

"Please," I croak, and I don't even know what I am asking for exactly, just that I want him to give it all to me.

"I stand out there on the court and try to practice but all I can do is think about you, and it's torture." He presses slow, burning kisses along the curve of my shoulder and then my collarbone as my head falls back against the wall behind me.

My hands find his waistband, and I pull him closer and then run my palms across the expanse of his thighs, finding his groin as he thrusts against me with a low moan.

"This needs to happen right now," I plead, insistent. Somehow I can feel the warmth of him through the distracting layer of clothes, and I want them off, immediately.

"What's the first thing you taught me about pickleball, Bex?" he asks as he takes a small step back, releasing my hair and tucking it over my shoulders.

"That's what you want to talk about right now?" I ask with a frustrated groan, as I nuzzle into the broad expanse of his shoulder. "Pickleball?"

One hand skates across my shoulder, finding the zipper at the back of my dress. He gives it a slow tug, pulling it down just an inch as his other hand glides up to my lower back, steadying me.

"Patience, Bex," he replies, his lips moving against my neck, a kiss coming between every word. "You said the key to pickleball is patience."

He gives the zipper another tiny tug as his lips drift across my cheek, planting painfully slow kisses along the way like he's trying to map each freckle with his mouth.

Before I even know what he's doing, his hands are at my waist, and he's lifting me in one fell swoop, sliding me up the wall until my thighs are around his waist, dress bunched around my hips.

"Do you know how hard it is to be patient with you like this?" His voice is gruff with want, but still steady. He knows exactly what he's doing, and he's going to take his time.

Me on the other hand? I'm a mess already.

"Because I make you crazy?" I ask, panting, my forehead resting against his as my fingers cling to his shirt like I'm hanging off a cliff.

"Because I want to be everything for you," he says, and as he does, I feel him relax against me as if just saying these words releases all the tension from his body. "And I can't wait any longer."

His words cause me to moan, and before I know what's happening, he's carrying me, pushing open the doors that lead to the courts. I'm so drunk on him, on the possibility of what's to come, that I can barely process the change of scenery. But sure enough, the night sky appears overhead, and somehow, a few steps later, we're in the middle of court 1, where he spends most of his days.

With every step he takes, I feel myself fall apart just a little bit more, piece by piece, limb by limb. Niko is built like a redwood tree, unwavering and rooted, and he is the first person I've let myself lean on in so long. But I still don't totally know how to ask for what I need. And so all I can do is show him, to try to give myself what I'm desperately craving.

The second my feet hit the ground, I pull away from him, and his eyes are confused, searching, until I reach my hands toward his face, giving him no choice. This time, when I greedily bring his mouth toward mine, he doesn't veer off course.

I part my lips, sliding my tongue against his, searching, asking, demanding.

"Please," I mumble desperately against him, and I can feel his entire body respond, his hands moving up my body and then back to the zipper, which he wrests undone in the most achingly slow, careful way.

He reaches up to my neck, gently pushing the dress off my shoulders, tugging it down to my waist. I take a step back and shimmy out of it and then slide my fingers through his shirt, fisting the cloth between the pearl-white buttons. Whatever the opposite of an out-of-body experience is, I'm having it. Every small touch, every brush of his skin against mine, seems to light me up from the inside. We're outside and completely exposed, and yet it feels like we're the only two people left in existence on the planet.

I pull him closer as he tears his shirt free from his waistband, yanking it over his head, while I wrestle with my bra and then the button of his pants. He groans as my hand grazes his stomach and then shuffles us closer so I'm flush with the net. He kisses me with abandon as I find his pants with the ball of my foot, halfway off to his knees, and push them all the way down to the ground.

He takes a moment to kick them away before hovering back over me, hooking his index finger into the black lace underpants I wore especially for tonight, toying with them playfully. I grab a hold of his ass and am pleased when I get the answer to one of my most burning Niko questions—he does, indeed, wear boxer briefs. I shift my hips, electric against his touch, and a small smile emerges on his face.

Niko's eyes trail across my brow, down my body and up again, asking me silently, one last time: *Are you sure?*

I dip my chin, the smallest of nods, and the second I do, he holds me to him as he hitches my thigh over his hip, tugging me closer as he kisses me deeply, thoroughly. His fingers tangle in my hair as it pools around my shoulders, and Niko, normally so focused, so precise, unravels against me as he crushes his lips against mine.

"Fuck," I moan as our tongues meet, slick and desperate. His hands are steady, learning my body as they travel down the curve of my neck and the slope of my spine.

"I love seeing you naked," he says, his fingers painting imaginary scenes across my hips and up my waist. I let out a little gasp as the pad of his thumb runs circles around my nipple. "But I might love seeing you out here, in your wild pickleball outfits more. When I close my eyes and think of you, I see a rainbow."

"I thought you didn't like all that color," I mutter, my hands enjoying every hard line of muscle until they find his ribs with a teasing poke. I've seen him shirtless enough to know that he is cut like marble, his body fat percentage nonexistent. But to feel his warm skin and the pounding of his heart against my palm is another thing entirely. My eyes shift over to his shoulder, where there's the faint hint of a scar, a relic of his past life and the havoc it has wreaked on his body. He is beyond beautiful, and I feel a deep ache of sorrow for him.

"I like everything you do," he rasps. "You keep telling me I have to have a soft touch, to stay calm when we're playing, but being around you makes me want to crawl out of my fucking skin."

He intertwines our fingers and drags our clasped hands just below his waist so that I can feel the burning need that's consuming him. "I can't focus out here when you're next to me. I can't sleep at night knowing you're alone, a couple of miles away. I can't remember my training schedule. Hell, I can barely play tennis anymore. I can't do anything but think about you, Bex. I know we never meant for any of this to be real, but it is now, at least for me."

His words make me whimper, an actual pleading sound that escapes my lips, as I grind against him, desperate to show him that I feel the exact same way. I don't want to think about anything but Niko, but us, but this very second in time, not a minute before or after.

He grunts as our bodies collide and move, and he leans forward, pressing wet kisses along my shoulder and across my collarbone before looking up at me, his eyes alight with fire. "You're so fucking beautiful, Princess."

"You're all I think about, too." The words slip out of me before I even know what I'm saying, and he pauses, clasping my chin between his thumb and forefinger.

"Tell me."

I press my lips together, teetering between self-conscious and wide open. Am I really going to do this, reveal my sweaty, dirty thoughts about this man to his face? I no longer loathe him. Niko is tender and kind, silly in his own way. And now he is here, naked in the middle of the racquet club, eagerly ripping my clothes off.

"I play back the memory of you kissing me constantly," I whisper, as he cups both my breasts in his hands, running his thumbs slowly across my nipples in the most deliciously tortuous way. "I imagine what it would be like to..."

"To *what*, Bex?" he asks, his lips curling into a devilish, pleased smile. "I've never seen you this quiet."

"To fuck you," I say, and the words come out like a plea. I want this so badly I can't contain it. "To feel you inside me. On top of me. Behind me."

Niko drops to his knees in front of me with a groan and slips my underwear down the length of my legs.

"Oh god," I whisper, because if he comes any closer, I might completely self-combust.

He grazes his hand softly down my calf, nudging my heel up as he helps me step out, first one foot, then the other. "Niko, please," I croak, dragging my fingers through his satiny hair. Touching him is like racing into the ocean on a winter day, shocking and thrilling. It makes me feel wildly, unabashedly alive. "I want to feel you."

"Patience, Bex." His words dance along the inside of my thigh, his breath a soft tickle on my skin. "It's all about going slow. Watching your opponent, learning their strengths and weaknesses, and being one step ahead of them."

I am so caught up in the all-encompassing sensation of his mouth licking my hip that it takes me a second to realize what he's saying. It's the exact thing I told him during our first pickleball lesson together.

He traces a knuckle over the tuft of hair between my legs, just barely touching me. "You want to have a light touch."

His hands glide up the backs of my thighs, cupping my ass. I lean into him, desperate for the sensation, but he scolds me, clucking as he pinches me lightly. "I learned this from an amazing teacher. She told me my grip was too tight, and if I just loosened up a bit, I'd be a much better player."

"I like your tight grip," I plead. "Holding the paddle lightly is way overrated."

"But maybe if I'm gentle now," he says, his touch feather-soft, "my opponent won't have any idea when I'm about to punish them."

He is using my words against me in the sexiest way possible. I am an ice cube melting in the sun, a ball of clay in his hands, begging to be bent and molded exactly as he wants.

Every thought that has been weighing on me for the last month, every bill and cracked court, drifts away as he presses delicate kisses to the inside of my thighs and then shifts one hand to softly stroke my clit, spreading me open so that he can replace his finger with his mouth.

"You're so wet," he says as his teeth skim the sensitive skin there, his voice a reverential growl. "I've never seen anything more beautiful than you like this."

"Niko," I say, pitching my hips forward, closer to him, craving some friction.

He lets out a *tsk*, and it vibrates against me in the most maddening, delectable way. "Moving too quickly, not waiting," he says, and I tug at his hair, frustrated. "That's how you lose a game, Bex."

He toys with one finger at my entrance, swiping slow circles inside me. "Do you want to lose?"

"No," I squeak, as my hands drag through his hair, holding on to him for support.

"Good," he says with a chuckle, still tracing me lightly with that maddening finger. "I'm going to need you to follow one very simple rule."

"What is it?" I gasp as his tongue gently twirls a circle against my clit.

"It's easy," he says as our eyes meet. This man is downright smoldering, completely in charge as he worships my body. "Do less."

With a soft push, he nudges my legs wider. Somehow he trusts that I can stand here like this, with him on his knees in front of me, and let go. I've never had sex with anyone outside of a bedroom—much less a bed—but suddenly with Niko, it feels like we're defying gravity. I lean against him, steadying myself, as he continues to rub me in small, deliciously slow circles. "Niko, I don't know if I can—"

"What?" he says. "Relax? But you're such a good coach."

"It just feels so good." I look down and watch as his brows twitch, eyes fluttering closed for a split second, a glimmer of something passing across his face. I know what it is instantly, a momentary loss of control. He slides one finger inside me, his gaze never leaving my face. The slow pace is agony. I want him fiery, full of aggressive, grunting rage. But this Niko reminds me of glimpses I've caught of him recently, and it hits me as he watches my body jerk against him with a smile on his face, orgasm pulsing through me, all my patience gone. He's giving, tender, generous—as a lover, yes, but as a person. And I realize something about myself too, a truth that's becoming harder and harder to avoid: I love these things about him, because, well, I…

Fuck.

I push the thought aside. *Don't even go there*, a voice in my head warns. But I know it's too late to stop myself, or these feelings for Niko. I'm already gone.

25

MY EYES FEEL like they're weighted with sand, and when I crack them open, he's back standing in front of me, stroking my bottom lip with his thumb. I wait for another coaching lesson, but Niko's quiet, studying me.

"The same thing I said from the other night still stands," he says in a rough, gravelly voice. "You say stop, and I do. Is it okay if I—"

I nod yes because my mouth has lost the ability to form words.

"I have a condom on," he says, guiding my hand down to feel him. I have no idea when he did that—probably when I was floating away on my orgasm—but the fact that he did and wants to make sure I trust him sends a flutter of adoration through me.

I glide my hand down the length of him, and he groans. His eyes are clenched shut, breath heavy, and this is the Niko I've seen so many times before, the one who seems on the verge of losing all control on the court. Like he's also dancing on the edge of it being too good. I reach a hand to his chin, drawing his lips to mine one last time before I turn my body, repositioning us so that my back is pressed against his chest.

"Fuck, Bex," he moans as I reach for his hands, guiding them up to my breasts. Wrapped in his arms, I feel both at his mercy and totally in control.

"I want to give you what you want," he says, as he gently pinches my nipples, his mouth frantic against the side of my neck. "I want to give you everything."

He nudges us forward a step, then another, as his hands find mine, bringing them to the top of the net. "Hold on," he says, and all I can do is moan in understanding.

I think about it, too, I said that night we kissed. *About you behind me, bending me over.* And here he is, patiently guiding me forward, one hand tangling in my sweaty, knotted mess of hair. *Outside, or sort of in public,* I told him, as we sat and sipped iced coffees together.

And now I am naked under an endless cover of darkness with Niko's knee gently nudging my legs wider, one hand on my hip as the other cups my breast. Slowly, he thrusts forward, allowing me to feel every inch of him, until he's fully seated inside me.

Then he starts to move. His pace is glacial, and with every shift of our bodies together, I moan. I stand slightly, still holding on to the net with one hand as I reach back for him with the other.

"How's this for de-banging." He pants the words against my skin, and I let out a throaty laugh.

"I think you could play a lot harder tonight," I tease, and he responds by lightly smacking me on the ass. It stings with the perfect amount of white-hot pleasure, and I grind harder against him, meeting his rhythm.

He's remembered everything I've told him, taking my fantasies and making them real. But this is better than I ever could have possibly imagined. The sensation of him pushing back into me, so maddeningly slow that we both cry out at the same time, is unlike anything I've ever experienced before. To feel so wildly open and vulnerable and yet so cared for and safe unfurls a new horizon in front of me, an awakening about what intimacy can and should be. My fingers wrap around the net, but even with that to steady me, I feel almost like I'm floating in space, living without gravity. But Niko's touch grounds me, the soft pull of his hand tugging at my hair, the firm hold he has around my waist, the way he fills me, completely, over and over again.

When it feels like I can't take much more, he releases my hair and presses his thumb against my clit in firm, deliberate circles.

"Niko, I can't," I sputter. "I'm going to—"

I'm going to come, I'm going to fall, I'm going to lose myself to you, I'm going to love you—

He pushes hard inside me one, two, three more times, and the words spill out of him, praising me for being a good girl, for taking him so completely, for driving him so crazy he can't hold on much longer. I love the way this man talks, and I love the power I have over him, the way he lets go of that intense focus and gives in to whatever lies at the base of his animalistic heart. This is pure, unadulterated fucking. It's both dirty and so sweet that I can't tell if I'm about to have another orgasm or burst into tears. Maybe both.

"I've got you," he says with one final, hard thrust, and that's all I need to hear to let go completely.

26

Monday, May 15

NIKO SLEEPS ON his stomach.

It's the first thing I notice as my eyes adjust to my still-dark bedroom. The clock on my phone reads 5:24 a.m., and I know the second I open my eyes that this is going to be one of those mornings where my body and brain are going to refuse to let me fall back asleep, so I turn off my alarm. Travis is scheduled to be here at seven with one of his workmen to do a more detailed walk-through and estimate based on the resurfacing we need to do, so I might as well just stay awake.

It's Niko's fault that I'm restless, of course. I can't stop staring at him, thinking about last night, together on the court and then again after, in my shower. He is a devious and generous lover, but now, tangled up in my sheets, he looks downright innocent, especially with one leg peeking out from under the blanket. Up close, I can see the small snowflake-like scars that dot his knee. They're mostly faded, pale white and unassuming, but they also hint at something, a cataclysmic event that disrupted his entire life, changing everything. It's strange to think that just around the time Niko was stumbling on the court, tossing his racquet and tearing up his knee, my mom was checking into the hospital, my world on the verge of changing in ways I never imagined.

How is it possible that our lives can exist in parallel worlds until one day they crash together through some strange twist? What was it that brought Niko here, to me, I wonder. Was it Loretta breaking her wrist? Was it the moment he fell on the court? Or did something set off this chain of events earlier, years before?

My brain is churning through these kind of exhausted, emotional thoughts as I watch him sleep, one arm wrapped around Baleen, the stuffed whale that my grandparents gifted me when I started kindergarten. He's the same man who stormed into the hospital and scolded me over Loretta's bed, but he's become someone new, a person I want curled up next to me every night.

Everything is going exactly as we planned it, and I can't help but let my optimism take over. Sure, we have to actually win at the Paddle Battle, but Niko's skill is unmatched, the stuff pickleball pros dream about. Angela seemed constantly charmed by our conversations, especially when Niko jumped in to care for me when I fainted, just like a real boyfriend would. Loretta's physical therapy is going well. Soon the courts will be repaired, I'll be able to focus on the club, and I'll get back to my quiet existence here in Sunset Springs.

But a giant *except* looms over me, a dark cloud blocking

my sunshine. *Except* now that Niko's a part of it, it's hard to imagine my days without him. I've settled into Niko, or maybe Niko's settled into Sunset Springs. His presence, once a nuisance, is now a comfort, and I've gotten used to having him here, battling the ball machine, taunting Ed into volleying with him, chauffeuring Loretta around, and being there for me, like, well, an actual boyfriend.

I scoot up against the pillows, taking my worries out on the cuticles around my thumbnails. Niko's not my boyfriend, and it was because of me and my one lapse in kissing judgment that got us stuck into the charade in the first place. But in just a few short weeks, it feels like we've gone from playing these roles to really living them. Especially after last night's date and having him here now, spread out in my bed. He's making one final attempt to get back on the tennis pro circuit. I have a business to run, and not into the ground. That's what we both want, why we're doing this. Once the tournament is over and the profile's out, both our paths will hopefully be back on their correct tracks.

I reach down and tug the blanket up over his bare shoulder, running the back of my knuckles against the soft expanse of his skin. It's pointless, stupid even, to acknowledge the voice in my head that won't shut up. It started as a whisper but is now screaming like a blaring siren.

I like Niko. More than I ever imagined I could. And I especially like him here, in my bed, with me. As my partner, my boyfriend, the person I fall asleep next to and wake up with every day.

I lie back down and snuggle myself up against him, letting

my fingers rest on top of his. If only, I think, as I let my eyes close for just a second, he was the real thing.

• • •

I wake up with a start to the sound of my phone ringing. The clock reads 7:10 a.m., and I have three missed calls from Travis.

"Shit!" I throw the covers off and leave Niko—who is still out cold—asleep in my bed, pulling on some sweatpants, a sports bra, and a T-shirt I find in the clean pile of laundry I have yet to fold and put away. I had big plans of greeting Travis at the door with some freshly brewed coffee, but instead, I am a chaos tornado, stumbling down the stairs while pulling my hair back into a messy ponytail.

I reach the front door and rush through the usual twisting of locks and button pressing before ushering him inside. Travis is alone, and I glance behind him, confused by his solo appearance.

"Hey there, Bex," he says, adjusting the sun hat on his head. For some reason, he's averting his eyes as I peek behind him one more time.

"Are we waiting for your guy?" I ask, pinching my nose just between my eyes, hoping I don't look as exhausted as I feel.

"Listen, Bex, this is awkward," he says, not moving an inch out of the doorway. "But I'm not going to be able to take the job."

Half of my body sinks into the floor. "What do you mean,

you can't *take the job*? The whole point of you being here is to update your estimate, for the job."

"Listen, you know I've always tried to cut your mom fair deals, but I'm about to put the twins through college in a couple of years." His face looks genuinely regretful, like he hates giving me this news. "Wilson's offered me triple to do some stuff for Starlight, and I can't turn it down."

I can feel the panic kick on inside my chest, like someone just turned the burner on the stove up to high.

"Starlight was literally just renovated like two years ago," I say, confused, scrambling to find some reason for Travis's about-face. "What could Wilson possibly need you to do?"

"I don't know what to tell you." Travis shrugs awkwardly, his face pained. "The money's too good to pass up, and the one stipulation he gave me was that I had to pull out of any upcoming jobs."

"But the contract—"

"We haven't signed anything," he says, and I immediately feel foolish, once again a clueless kid who stumbled into running this place and thought she could handle it. "It's not binding. You haven't even put down a deposit."

Wilson is trying to ice me out, I think immediately, even though that seems like something a movie villain would do, and not some sixty-year-old tennis club maven. But it makes perfect sense. He's already offered to buy the club, and now he's backing me into a corner.

"So what am I supposed to do now?" I ask, my clothes itchy against my skin. It feels like everything is closing in on me—the walls, the bills, the cotton of my shirt. "Every other estimate I got was more than I can afford."

And even Travis's offer was more than I have right now. But at least it was what I can handle if we win at the tournament, something I could stick on a credit card and then pay off quickly. Now I am back at a very expensive square one.

"I can refer you to some folks," he says kindly, but it does nothing to assuage the dread shaking me to my core. "I'll reach out to some people I know, see what they're charging these days."

"This is really screwing me over, Travis," I say, unable to hide how furious I am, my lip quivering. Something about this feels like it's all too much. I've been juggling so many things for years now, and I don't want to carry this stress anymore. I just want something, *anything* to be easy.

Last night with Niko felt easy, but that peace was short-lived.

"I know, and I'm sorry." I can hear the sincerity in his voice, but it's a tiny bandage that barely covers this giant, open wound of a situation. "It's not personal."

But everything about it feels deeply, pointedly personal.

"Oh yeah? Tell that to Wilson," I snap as I force a pinched smile. "I'll figure it out."

"Your mom always did," he says with a look on his face that I know he intends as kind, but appears way more like pity. "If you got anything from her, I know it's that."

I manage to hold it together as I let Travis out the door and lock up behind him, but once I check my watch and see I have exactly forty-five minutes to fall apart before we open for the day, the tears come sliding down my face. I lean over the desk, elbows bracing me as I sob into the palms of my hands.

"Why didn't you do any of this?" I ask my mom out loud, though I know it's impossible to get an answer. For all the ways my mom taught me to play pickleball and run the club, the finances were a thing she kept tight to her chest. I always thought it was because she didn't trust anyone else to handle it, but now I wonder if she was trying to protect me from the reality of our precarious financial situation.

"Goddamn it," I swear at her, at our dwindling bank account, and the universe. I can't help it. I'm angry that she didn't better prepare me and mad at myself for all the ways I didn't pay attention, didn't learn.

I know it's no one's fault, not hers, not mine. And I know the anger isn't really about any of this. The anger is my grief. I can't shake it, even two years later. I am just so mad she's gone and furious at myself for not knowing how to pull myself out of this situation.

● ● ●

I'm peering into the darkened bedroom at Niko, still rumpled in my sheets and out to the world, when a text pops up on my phone. Hilariously, my first instinct—even though I am staring directly at him laid out in my bed—is to hope it's from Niko. Over the last few weeks, seeing his name appear on my screen has been a bright spot, a shiny little moment that breaks up the mundane stretches of my day-to-day.

The last name I expect to see on my phone is Freddie Alwin.

Hi Bex, it reads, as a photo of Freddie grinning in his BIG DINK ENERGY shirt pops up underneath. How are things? Loving the shirt!

I stare at the words, unsure of how to even reply. *How are things? Well, for starters, I have a man in my bed who I'm pretending to date when actually I'm developing very real feelings for him. That's how things are right now. Thanks for asking!*

As if he knows I'm thinking about him, Niko lets out a half groan, half yawn, dragging a hand across his face as he leans up on his elbows and surveys the room. It is undeniably sweet, like watching a baby deer try to walk for the first time.

"Hey," he says in a scratchy morning voice as his eyes land on me standing in the doorway. "You need to get naked and get in this bed with me."

"You're bossy when you wake up." I shuffle into the room and flop down next to him. His hand finds my stomach, and it's warm and comforting against my skin. I roll closer and hook my leg over his hip as I press a kiss to his nose.

"I'm bossy all the time," he corrects, snuggling in closer to face me.

"That's very true." I tweak his earlobe, run a finger over his eyebrows, and smooth out his hair. "You're also a cute sleeper."

Now that I can touch him freely, I can't get enough. I'm like a kid who's just had a soda for the first time and now won't stop asking her parents when she can have a Coke again. Niko's mouth finds my neck, and his lips flip on every switch in my body.

"Have you been up for a while?" he asks.

"I had to meet Travis about the court repairs," I say and immediately my body sags with the stress of it all.

"Oh good," he mumbles into my skin, lips electric against my collarbone.

"Not good. He just pulled out of the project. Wilson hired him and is paying, like, triple what the job here would have paid. He was the most affordable contractor by a mile."

I feel him pause, and then he shifts to look at me, concern evident in his face. "What are you going to do?"

"What can I do?" I shrug, defeated. I dig around for some optimism, a glimmer of hope in my chest. Normally, I can find a silver lining somewhere. But right now, I come up empty. "Wilson's already offered to buy the place, and I refused. I'm sure this is all part of his plan to push me out somehow."

"Oh no." He brushes a strand of hair away from my face, and once again I'm reminded of how nice it feels to be tended to, cared for. "Until a month ago, I really had no idea how cutthroat pickleball was. You all are like the mafia."

I snort out a laugh. "He's gonna make me an offer I can't refuse," I say, doing an absolutely abysmal Godfather impression.

"Seriously though," he says, "how can I help you fix this?"

I fall back onto the pillows. "I don't know," I admit. "I have to think of something, because even if we win at the Paddle Battle, that money's not going to cover everything I need to do here."

He strokes the inside of my arm, a quiet touch of reassurance.

"I could ask Freddie Alwin," I say and immediately feel Niko's body stiffen and his hand pause. The panic is causing me to spitball, shooting out ideas I've never let myself think before. The desperation I felt a few weeks ago is nothing compared to the sinking feeling wrecking my insides.

"Bex, trust me," he says, sounding resigned. "That guy is no good."

"I know you don't like him, but he's practically pickleball royalty," I explain. "Maybe he has some ideas on how I can raise the money for this place. Besides, you know, letting us kick his ass."

"First of all," he says, his voice returning to something slightly more playful, "*you're* the Pickleball Princess. He's not deserving of any title other than King Asshole."

"Okay, Tennis Prince." I ruffle his hair affectionately. "But at this point, I need to try to work every connection I have. I can handle him."

"I know you can." He pushes himself up to sit, and it's hard not to be completely distracted by his bare chest and the way his stomach muscles literally ripple as he moves. If we weren't in the middle of this slightly awkward conversation, I'd straddle him and beg for a replay of last night. "I just wish you weren't even entertaining the idea."

"Why?" I ask.

"Because he, because we're..." he starts, and then goes silent for a second before starting again. "I want to be the one to help you."

He's stumbling over his words like he's not sure which one he wants to say first.

"You have helped me," I say, squaring myself so that I'm sitting, legs crossed, directly across from him. "But this is something I need to figure out for myself."

"But we're in this together." He says this with a touch of frustration, like I'm just not getting his point.

"But we got into this whole mess *together* based on a lie," I remind him.

"Last night wasn't a lie," he says, and I can tell he's exasperated. "That wasn't me trying to pretend to date you for Angela's sake. That was me, the real me, wanting to take you out. To do something special for you."

"Yeah, and it was amazing," I insist. "It was the best date of my life. If I'm being honest, it was kind of the only date I've been on, unless you count, like, tagging along to frat semiformals in college, which I don't."

Niko watches me, his fingers twisting with mine. He gives my hand a tug, and my eyes shoot up to his. "When you kissed me, that wasn't a lie."

He's got me there. "No, it wasn't. I've wanted to…I don't know. You've maybe always been under my skin in some way. But you're leaving soon to go off to that qualifier, and then what? Do you even know where you'll be in a month? Because I'm going to be here. I'll probably *always* be here."

Niko is quiet, and for someone who puts so much thought into everything he does, I can tell he hasn't actually thought about this.

"I am going to be as plainly honest with you as I can," he

says finally. He's all flustered now, dragging his hand across his face. "I don't know where I'm going to be in a month, no."

Even though I'd just said this exact thing, the words sting more coming out of Niko's mouth.

"I don't know what I want to do with my life, Bex," he says. "I don't even know about next month."

"You want to go back to playing tennis," I tell him, because isn't that what this whole thing has been about? "You're going to get some publicity from this article, and the Paddle Battle, and then go do the qualifier in Miami, try to get into the draw. Go back on the road. Isn't this the plan?"

He looks absolutely miserable. "I thought so, but then I met you and..." He pauses. "I've spent my whole life trying to prove something. When I was a kid, all I wanted was to show my dad that I was worthy of his attention. Then that worked too well, and I became a better player than he ever thought I could be, and so I kept going, because I wanted everyone to know that I deserved to be there. I fought so hard just to be considered worthy, and then just when it was all starting to happen, my brain betrayed me, and my body..."

He trails off and looks up at me, and it registers on his face that I'm not totally following. "What does your brain have to do with your knee injury?"

"In that match, I didn't throw my racquet because I was angry with Freddie," he explains with a pained look on his face. "That's what I tell everyone, because it's easier to explain..."

He lets out a long breath before continuing. "I was angry with myself. A few weeks before that, it just started happening.

I knew what plays I needed to make, but I couldn't get my body to cooperate."

"You had the yips?" I ask, as parts of Niko's story that never quite clicked for me suddenly fall into place. Immediately, I ache for him, a deep and raw sympathy that makes me want to scoop him up and hold him in my arms.

The yips are a real and painful thing—your anxiety basically stops your body from being able to play—and are still so stigmatized. I remember my mom explaining it to me at a Dodgers game when I was a kid, when the pitcher just suddenly started walking every batter, failing to throw in the strike zone. They were the reason Simone Biles pulled out of the Tokyo Olympics—in gymnastics it's called the twisties—and she'd received so much unfair criticism for simply taking care of herself. They are a mental health crisis still often treated as a joke, and that persistent stigma must have made it that much harder for Niko.

"Had, or have," he says with a bitter laugh. "I guess I'll find out at the qualifier."

"You know you could have told me this, right?" I tell him. "I'd never judge you about it."

"I know you wouldn't, that's why I like you," he says. "But you're not the rest of the world. You're not the press or the guys I used to play against, like Freddie. You're not my dad."

"Thank god for that," I say, trying to lighten the mood. It's a protective move, one I did so often when my mom was having an especially hard day.

"Can you believe that my dad was mad when I called and

told him I wanted to stay here to help out Loretta?" Niko is visibly upset now, pent-up anger seeping out of him. "She's his *sister.* He literally said to me, 'What about your training?'"

I suck in a breath, remembering that phone call at the hospital, Niko muttering in Greek. I'd assumed he'd been the one trying to get out of staying. "Your dad sounds like a real jerk."

"Yeah, he's a piece of work." He lets out a sad laugh. "You'd think his move across the ocean would make me less stressed, but I guess it's hard to let go of wanting to make your parents proud."

His words hit me instantly, reminding me of my mom wrapped up in blankets, sitting out on the court one last time. I'd been doing all of this for the very same reason.

"It is," I say, stroking his arm. "You're not the only one who has something to prove. But I also don't think this is necessarily about Freddie, or old rivals, or bad news stories, or even your dad. Maybe you're trying to prove something to yourself."

"So what are you saying?" He looks up at me through soft, hooded eyes, and the sight of him like this, so unguarded and raw, threatens to split my heart right open.

"I think we both need to figure out our own shit." My voice cracks, the words physically painful to say out loud. "And not by lying or pretending to be something or someone we're not."

"What about the Paddle Battle?" he asks.

"It can be our last hurrah," I tell him. "But I don't think it's the solution to my problems. If we lose, then what? I need to figure out a real way to save this place. And I think Freddie can help."

"Bex," he says, wincing, "this is not how I want things to go between us."

"I know," I say, putting on a brave face. The urge to cry rushes through me, catching me off guard. "But it's okay. You've helped me figure out what I need to do, and that's been a huge gift."

"Are we breaking up?" he asks me, and even though he's got a slight smile on his face, his eyes look defeated, sad.

"I think so," I say, nodding. I swallow the lump in my throat, pushing it down and trying to hide it away next to all the very real feelings I have for this man. "Though I'm not sure we can when we were never really dating."

"Well." He leans forward to kiss me, and I duck so that his lips land on my forehead. I don't want him to see me cry. He wraps his arms around my waist, and I lean against him one last time.

"This was the best fake relationship I ever had," he says.

27

AFTER NIKO LEAVES, I drag myself downstairs to the computer. It's still early, and my body feels like a bag of bricks, the emotional exhaustion weighing me down just as much as the physical. The last twelve hours have flung me from the highest high down to the lowest low, and I just want the roller coaster ride to be over.

I open Wilson's email with his offer to buy the club, and the sight of it fills me with an agonizing sense of dread. I hover the mouse over the PDF of the contract he's attached. Selling the club is the logical answer to all my problems, but actually committing to it, truly ceding this place to someone else, someone with no care for the meaning or true beauty of the club, hurts too much.

I know, in my gut, that I want to hold on to the club. I'm not ready to give up on it.

Not yet.

I close my inbox without opening the contract. Instead

I find myself wandering back up to my apartment and standing face-to-face with the wooden urn, the one that I'd been holding in my arms on the day I first met Niko.

I'd been carrying it with me everywhere I went since the moment Mom died—not in my hands but in my heart, in my mind, in every second I spent trying to keep the club alive in her honor. But stumbling along like this, anxious and upset, doesn't seem like something that captures her spirit, her love of this place, her love of me. This isn't what she'd want for me or for the club.

"But what about what I want?" I say out loud to the quiet apartment. Who am I doing this all for, besides her, besides the members, besides this obsession with our family's legacy? Am I doing any of this for myself?

I'm not sure. The only thing I've done solely for myself lately is, well, kiss Niko.

"I need you to tell me what to do," I beg the urn. I've talked to Mom before like this, driving alone in my car or muttering under my breath after a challenging lesson. At first, it had felt utterly bizarre to speak out loud to someone who wasn't physically here anymore. But after a few times, it started to feel oddly comforting and natural. I never expected a reply, obviously. What I craved was the feeling of still being her daughter, still letting her comfort and hold me and help me figure things out.

"Come on, Mom," I plead, but the only response I get is the whir of the air conditioner begrudgingly clicking on as the morning heat rises.

I think back to that first moment I ran into Niko at the

hospital, how she'd been with me then because I'd been out trying to fulfill one of her last requests. I'd all but forgotten to do it since, so wrapped up in the last month and a half with Niko and trying to course correct the future of the club before it was too late.

It was Deb's call that stopped me from sprinkling her ashes there on the beach, the same call that sent me speeding back down to Sunset Springs to the hospital, to Loretta, and directly into Niko. All these little things coalesced into one big, coincidental chain event, all leading to this very moment.

I don't know how to save Sunset Springs Racquet Club any more than I did that day. But I do know what I need to do right now.

I grab the urn off the shelf and bolt downstairs, still in last night's pajamas. The second I push through the doors to the outside, I'm reminded that it is unforgivingly hot today, with a gusting wind. It's not a cool breeze, but rather a punishing, abrasive jolt of hot air that reminds you just how hard it is to live in the desert sometimes. But it doesn't deter me, not today. Instead I stop right in the middle of court 8, exactly where my mother and I had sat so many times throughout my life, and tug at the lid of the container.

"I can't think of any place that means more to us than this," I tell her, my voice wavering as I unscrew the lid of her urn. The wind wails a reply, sending my hair every which way as I tip the container slightly forward, tapping out the tiniest bit of ash. I fully expect it to blow back in my face, but almost as soon as it puffs up into the air, the wind falters and dies, and the dust settles and slowly scatters across the fissured, weather-beaten court. The ashes come to rest in the cracks that I've been so desperately trying to fix, and as the wind shifts and picks up again, they spread out even farther, disappearing into every corner of our favorite place.

"I know you'll watch over the club, even if I'm not here anymore," I tell her. I don't cry. My voice is now strong and steady because I know that the hardest thing to do is also the right thing. But I'm not ready to let this place go, not yet.

"I promise," I reassure her and myself. "I'm going to try really hard to figure this out."

28

Thursday, May 18

"**DRINKS WITH THE** competition. Are you sure your teammate is cool with this?"

Freddie swirls the whiskey in his glass, clinking the lone square cube back and forth before taking a slow pull of the murky brown liquid.

Niko relies on pure, icy focus and strength against his opponent to win. I've gotten used to being around this energy, enjoy it even. But Freddie's offensive strategy is all charm, oozed all over whoever is in his orbit, and right now that happens to be me.

I've carried the heavy stress of the last few weeks and, frankly, the last few years just underneath the surface of my skin. But after Travis bailed on the job, I could feel it erupting, hot lava spilling out in every movement of my body, every word that comes out of my mouth.

"Niko doesn't care what I do," I say with a confident

smile. The truth is that I'm pretty sure he does care, and *I* care that he cares. But there is a layer of confusion on top of all the real feelings that have bloomed between the two of us. "And if he did, I'd put him in his place. Anyway, I'm not here to talk about Niko. I'd actually love to talk business."

I pinch the orange peel in my glass and bring it to my lips, nibbling on the alcohol-soaked fruit, enjoying the immediate effect of it relaxing my shoulders and tamping down my nerves.

Freddie shifts in his chair, recrossing his legs before he settles in a little closer to me. His shirt is the palest of pinks, and his sleeves are cuffed in precise rolls, showing off a different, glitzier watch this time. He's one of those men who's just a little too comfortable taking up space, and even though I've never seen him on an airplane, I know instinctively that he spreads his legs wide and hogs the shared armrest. "Okay, now I'm curious."

I take a deep breath.

"The Sunset Springs Racquet Club is my family's legacy." I've practiced this little prepared speech all afternoon, but that doesn't make it any easier to say. "First, it was my parents' together, then my mom's on her own, and now it's mine. And it's struggling. I'm struggling."

He nods, giving me a sympathetic look. "You're looking for someone to buy the place?"

"No." I place my palms flat on the table in front of me, steadying myself. "I'm looking for an investor."

A flicker of something passes across his face, and I race to identify it. Is it intrigue? Amusement? Before I can get a good read on him, it's gone, and he's back to that easygoing, steady gaze.

"Pickleball is expanding rapidly. You know this better than anyone," I say, and though I can feel my heart thumping through my chest, my voice is calm and even, the projection of a professional, which is desperately what I want Freddie to see. "Well, anyone else besides me. The demand is there, but the club needs work in order to catch up and be competitive."

"So you want a silent partner." He says each word slowly, like he's processing the idea. I take this as a good sign and continue.

"Yes. A co-owner, though I'd keep the majority share of the place."

"And what does your boyfriend think of you approaching me about this?" His eyes are warm and unassuming, but his words grate. They're infantilizing and insulting. I'm here to talk about business, not Niko.

"He's *not* my boyfriend." I say this plainly, and the words feel strange coming out of my mouth, probably because I have not confessed this to anyone else. But also, maybe, because he really had come to feel a lot like a boyfriend. A very, very real one.

"Did I miss something?" Freddie squints in confused thought. "When did you break up?"

I brace my hands on the edge of the table, trying to figure out the next right thing to say to keep our story going. But all I can come up with is the truth. "Cone of silence?"

He nods. "Of course. We're friends."

I restrain the urge to roll my eyes and continue.

"Niko and I have a deal. He's being profiled by Angela Rakkas for the *LA Times.* He wanted to get some good press before this qualifier. She's been covering him for the last few weeks. So we exaggerated our relationship a bit to make the story better and get the club featured in the piece, too."

Freddie's mouth drops open slightly. "Wow," he says finally. "I have to hand it to the two of you. That's a brilliant little scheme you've concocted."

He tilts his tumbler toward me, a toast, a gesture of respect, and we clink glasses, the liquor burning its way down my throat. "And quite a business arrangement."

I know I should feel guilty for sharing our secret, much less with someone Niko loathes. But it feels so good to speak the truth, like a stack of bricks has just been lifted off my back. I can't save the club without first being honest about what I need and what I want to do.

"That's exactly what it is." I start to fidget with my hair and then stick my hands in my lap. "You can probably tell that the racquet club is my life. At this point, I'd do anything to save it."

"Like partner up with me," he says, cocking his brow ever so slightly, like he's enjoying this discovery.

"We're underwater financially, and I need something to change. Obviously being featured in the *LA Times* could get us some buzz, help bring people in. Paying customers. Which I need, especially if I don't win the prize money in the tournament or the exhibition match."

"I thought you were going to kick my ass," Freddie says conspiratorially.

"Well, obviously, I'm planning on doing that." It's a joke, of course, but also it *is* the plan. "But, you know, I'm trying to cover all my bases."

Freddie crosses and recrosses his legs, and then tents his fingers, tapping them against his chin in thought. "Maybe you don't need a partner, though."

"What do you mean?" I ask, slightly caught off guard.

"I don't know," he says, but he sounds anything but uncertain. "It sure does seem like selling the club could be the kindest thing you can do for yourself."

"Trust me, I've thought about it," I sputter. "The club is work. Just me, doing everything, all by myself."

I don't think I'd realized how lonely and hard the last couple of years have been until I'm saying it out loud to Freddie.

"The only thing stopping me from selling it, throwing in the towel, is that I truly love it more than anything else in the world. And not because of my parents or mom, or even the members, though they're everything to me. It's because it's a part of me, above all. I really want to do this myself."

"Jesus," Freddie chuckles, giving me an admiring look. "If you're this determined about saving the club, then you really are going to kick my ass in this exhibition match."

Finally, it feels like he's getting my point, and I scoot forward in my seat, trying to land this pitch confidently.

"I know I can pull it off. I know this place better than anyone. I just need the financial support to make it happen. And with an investment that makes improvements to the club, you get to be the hero who saves the day. If, of course, you're interested."

He considers this for a moment, tapping his index finger on the rim of his glass in thought.

"Well, I appreciate you telling me all this," he says finally, and his blue eyes are angelic, almost translucent, his face genuine and kind. "And frankly, I'm flattered that you'd want to go into business with me, of all people. I mean, it's no secret your—*Niko* doesn't like me."

"Well, just because the two of you have history doesn't mean we can't get along," I say diplomatically.

This morning, I dug up YouTube clips of Niko's last match, and sure enough, there was Freddie on the opposite side of the court. These days, they both look a touch older, broader, stiffer even. Niko's hair was shaggier three years ago, but his obsession with white sweatbands was evident then, too. Freddie's now-trimmed blond hair was also longer during that last match, tucked under a white cap. It's not an especially extraordinary match, from what I can tell. They're both close in score and skill. But there's a moment when Freddie says something, and Niko grows more and more agitated until that final second when he slams his racquet and stumbles and the course of his tennis career changes in a quick, brutal instant.

"He was always my favorite person to play against," Freddie says. "Like oil and water, the two of us, but sometimes we actually mix together well."

"Yeah, I know the feeling," I admit, and my body does that hot, flushed thing it always does when I think about Niko.

"Well, he's lucky to have you." Freddie shifts in his chair, dragging a finger along the rim of the crystal tumbler in front of him. "As…" He waves a hand like he's a magician casting a spell. "His pretend girlfriend and sort-of-real doubles partner?" he says, crinkling one eye at me in the quickest of winks.

I laugh at the absurdity of it all. "Yeah, sure, that works. But it's just for the Paddle Battle. He's determined to get back to tennis, I think."

"Yeah." Freddie considers this for a second. "But when you're injured like he was, it's hard to bounce back."

I feel immediately defensive of Niko, protective even. "Well, he's definitely put in the work."

"Sometimes it doesn't matter." Freddie shrugs. "There's always going to be someone younger, better, waiting in the wings for you to literally fall."

He takes a gulp of his drink and continues. "I'm just glad I figured it out before I hurt myself to the point where I couldn't play. I'm way happier playing pickleball. And the money, the growth, it's so much bigger and better than tennis."

"Exactly." I try to steer the conversation back to my original goal. "I hope this means you'll consider discussing my offer further?"

"Let me think on it," he says, and his face is friendly but utterly unreadable. His poker game must be impeccable. "But I hope, after all of this, we can stay friends." It's a strange thing to say, but before I can question it, Freddie lifts his glass toward me again.

"Cheers," he says, and when our glasses connect, he winks before throwing back the rest of his drink.

29

Friday, May 19

MY ALARM IS loud and thumping, a new sound I don't remember programming. Normally, it's a high-pitched bird chirp, but this morning it's a steady beat, like thunder, and I swat at my phone to turn it off.

Except it keeps going, persistent and irritating. I drag a hand through my hair, which is damp with sleep sweat, and grab for my phone again, the screen painfully bright. The time reads 5:45, almost an hour before my alarm normally goes off.

That's when it hits me. It's not my alarm that I'm hearing at all. It's the door to the racquet club downstairs, and someone is banging on it. Loudly.

The few people who have the front door code know it's not set to unlock for them until 6:00 a.m., and I leap out of my bed like it's on fire, hands flailing to my chest, then my thighs, to make sure I have pajamas on. My mouth feels like a stack of newspapers, dry and stale, and there's a low thrum of a headache pulsing at the nape of my neck. It's a light hangover, which in my experience, is one of the worst kinds—barely there but bad enough to ruin your day.

The incessant knocking is only making it worse.

I stumble my way downstairs, and even though it's still dark outside, the figure in the glass is lit up from the security lights that loom brightly over the entrance. Niko is there, palm pressed against the door like he's being chased by zombies and is desperate to get inside. Something seems very, very wrong.

He pushes through the door the second the lock clicks open, and I've never seen him this unraveled. He's disheveled, like he drove here still half-asleep, and my mouth falls open a bit in surprise when I notice that he's in a gray T-shirt and navy shorts. But he hasn't totally lost his mind, I realize, looking down at his feet. He's still in ice-white socks and those pristine sneakers.

"What the hell is going on, Niko?" I ask, suddenly worried. "Is Loretta okay?"

He shakes his head. "It's not her," he says quickly, and I immediately feel reassured. But then my stomach sinks. He passes me his phone, and before I glance at the screen, I catch a glimpse of his face. He looks sickly, a ghostly, greenish pale, and even though I've seen this man almost daily for a month and a half, I have never once seen him like this.

"I'm so sorry for dragging you into this," he rasps.

I look back down and read the email on the screen.

Hello Niko and Bex,

Due to some new information we received, we're going to publish the profile online today at 10 a.m. and in print tomorrow, earlier than planned. I wanted to give you both the opportunity to comment on the following:

Your romantic relationship is fabricated. The two of you have been pretending to date to generate publicity.

"Holy shit." My voice quakes with unbridled panic. I don't need to keep reading to know what the rest of the email says. Freddie's told her everything, and it's all about to be in print. "Did you respond?"

Niko nods. "I did."

"And?" I ask, even though there's no answer he can give me that will fix this.

He reaches for my hand. "What else could I say? I told the truth. That'd we'd been faking, for the sake of trying to boost my career and help the club."

My body freezes, but the absolute panic that courses through me is red-hot. "I'm going to throw up," I say, dropping his phone on the counter and racing toward the bathroom.

"Bex"—Niko chases after me—"let me stay with you."

"Leave me alone, please," I croak as the bile in my throat rises. I barely make it to the toilet before I am sick. My sweat is clammy, and I'm blinking back tears as I crumble on the floor.

Luckily, I don't heave up last night's dinner—or cocktails. My stomach settles into something hard, and tears begin their steady stream down my face as I back up to sit, cupping my head in my hands. The motion-sensor light shuts off, and I hug my knees in the darkness, flushed with a sadness so deep I don't know my way out of it. I don't need to read the rest of the email to see the writing on the wall. We've been found out, exposed, and humiliated, our plan foiled before we even had a chance to finish it. I was foolish to think that I could save a business by pulling off some sort of concocted juvenile scheme.

No, I was foolish to think that I could save a business, period, much less run it.

I don't know how much times passes before I hear the door creak open. "Can I come in?"

"Okay," I mumble, as the overhead light flickers back on. Niko slides down onto the floor and sits across from me. He reaches for my hands and gives them a squeeze, and I look up at him through eyes that already feel swollen from the onslaught of tears.

"We can figure this out," he insists. "Tweak our plan."

"No," I say hoarsely, my body dried out and exhausted. "No more plans."

"I'm so sorry I got you into this mess," he says. "Seriously, Bex. I didn't mean for it to blow up like this."

"It's my fault," I start, the guilt overwhelming. "I was trying to explain to Freddie the lengths I'd go to save this place, why he should invest in the club. I fucking said 'cone of silence' and everything."

I watch as he processes this information, anticipating the worst. But he just shakes his head while stroking his thumb softly over the curve of my wrist.

"Well, you know the first rule of saying 'cone of silence' is that nobody ever actually follows it." His voice is kind and soothing, and he gives me a sympathetic smile. "Especially Freddie. He used to always send in terrible things about me to all these tennis websites, trying to get them to print ridiculous stories about me. It was his form of psychological warfare, how he'd try to win matches off the court. Clearly his ego can't handle playing either of us in this exhibition match."

"Are you serious?" My eyes widen in horror. "So you didn't tell people you lost a match because of bad socks?"

Niko chortles at this. "Bex, I complain about a lot of shit, but have you ever heard me say a word about *my socks*?"

I shake my head before letting it drop back into my hands.

"Why are you being nice to me?" I grumble. "I fucked this whole thing up."

"This has nothing to do with you," he says firmly. "I get why you told him. It wasn't a bad idea. He's just a scumbag. There's no reason we can't still play this match tomorrow. Or in the tournament."

I appreciate that he doesn't even hint at an *I told you so* about Freddie.

"I don't think I can," I mumble, still sniffling. "This is so fucking humiliating."

"Bex, I think I know you pretty well by now," he says,

"and I know you don't give up this easily. We can still win the prize money, try to save this place. I know we'd kick his ass, especially if he's playing with someone who bought the spot to play with him."

Niko's a good person. He didn't need a write-up in the *LA Times* or some pretend pickleball career to prove that. Niko isn't perfect, and I wouldn't want him to be. He's human. Insecure and arrogant, sure. But kind, loyal, and determined. Someone I would want by my side on a regular basis.

"I can't show my face there, Niko," I say flatly. "Everyone will have read Angela's story. I'll be a joke. *The club* will be a joke. I'm going to take today to review the offer Wilson sent over to buy the club. I think that's the only way out of this mess."

"Bex." He winces, his face pained. "I don't care if my image is fucked or if I'm irredeemable after this stupid article. That's not why I'm doing this anymore." He reaches a hand up to my chin, tilting my gaze until our eyes line up. "You get that, right?"

"I do," I tell him. "And I love that about you. But this is something I need to do on my own."

He's quiet for a moment, thinking. "You know there are so many people who want to help you," he says finally. "Me, most of all."

"Well, you of all people should know what it's like to not want to rely on anyone else, Mr. Never Played Doubles before," I reply. Despite my tears, there's a saucy edge to my voice, and he lets out a quiet chuckle.

"That's fair, I guess." Even in moments of despair, I love when he admits that I'm right. He brings my hands up to his lips, kissing them softly. "But where does that leave us?"

"I was never pretending," I admit. "Even when I said I was, I knew all along that everything I did, everything I felt, was real. I know you didn't get the profile you wanted, but if it's any consolation, you definitely changed one person's opinion about you."

Niko sighs, and it hits me in that spot where all his sounds do, in the funny bone of my heart. "I don't care what Angela prints in that story. That's all that matters to me."

"I don't know what this is, between us, when we started it on a lie just to get things we wanted." I pull away from him and wrap my arms around my legs, leaning my head against the wall. "That doesn't seem like a relationship. I just want something honest."

Niko stills and then clears his throat. "Then I have one more thing to tell you."

I stare back at him, and his face is stricken with sorrow. He looks unsure of himself, and I'm overcome with the urge to pull him into my lap and hold him close.

"What is it?" I am drained of every bit of energy I once had, and I'm not sure I can take more revelations today.

"I know I told you I signed up for the Paddle Battle for the article and to beat Freddie. But it was also about proving to myself that I could still get out there and play *something.* I was terrified of showing up at the qualifier and finding out that even after all this time and all this work, my body and brain are still broken."

His words chip off pieces of my heart, bit by bit. "That must feel so awful."

"I'm still scared." Even though his voice is low, this

confession echoes off the walls of the bathroom. "I don't want to find out what happens if I can't play tennis."

I know nothing I say will reassure him, but I still try. "I played against you enough to know that whatever happens with you and tennis, you sure as hell can play pickleball."

"But also," he interjects, "it wasn't just about that. I think it was about proving something to you."

"Me?" For the first time all morning, I smile. "No way."

"It didn't hit me until the other night, standing next to you at the museum," he says softly. "That all of this—the game, and pickleball, and trying to win—has just been to show you how much I like you."

"Oh, Niko." I drop my head into my hands with a groan. I don't know if hearing this makes me feel better or worse. "That is a really fucked-up way to try to go about doing it."

"I know," he admits, his face sheepish, guilty. "I realized that the other night, too. At least let me make it up to you, if you just play—"

But I shake my head. I don't want to get sucked into another scheme. I just want to be done.

"It was silly of me to put both of us in this position," I tell him. "I have a solution, and it's the one that hurts the most. But I think sometimes you have to let go of the things you love so they can go on to thrive on their own."

The words actually hurt to say out loud, causing an ache so deep in my chest that I'm not sure it will ever completely go away.

He nods, and I know he understands what I mean, even if I'm not quite saying it.

I'm letting the club go. But I need to let him go, too.

"I do need you to do one thing for me," I say finally.

"Of course," he agrees, leaning closer.

"Could you put a sign in the door telling people the club is closed until Monday?" I ask, smoothing out my hair, trying to collect myself. "I'll send an email out to members now."

If he hates this idea, he doesn't let on. Instead he just gets up to stand as I stay put on the bathroom floor. "Anything else?" he asks, reaching a hand down toward me.

I grab hold of him one last time, and he pulls me up off the floor with ease, like supporting me is second nature to him.

"Yeah." I straighten out the collar of his T-shirt and try to swallow back the lump tightening in my throat. "Go have that comeback. Win your qualifier. You've earned it. Show everyone how great you are. And don't worry about proving it to me. I already know."

He laughs at this, but it's hollow and so deeply, deeply sad. He runs the back of his hand gently across my jaw and then leans forward like he's about to kiss me before pulling away. "If anyone asks," he says, "I'll say I owe it all to my pickleball coach."

30

I GIVE MYSELF twenty-four hours to think it through. Texts and calls pop up all day on my phone—Loretta, Deb, even Ed gives me a call—but I don't answer. The only person I do reply to is Angela.

Twice.

My first email, sent immediately after Niko left, read, I have no comment.

But then, a few minutes later, I sent another.

> Actually, I do have a comment. I hope people can forgive me for acting foolishly and understand that everything I did was out of love for the Sunset Springs Racquet Club, my family's business and livelihood. And for the record: Niko Karras is an excellent pickleball partner and fake boyfriend.

She responded with a simple Noted, thank you, and that's all I hear from her before the piece publishes. When the clock on my phone switches from 9:59 to 10:00, I feel a sick, miserable relief. At least now everyone knows the truth.

Niko's name never appears in my texts, and I try to tell myself I have no right to be disappointed. I asked him to leave, told him to go back to Miami and chase that final dream of his.

But I can't help it. I'm annoyed that he's respecting my wishes because his is the name I want to see the most.

I don't read any of the texts or listen to the voicemails that accumulate. I want to make sure I am going into this decision with a clear head, without any other influences around. And so I spend hours cleaning with care, power-washing the courts, wiping down the bathrooms like they're made of precious stones, scrubbing every counter and shelf. This place may never sparkle on the surface, but to me, it shines.

When I'm done, I pour a bowl of cereal for dinner and then crawl into bed, telling myself I'll sleep on the decision for one more night. But the hours pass with hardly any rest, and by 7:00 the following morning, I know it is now or never.

I drag myself out of bed and slowly lumber into the kitchen, craving coffee. When I go to grab the milk out of the fridge, I come face-to-face with my calendar, the same one I'd marked up with Niko that night after our kiss. That giant *X* I scrawled across May 20 stares back at me, a reminder of what today is.

Twenty minutes down the freeway, hordes of people are about to descend on Starlight for the Paddle Battle. Freddie will flaunt his skills for the crowd, money will flow, and

Wilson's stupid juice bar will crank out a thousand protein smoothies. And any mention of the Sunset Springs Racquet Club and Bex Martin will be made with horrified pity or as part of a punchline.

Wilson will know how to run this place. Sure, he'll do away with mom's ancient potted plants, some of which are older than me, and the tacky glass block wall the previous owners installed in the eighties. The towels will be fluffier, the daily rates inflated. But he'll keep the place going, in some form. It is the best I can hope for.

My coffee tastes like nothing. It's as if my taste buds have gone numb along with the rest of my body. I make my way downstairs, and from my place behind the front desk, I see the Paddle Battle flyer still hanging on the wall, taunting me like a mean kid on the playground. I do my best to ignore it and fire up the computer. A lump immediately blooms in my throat as I open up my inbox, and I wait for the predictable deluge as I scroll back to find Wilson's old email that I've left sitting there, unanswered, for weeks. But my eyes stay dry. Maybe I really have run out of tears.

I scan the old message and find the PDF attached at the bottom. I expect some sort of lengthy document, hundreds of pages of tiny print, and I'm surprised to discover it's short. I guess I've never seen a contract to sell a business before outside of the movies, and Wilson, I realize, is no big-screen villain. He's just a businessman trying to make a deal.

I scan the numbered stipulations—I'd need to go over these again later with more focus on detail with my lawyer—and seek the one thing I'm looking for, the number that could change my life. There it is, seven digits long, and it's such an absurd amount of money that I let out a high-pitched laugh. It is an astronomical sum and more than what I assumed the property would be worth after an assessment. He'd gone high to prove a point but to also make it worth my while and to not make the negotiations difficult, I realize. With an offer this massive, there was no need to push back or to go through the formality of inspections. It was an easy way out, for both of us. I'd be an idiot not to sign it.

At the bottom, I see the line for my signature, my name printed above it. Next to it are two spots for the buyers, which at first strikes me as odd until I remember the message that had accompanied the offer. I have a new investor on board who's hungry to start a pickleball empire, he'd written in his email, and brings cash equity and experience to the table.

That person's name stares back at me on the document, directly below Wilson's.

Frederick James Alwin.

"That fuck!" I yell out loud, slamming my hands onto the desk. He isn't just Wilson's star client; he's his business partner. The last month replayed in my head in an entirely new light, like I was a detective who had finally stumbled upon the motive for a crime. Wilson and Freddie had been teaming up to try to push me into a corner from all sides. The friendly surprise visits, the eagerness to tour the club, the exhibition match, the vague, chipper banter over drinks the other night. This whole time the two of them had been playing to win while I'd never even realized I was in a game against them—until now. And there's no way in hell I'm going to lose.

31

I FLY UPSTAIRS to my apartment, racing into my bedroom and shoving the first sports bra I can find over my head.

It's not too late to get to Starlight. And it's not too late to win. The thought of standing center court, clutching a giant check as Freddie Alwin sulks off to the locker room, electrifies me as I move. I add another scenario to this fantasy: Wilson standing off to the side, grimacing as I toss his stupid contract back in his face.

Niko is there too, I imagine. I let myself envision our kiss, the crowd of adoring pickleball fans hollering in celebration, before getting back to the reality in front of me: I have to track down Niko. But I have no idea if he is even still at Loretta's. Maybe he left for Miami early. *I should call him!* I think, and then remind myself to multitask—I can dial him while driving to Loretta's to find him.

I grab my bag, tossing my keys and phone inside, and race

back downstairs, locking up at warp speed and dashing outside to where my car should be.

My still-dead, not-fixed, sitting-at-the-shop car.

I refuse to let myself panic, even if this plan was feeling flimsier by the second.

"Niko!" I say out loud to myself. He can drive here, and I'll explain it all on the way to Starlight. We'll be late, of course—the tournament will be starting soon—but maybe there's still a chance we can make it in time to play the exhibition match. I speed-dial his number and pace around the parking lot, waiting for an answer from him. When it doesn't come, I do the next most logical thing I can think of in the moment.

I text Loretta and then take off running for her house.

One very sweaty mile and a half later, Loretta opens the door before I even have a chance to knock. She must know from the frantic look on my face and the fact that my shoelaces are trailing after me like kite strings why I'm panting on her front steps in a panic.

"Oh, honey," she says, her face falling sympathetically, "he's not here."

I catch my breath on her steps, waving a finger to say *I need a sec* as I bend over, hands on my knees. My exhale comes with the overwhelming urge to cry. In my rush to her house, I completely neglected to consider what I would do if Niko wasn't here.

"Crap," I huff, trying to reset and calm myself down. But that ship has sailed. I am in full-on freak-out mode, and this discovery has only made things worse.

"I think he's one step ahead of you, actually." She wraps her good hand around my shoulder. "He left about an hour ago for Starlight. He said he'd meet you there."

"Goddamnit," I say with a laugh that cracks with the touch of a sob. He knew I'd show up to play even before I did.

"He takes everything extremely seriously," Loretta says as she tugs me closer, pulling me into a hug. "I'm sure you've figured that out by now."

"I have." I nod against her shoulder, inhaling the musky scent of her perfume. Everything about her is comforting, and I let myself be held. "Would you believe it's something I like about him?"

"I would," she says kindly. "It's also something you have in common with him, you know? You both do everything from the heart. I get why you're so good together."

"Oh god, Loretta, you must hate me," I say as I step back, choking out another sob-laugh. "I know you wanted the two of us to be together, but it all started as an act. You read the article, I assume?"

She shakes her head no and gives me a resolute look. "I don't need to read it to know who Niko is, and who you are."

"But we lied to you," I protest. Surely I do not deserve sympathy for tricking her into thinking I was in a relationship with her nephew.

"Did you really, though?" she asks. "Maybe the two of you weren't honest about your feelings for each other, but they seemed pretty straightforward to me, and everyone else."

She's got me there. I liked Niko long before I ever admitted it to myself. I was never completely faking it. I was simply hiding it because it felt too terrifying to actually admit the truth.

"Bex," she says, "he came out to Sunset Springs because he cares about me, in his own protective way. And he rushed out of here this morning to go play pickleball because he cares about you in the same exact way."

"And I'm here only because I care about the club," I mutter. "God, that makes me sound so shallow."

"Shallow to whom?" she asks, ushering me inside her house. The smell of coffee wafts over me, and when my eyes focus, I see Ed packing a bag on the dining room table. He's here, just like on our game nights, only it's the morning, and Maureen and Deb are nowhere to be found. Oh. *OH.*

My heart swells with happiness for them.

"Hey, kid!" he says, giving me a jovial wave. It feels a bit like what I imagine walking in on your parents having sex does, and I'm determined to play it cool.

"Ed! Hey!" I say a little too loudly, and it's obvious that I am, in fact, not going to be cool about this at all. But it's not because I'm embarrassed for stumbling upon them in an intimate moment. It's because joy has flooded my body at the sight of the two of them together, so touched by the obvious adoration they feel about each other.

"We're driving you to Starlight?" he asks, like I already know the plan.

"Yes, we are," Loretta answers for me as she rushes around the kitchen industriously, turning off the coffee and swiping the milk from the counter and shoving it back in the fridge. "We need to hit the road. Do you have the shirts?"

"They're in the trunk." Ed nods as I look between the two of them, utterly confused.

"What shirts?" I ask.

"Honey, did you check any of your messages from us?" She stops what she's doing and stares at me, and I can't tell if she's alarmed or about to burst out laughing.

"No," I reply. "I didn't read anything because I wanted to make a decision about the club with a clear head."

Loretta lets out a laugh like she can't believe what she's hearing.

"Oh boy," Ed says, as he guzzles whatever is left in his coffee cup and slams it down on the table. "Today is going to be fun!"

"I thought we already had fun." Loretta's voice is as mischievous as her grin, which sparkles from the kitchen. She opens up a cabinet and grabs a box of crackers, tossing it into Ed's tote bag.

These two are obviously baiting me, and I bite the inside of my lip.

"Oh, we did," Ed says with a wink, giving her a peck on the cheek as he grabs the bag and heads toward the front door.

"My god," I blurt out, unable to keep it in anymore. "Are the two of you going to just keep saying inappropriate things in front of me? I know what you're doing!"

"And we know you and Niko have feelings for each other." Loretta tries to say this with a serious face, but she cracks into a smile. "Even if you both think you were pretending for the sake of some stupid article!"

They've got me there, and I keep quiet as the two of them

putter around the house for a couple more minutes, grabbing sun hats and pulling phone chargers out of sockets, tossing them into the bag. They move with comfort, like they both feel unconditionally safe in the other's presence. It's absolutely wonderful to see them together like this, not just enjoying each other's company but existing in it.

Once we're in the car and I'm strapped into the back seat with nothing to distract me, my nerves turn back on at full blast, and I gnaw on a fingernail, staring out the window in between glances down at my phone. There are still no messages from Niko, and a nagging doubt starts fogging my thoughts. What if he's not there after all? What if he is there and is now mad at me?

What if he is there and mad, and we play the matches, and lose?

"We'll get you to the game, Bex," Ed says reassuringly, sensing the anxiety obviously radiating off me. "This isn't just important to you, you know. It's important for all of us."

"Thank you," I say softly. "It means a lot to me too."

"Have I ever told you how I found pickleball right after Terry died?" Loretta asks, as she turns around in the front seat to give me a tender look. "It was the only thing that brought me joy for that first year or two. I spent all of that time either crying or playing pickleball."

"Oh, Loretta, that sounds so hard." She talked about her husband often, but I'd never completely connected her loss to her time at the club until now, and her grief feels familiar, even if it's not the exact same as mine.

"Thank you, honey. It was," she says. "But it's also how I got really, really good at pickleball."

Ed laughs and reaches his hand across the console, finding hers. It's a simple, comforting gesture. He's checking in, making sure she's okay, and I long for Niko to be here next to me, for me to be able to do the same with him.

"Running the club definitely helped me after my mom died," I say, the realization hitting me. "It's given me somewhere to channel all that sadness, you know?"

Loretta nods in agreement. "I should say that I may have started playing to distract me from my grief, but now I'm there to kick ass and destroy the very fragile egos of the retired men of Sunset Springs."

"And I enjoy watching you do it," Ed adds with an affectionate glance.

"But my point is, Bex, the club *saved* me," she continues. "The place is a gift. And we'll do whatever we can to help you hold on to it."

"Especially because I literally count on it to keep me alive," Ed adds. "My doctor told me to play pickleball because it's good for my bones *and* depression."

"You two are amazing," I tell them. "And I appreciate it. But I don't have a plan anymore. It was stupid to think I could bank the future of the club on winning some game."

"It's what any person who loves their community would do," Ed says. "You're figuring out your own way as a business leader."

I try not to let out a self-pitying laugh at his assessment. If anything, I am still lost, not leading. But maybe I can change that today.

"Well, I appreciate you two not taking me to task over

it," I say. Then I remember the other half of our little friend group and let out a groan. "Though I suspect Deb is going to have a field day."

Ed *hmms* in agreement.

"Oh, you don't know the half of it," Loretta says with a chuckle. "She's already at Starlight, ready for you with her tripod all set up."

"What?" I squeak, practically bouncing out of my seat. "What is she doing there?"

"Oh, honey, just you wait and see." She gives me an easy grin, like a person with their mind made up, who's not worried about anything stopping them. "We're all here to help you save the club, no matter what happens today."

32

MOM ALWAYS CALLED the club's members our family, and I have followed in this tradition. But I don't think I've ever thought about what she really meant by that until Ed pulls his car directly in front of Starlight and yanks it into park.

They both turn around to look at me in the back seat. "Go find Niko," Loretta commands. "And we'll be right behind you."

They love the club just as much as I do, not in spite of all its cracks and quirks but maybe because of them. It isn't fancy or shiny, but it is theirs, and mine, and it is home. Even if Niko and I lose today, even if I never figure out how to save the club, it will always, *always* be our place.

I move like a person on fire, jogging past the DJ spinning amped-up dance tracks right outside the front door. Racing through the check-in in the foyer, I grab my branded tote bag full of granola bars and Vitaminwater, pocket my coupon for a free post-game smoothie, and rush outside toward the players' tent. Hordes of players are gathered under the giant white canopy, chatting and gnawing on the spread of free food that covers one long banquet table in the corner.

It's packed, bumper to bumper with people. For a second, I think of my mom and how the sight of this many people gathering to play a sport she loved so much would make her toss her paddle in the air with glee. She'd loved pickleball as much as she'd loved tennis, and I understand now that it was never really about what game she was playing. She loved the fun, the community, and the joy that came from the competition, and the camaraderie.

That was the legacy she wanted me to continue, no matter where or how I do it.

I shake the memory aside and search the faces around me frantically, trying to land on a brooding man begrudgingly holding a pickleball paddle in head-to-toe pristine tennis whites. But it's an impossible feat in this crowd, which is packed wall to wall with people in neon lime-green shirts. A pang of annoyance hits me—am I the only player here not to get gifted this T-shirt? I dig around in the bag I just received to see if I've missed it under the packets of electrolytes and flyers, but I come up empty.

How did everyone know to wear the same shirt?

"Excuse me," I say as someone bumps my shoulder. I glance up, and the words BIG DINK ENERGY stare back at me.

This isn't just any shirt. It's the shirt I designed. I blink and refocus on the people milling about around me as it hits me: Every single person in the room is wearing one.

I grab frantically at the sleeve of the person I'd just knocked into. "Where did you get that shirt?" I ask as they take a step back and give me a strange look. I must be in an alternate dimension because nothing about this could possibly be real.

"Wait." The woman's face registers something and shifts from confusion to elation. "Aren't you the woman who designed them? I'm so excited for you! That video is everywhere."

"What video?" I ask, even more perplexed. But she's swept off into another conversation, and I push forward through the crowd, determined to get to the bottom of whatever the hell is going on.

"Excuse me!" I bark, trying to maneuver through another group conversation.

One of the men—a bearded older guy—taps me on the shoulder. "I donated," he says. "Good luck today."

"Donated to wha—"

But before I can even finish my question, his group parts, shuffling just a few steps over in one direction or the other, as if they all received a text alert at the same exact time, instructing them to move. My eyes follow the narrow path that's opened up in front of me, straight down to the strikingly handsome man standing all the way on the other side of the tent.

I was wrong. He's not wearing tennis whites today. He's in the exact same shirt as everyone else, the shirt he unceremoniously tossed back at me a few weeks ago, and he looks… proud.

Maybe I've fainted again, and this is the lucid dream I'm having while splayed out in front of Loretta's house.

But the closer Niko gets, striding through the crowd, the more it becomes obvious that I am very awake and that this is all very real.

"I was hoping you'd show up," he says when he reaches me. The man is downright beaming. There's no trace of the worried, tense person who comforted me on the floor of the bathroom.

"Niko, what the hell is everyone doing in my shirt?" I gasp, reaching out for his arm to steady myself. "I mean, what the hell are *you* doing in my shirt?"

"Well, technically, it's my shirt, Princess," he says, those dark eyes alight with mischief.

"You gave it back to me," I remind him, still utterly confused. "You didn't want to wear it." For some reason, this only makes his grin deepen.

"Well, I changed my mind, and took it back the other night when I slept over," he explains, like this should be obvious to me. "I figured it might come in handy today."

Suddenly, I notice that Deb is there next to us, walking in a slow circle, holding her phone directly out in front of her.

"Okay, you need to tell me what the hell is going on," I demand. "This feels like I'm on some prank show from my childhood."

"She hasn't seen the video," Deb tells him, her eyes still focused on her screen as she films, and understanding ripples across his face.

"I need you to listen to me." Niko's voice is warm and steady, as he takes my shaky hand and pulls it close to his chest. "After I left the club yesterday, I called Deb and Maureen," he explains. "They helped me make a reaction video about the article, and us."

"It was a good ten minutes that we had to edit down to three," Deb says, never breaking her focus on the screen in front of her.

"I was nervous," he says with a shrug. "I've never made one of those before."

"What does this have to do with the shirts, though?" I ask, trying to keep up with what he's telling me.

"You should probably watch it," he says, just as a voice comes over the loud speaker announcing the start of the tournament.

"But maybe not now," he rushes.

"Just tell her about the video!" Deb says.

"Okay, okay!" He laces our fingers together, giving them a squeeze. "I explain that I'm madly in love with the woman who designed that T-shirt, and I talk about how she's been busting her ass to save the most special place in the world, the Sunset Springs Racquet Club."

I'm trying to absorb his words over the loud thump of my heart beating in my ears.

"I also said she was a real hero for taking on this nightmare," he says, gesturing at himself, "as a pickleball partner and boyfriend, all to help me. And I said that the least I could do was make the shirts available and try to go viral to help raise money for the club."

"I'm so confused," I say, trying to make sense of everything he's telling me.

"About which part?" he asks, and he's so steady, so calm,

so not scowling that I can't quite believe what I'm seeing. "The part about me being in love with you or about how we've sold twenty-two thousand dollars' worth of shirts in twenty-four hours and all of that's going to go toward repairing the club?"

"All of it," I manage to squeak out, and it takes me a second to realize I'm trembling, my body lit up in what feels like unbridled ecstasy. "Who the hell bought all those shirts? How did you make them for everyone here? Where did you even post a video?"

"I have over four hundred thousand followers on TikTok, Bex!" Deb says, exasperated, finally putting down the phone. "And it's already got over a million views. Turns out, a hot tennis player spilling his guts to the camera does very well in the algorithm. And I called in a favor with the local T-shirt printer."

"Who just so happens to be one of the vultures from the Six AM Club," he tells me. "She was excited to help out."

"But why would so many people want to do all this for me?" I ask, heart racing to keep up with my mind as it works to process what he's saying.

"Bex, I think it should go without saying that you're amazing." He smiles down at me, searching my face for something. "And not to toot my own horn, but I did a pretty great job explaining just how incredible you are. And the club."

"You're bragging." I smile. There's no hiding it on my face—I love the cocky side of him, and, it turns out, I especially love it when it comes out in support of me.

He nods and gives me a satisfied smirk. "I definitely am."

Around us, people shout greetings at each other, twist open bottles of water. I'm both acutely aware that we're standing in a sea of people, including our friends, and also feel like we're the only two people in the world. My body hums with emotion, but the fear that filled me earlier quiets, replaced by an overwhelming sense of serenity, and pure, unbridled love.

"You didn't have to do that," I tell him, and now my tone is anything but teasing. My eyes sting with the pressure of looming tears. It's like the happiness within me cannot be contained and is springing forth in the form of waterworks.

"I didn't do it because I have to," he explains, and his gaze is the warmest I've ever seen. "I did it because I love you. Because we're a team, and teammates show up for each other. Take care of each other."

"Niko." It's all I can say as I try to digest his words. When nothing coherent comes out of my mouth, I drop his hand and reach both my arms around his neck, pulling him into me. "Thank you."

His hands find my waist, and I press my cheek to his chest, breathing him in, as I let him hold me. Of all the intimate moments we've shared, something about this simple gesture is the most vulnerable. To hold, and be held, to care and be cared for. It's terrifying and wonderful all at once.

"I should be thanking you," he says, planting a soft kiss on the top of my head.

I pull back and peer up, giving him a questioning look.

"'Niko Karras is an excellent pickleball player and boyfriend'?" He quotes my statement to Angela with a pleased smile, almost word for word. "What a glowing review."

"I'm pretty sure I told her you were an excellent *fake* boyfriend," I remind him.

"Oh, I know," he says. "And after I read that, *I* told her

that hopefully I'd get a chance to try out being a real one someday. Who knows, maybe we can give her a reason to write a follow-up story."

I stretch up on my tiptoes, lips close to his ear. "You've always been the real thing to me."

Loretta and Ed appear next to us, and in the minutes since I last saw them, they've also changed into BIG DINK ENERGY shirts. "Oh good. You found each other," Loretta says, and for the first time today I notice that she's dressed like she's about to meet me for a pickleball lesson.

"Don't worry. I got it all," Deb quips, still behind her camera. "This is going to make an amazing part two."

"Niko," I say, suddenly remembering the urgent reason I'm here, "Freddie's trying to buy the club with Wilson. They're business partners."

He grimaces at this, but nothing about him looks shocked. "That fucking guy."

Niko immediately begins scanning the crowd, like he's about to hunt Freddie down, and I tug at his hand, bringing his attention back to me.

"You know I don't like to tell you when you're right, but you were right," I admit, and he chuckles, shoulders relaxing the teeniest bit. "He does suck."

"I'm going to remember this so I can gloat later," he promises.

"I expect nothing less." I level a look at him, and he gives me a playful squeeze.

"But first we need to go kick his ass," he says.

"And have some words with Wilson," I add. "I'm not

going to accept his offer now, obviously. Not that I know what I *am* going to do, but it won't be that."

"Well, we're on track to raise a lot of money," he assures me. "I bet, at the end of next week, we'll have double what Wilson's forking over for prize money. So we don't have to do anything. We can play if we want to. And we can lose if we want to. But that's not really my style."

Double. The word bounces around my brain as I try to make sense of it. Not just the dollar amount, but the overwhelming outpouring of unconditional support. "This is way too much, you guys. You don't have to do this for me."

"Bex, we all love you," Loretta says, standing closer to Niko. "We don't want you to do this all on your own."

"We're at the club for pickleball, but we're also there because it's such a special place," Deb adds, finally putting down her phone. "And you did that. You made it that way."

"I know it's really hard to rely on other people," Niko says, pulling me a step closer to him. "You know I get it. But if you can get me to like pickleball, then hopefully I can convince you that you don't have to solve every problem on your own. Especially when you have a great partner."

"Excuse me." Loretta nudges him with the hard edge of her cast. "A great *team*."

"You all are the best teammates I could ask for," I tell them, before leaning into Niko's shoulder, my hand finding the nape of his neck.

"You said you're in love with me," I whisper, as he nods, wrapping his arm around me as he tugs me closer for another hug.

"I've already told the *LA Times* and social media," he says in my ear, and I can feel his face shift into a smile, pressed against my cheek. "I figured I should let you know eventually."

"I always thought it was stupid that love means zero in tennis," I tell him, taking a small step back so I can admire his face. "It makes *zero* sense."

"No, it makes perfect sense," he says matter-of-factly, with that slightly peeved tone I've come to adore. It means I am exactly where I want to be—right under his skin. His eyes narrow ever so slightly. "It's because a zero looks like an egg, and the French word for egg sounds a lot like love."

"I took French in high school," I scoff. "The French word for egg is *oeuf.* And you think pickleball is ridiculous? You tennis people need to look in the mirror."

"*Laaaaa* oeuf," he says, dragging out every sound. We're both grinning, relishing being right back where we started—bickering about the merits of tennis and pickleball. "L'oeuf. *Love.* I don't understand how you can't hear it."

"I don't understand how you can't hear how ridiculous you sound," I reply as he pulls me back into an embrace, arms tight around my back.

"I l'oeuf you, Bex," he says quietly, muffled against my neck, just loud enough for me to hear.

"I egg you too, Niko," I say back with a giggle. "So much."

I can feel the energy of the world around us—people chattering, bumping into us as we hold each other—but it all falls into the background. All that matters is him.

"So what happens next?" I ask finally, and as I pull away, my arms still rest on his shoulders, solid and reassuring as always.

"We play today," he says, as he finds my hand, "and when we win, you can use that money for the club, too, or we can donate it wherever you like. Then I fly out to Miami for the qualifier, play like the fearless asshole that I am, and well, after that—who knows. But I think we can figure it out, together."

Our group starts walking slowly through the mass of people heading toward the courts.

"Wait," I say suddenly, tugging him to a stop next to me. Everyone follows suit, eyes centered on me. "I don't know if I can go out there and play. What if we lose?"

"Then we shake their hands and say 'good game,'" Niko reassures me. "Or we smash our paddles and curse. Up to you. But I'm not worried about losing."

I let out a nervous laugh. "Always so self-assured, aren't you?"

I hate that the doubt has crept back in, but I also only want to be honest with Niko. And the truth is, there's a part of me that's still scared: of losing the tournament, the exhibition match, the club, him. All of it.

"If you want to leave, now, we can leave." He reaches a hand up and gently toys with the end of my braid. "But you gotta embrace the risk of losing if you want to win. And I think we can win this one, Princess. I think we can win it all."

He raises his brows in silent challenge, and something about his unbridled confidence settles me.

"Okay," I say with a firm nod. "But damn, whoever bid on the chance to play with Freddie is in for a rude awakening when you start banging balls at them on the court."

"He better not!" Loretta says, holding up her broken hand.

I look from one Karras to the other as Niko shakes his head. I can see a familiar shadow of worry on his face, just like that day we met in the hospital. But this time, I'm the one to protest.

"You should not be out there playing," I tell Loretta, before turning back to Niko. "Didn't you give me a big speech about how dangerous pickleball was when we met?"

He shrugs like it's no big deal. "Some people have convinced me otherwise."

"I'm very persuasive," Loretta chirps, clearly pleased with herself. "And I threatened eviction if he tried to stand in my way."

"Loretta, this seems…I don't know, reckless?" I say, still trying to wrap my head about this plan they've concocted. "And also, I thought we agreed no more schemes to try to win."

"Oh, shush." Loretta swats at me to be quiet. "I'm not going to purposefully play bad. You know my ego couldn't stomach that. It just so happens that my dominant hand is broken, so I'll do the best I can with the left. Besides, the donation goes to the food bank. That place meant a lot to your mom. She was always looking for a way to help out there."

I soften at the memory of my mother, always showing up

for me, for clients, for her community. It was never transactional or done to curry favor. She simply cared.

"Do I even want to know what that highest bid was?" I ask, reaching for Loretta's hand, trying to convey my gratitude.

"We all chipped in," says Ed. "You're not the only one who wants to keep the club around forever."

"I don't know what to say," I tell them, so overwhelmed with emotions that no words even come to mind other than "Thank you."

"You don't have to say anything," Niko says, wrapping an arm around my shoulder. "You just need to go play some pickleball."

I'm still for a moment, admiring this bighearted group of people surrounding me, rooting for me, supporting me. This is the legacy my mom left behind, and it's what will last, even if the club does not.

Finally, I nod, eyes sparkling. My answer, of course, is yes. I'm all in.

"I don't just want to play," I say, sliding my hand through Niko's. "I want to win."

EPILOGUE

Tuesday, May 30

IT'S WELL PAST seven o'clock, but this means nothing in the desert. The sky is every shade of orange imaginable, the sun resisting setting for just a few minutes longer. I've told myself to stop checking my phone, but I can't help it. I give it one more glance before shoving it into the cup holder that dangles from the camping chair armrest.

Niko's shared his location with me, and I can see he's about to turn off the main drag of Sunset Springs. In a minute, maybe less, he'll be pulling up in front of the club.

I chomp my gum nervously and shift in the chair. It's still close to ninety degrees out, and my skirt—a mix of old Lilly Pulitzer patterns I found in Loretta's storage closet—sticks to the back of my thighs. Niko's qualifier in Miami wasn't televised, and I purposefully avoided searching for the results online and told him not to tell me anything. I wanted to hear it all from him directly. We'd agreed to take these nine days apart as a break, no communication, so we could each simply focus on our own lives, figure our own stuff out.

With the money we won in the Paddle Battle, plus the T-shirt orders and donations still coming in, I've gotten my wish—the club isn't going anywhere, and neither am I. I spent the last several days drowning in tedious paperwork, hammering out payments and financing and budgets. I am grateful for every second of it.

But I didn't need nine days or even nine minutes to figure out how I feel about Niko. I want him. And I am growing impatient.

His flight landed in Los Angeles earlier this morning, and the text he sent was our first communication since he'd left. But all he'd said was that he had "something to take care of" and he'd see me later tonight.

I hear the familiar creak and thud of the door, and it's a sound I know better than my own breath.

"I'm on court eight!" I holler, knees bouncing with child-like excitement. He left for Miami the day after we won the tournament and beat Freddie and Loretta in the exhibition match—"a walloping" is how Angela described it in the follow-up piece she wrote—and I am downright giddy to see his face. Nine days have felt like, well, nine very long days, and I hop up and run across the court, desperate for a glimpse of him.

Niko turns the corner and appears just when I hit the kitchen line, and I freeze. He's in his usual white—a crisp polo and shorts—but in his hands is a bouquet of flowers, a rainbow of colors, in a strange container.

"What is that?" I ask as he takes those last few steps toward me. He holds it up so I can get a better look, and that's when it hits me. He's brought me a bouquet nested in a vase made entirely of crayons.

"It's a very hard craft project from Pinterest that I had a lot of help with," he says, looking down at the creation in his hands. "I had no idea what a glue gun was until two days ago."

"You glued." I tilt my head to marvel at the arrangement in his hands. "All these crayons onto the va—*Holy shit.*"

He chuckles because he knows exactly what I'm gasping at.

Every single crayon that makes up the outside of the vase—all perfectly symmetrical, I might add—is burnt sienna.

"Maureen coached me over FaceTime," he adds, placing the flowers in my hands. "She's extremely crafty, it turns out. And I'm a perfectionist. So you can imagine how that conversation went. She and I had to do some touch-ups before I came over."

I grin at the thought of the two of them going back and forth over an art project.

"Niko, I love this. No one's ever made anything like this for me in my entire life." I lean down to inhale a rose, lost in the magic of the moment before remembering the whole reason I'd been missing him in the first place. "Wait, how was the qualifier? Did you win? What happened?"

My eyes dash across his face, looking for any sort of hint as to how he did, but his smile gives nothing away.

"I won my first match," he says finally, running a hand through my hair. "I beat this twenty-year-old kid from New Zealand with a wicked backhand. You would have loved it."

"I'm very proud," I say, heart bursting. He did it. Not that I ever thought otherwise. This is Niko, after all.

"And then I did what I should have done two years ago,"

he says, his hands finding my hips, fingers twisting in the soft pleats of my skirt. "I retired. Officially."

He's quiet, and I use this moment to take in the sight of him. His hair is still damp from the shower, the smell of Dove soap lingering on his skin. I balance the flowers under the crook of one arm and use my free hand to stroke the soft expanse of his cheek.

"But you love playing tennis," I tell him, and he chuckles.

"I do," he agrees. "But I've also learned how nice it is to love other things, too."

L'oeuf.

"Also, Bex," he says solemnly, "you might not believe this, but I can play tennis here in Sunset Springs."

"I know that," I say. He leans into my hand, and I notice for the first time how utterly relaxed he seems.

Niko shifts so that his lips kiss my palm, and then he grabs the flowers from under my arm, placing them gently onto the chair next to us.

"I remember what you said, that you'd bring me a crayon bouquet on our first date," I tell him, admiring his handiwork. "So is this it?"

"No, this is not our first date, Princess." His lips curl into a smile, and his hand finds my cheek, his thumb rubbing gently along my bottom lip. "This is just me trying to butter you up before I ask you if you'd be okay if I stick around."

"Here," I say as I wrap both arms around his neck, and he nods slowly.

"Here, in Sunset Springs. But also here, as your boyfriend. Here, in your life. Here, with you."

I can see the slightest crease of concern on his forehead, and I know him well enough to know now that he's unsure, taking a risk in being this forward. I love this about him, that he's most likely scared, but he's doing it anyway.

"Well, you're going to fit right in here in Sunset Springs," I tease, as I reach up and run my thumb gently across his brow, as if I could simply wipe the worry away. I brush my fingertips along his temple, until they find a tendril of wet hair. "I can already see your grays coming in."

"Well, that's a relief," he says, his head dropping to the crook of my shoulder. "Maybe I can fool the intake staff at one of these retirement homes and get an apartment. I don't think Loretta's going to let me squat at her place forever."

My hands move through the waves of his hair down to the nape of his neck, savoring every bit of him, the hard and soft, the beautiful contrasting parts that make up this man that I love.

"And all that wicker is a lot for one person to handle," I say solemnly.

He chuckles, and the vibration of his laugh sends the smallest of shock waves down my back. "That's true."

"So you stay here, and..." I trail off, still trying to figure out his plan.

"Well, I've loved the clinics I've taught recently," he says, lifting his gaze to mine. "Maybe I do more coaching."

"Tennis or pickleball?" I ask, raising both brows skeptically.

"Ideally, both," he says. "But it's really up to my future boss, Princess. Hopefully, the Sunset Springs Racquet Club will be hiring. If not, I guess I can hit up Starlight. I hear that place makes a mean protein shake."

"Hey!" I thwack him playfully across the shoulder.

"What?" he asks, feigning innocence.

"As long as you agree to keep playing pickleball with me, I'll think about it," I agree, and he grins at my answer. "Because I love playing pickleball with you, like I love doing everything with you."

"I told you I'd win you over eventually, Princess." His voice is a purr, as he leans down and plants a kiss on the top of my head. I hold him tighter, relishing the feeling of having him back, having him here, for good.

"I've spent so much time worrying about how to keep my mom's legacy alive with the club that I never let myself think what other ways she might want me to honor her." My voice cracks slightly. There's a weight to my words, but it's not the sadness I've been carrying with me for so long. It's something new. Hopeful. "But I think loving you, and letting myself be loved, is a good start."

He tugs me closer, so close I can almost feel the tender ache of love in his chest as it rises and falls. The longer he's wrapped around me, the more I feel both of our bodies relax. "You're stuck with me. I hope that's okay."

I scratch my nails gently along his neck, right at the hairline, and he lets out a satisfied moan.

"When you do that, there's no way I can say no," I say with a laugh.

"Do what?" he asks, in between slow kisses along my neck, just under my ear.

"Make those sexy noises!" I say, and my voice becomes more breathless with each syllable. "You know what that does to me."

"I do," he says, his voice a rough growl. "But I think you need to tell me again."

But I don't say a word. Instead I bring my lips to his and let him know exactly how I feel.

It's our second first kiss.

After a few minutes, I pause and rest my forehead against his. "Of course I want you to stay."

He glances down and then gives me the most devious pout. "Then can I take you out of this very sexy little skirt?"

His fingers curl into my waistband, teasing me. "Yes," I say, my voice on the precipice of a moan. "But if you take off my clothes, you're going to have to play with me out on this cracked court, and I think you once told me they were dangerous."

His laugh is warm against my skin. "Dangerous because every time I'm around you, I want to throw you to the ground and have you a hundred different ways."

"So what you're saying is, you love playing pickleball," I say, finding the hem of his crisp white shirt and giving it a tug upward, signaling to him that I want it gone, immediately.

"I love it more than anything in the whole world," he says as he obliges, yanking it over his head and tossing it behind us. "But only when I'm playing with you."

ACKNOWLEDGMENTS

I am so grateful to get to do what I do and am indebted to many wonderful people who help make it possible.

First and foremost, Jim Spencer, who introduced me to pickleball in 2021. I teased him about it, and then, of course, I got hooked. You were right, Dad! And you know how much I hate to admit that.

My pickleball coach, Roland Sunga, who has been a mentor, a friend, and a very helpful adviser during the writing process. Thank you for your wit and wisdom, and for coining the phrase "de-bang the bangers."

Jen McCreary, Annie Mebane, Gwen Mesco, Matt Rocheleau—my pickleball partners in crime. May we swear together on the court for years to come. Thanks also to Maribel Sunga, the staff and fellow pickleball players at the Burbank Tennis Center, and the folks at the Courtside Caffe. (Get the Greek salad.)

Holly Root, for everything, but especially for suggesting

that the world needs more pickleball in romance. You were obviously right.

Alex Logan, thank you for saying yes to this story and being an incredible partner in bringing it to life on the page.

I'm fortunate to have so many fantastic folks on my team, including Estelle Hallick, Dana Cuadrado, Grace Fischetti, Anjuli Johnson, Lori Paximadis, Alyssa Maltese, Kristin Dwyer, Molly Mitchell, Genesis Reyes, Heather Baror-Shapiro, Mary Pender-Coplan, Grace Kallis, Daniela Medina, Caitlin Sacks, Rebecca Holland, Jeff Stiefel, Erin Cain, and Maya Chessen.

Additionally, the following superstars provided vital editorial, professional, and/or moral support throughout this process (listed in no particular order because I am an agent of chaos): Alexa Martin, Zan Romanoff, Tara Copeland, Angelika Rougas, Anna Lane, Doree Shafrir, Sarah Enni, Elissa Sussman, Maurene Goo, Falon Ballard, Courtney Kae, Erin La Rosa, Taylor Hahn, Derek Hoyden, Danielle Nussbaum, Liz Grubin, Rebekah Weatherspoon, Lauren Kung Jessen, Kate Sweeney, and Lacie Waldon.

To the many friends who keep me laughing every day, thank you. I am beyond lucky to have you in my life.

My dear husband, Anthony, and our amazing daughters, Eleanor and Lydia, gamely put up with having a stressed-out romance writer in their midst at all times. I love you all more than is humanly possible to imagine.

And to all the "book people" out there—the readers, booksellers, librarians, reviewers, book clubs, and podcasters; the folks sharing books on Instagram, TikTok, and all the other forms of social media I can't figure out; the people who come to signings and panels and say hi and trade bracelets and champion these happily-ever-afters—thank you, thank you, thank you. Your support means the world.

I carry a piece of my mom, Martha Spencer, with me wherever I go, including in the pages of the books I write. When I started drafting this story I never expected to touch on cancer, grief, and mother loss. But characters have a way of revealing themselves as you write, and it has meant so much to me to get to do so through Bex and her mom.

Finally, a note of gratitude to those who have shared their personal ADHD stories with me. Understanding and nurturing my own neurodivergence has been one of the greatest gifts of my adult life, and I honor anyone reading this who finds themselves on a similar path. May we all cherish and celebrate every unique part of ourselves and each other.

ABOUT THE AUTHOR

Kate Spencer is the author of the bestselling novel *In a New York Minute*, *One Last Summer*, and the memoir *The Dead Moms Club*. As a former podcaster, she won two iHeartRadio Podcast Awards for her work on *Forever35*. Her writing has been published by *InStyle*, *Cosmopolitan*, *The Washington Post*, *Rolling Stone*, and numerous other places. She lives with her family in Los Angeles.